L-One _____

L-Two _____

N _____

J _____

C _____

New York:
Alfred A. Knopf
1971

L-One

L-Two

N

J

C

the last
writings of

J. J. sephoJ

THIS IS A BORZOI BOOK
PUBLISHED BY ALFRED A. KNOPF, INC.

ISBN: 0-394-47173-3

Library of Congress Catalog Card Number: 76-154918

Manufactured in the United States of America

First Edition

to **C** to see

"Even a chameleon can't stop being a chameleon."

Anonymous

In order to be profound, all you have to do is just tell the truth.

But I don't know the truth.

That's very profound.

L-One	
L-Two	
N	
J	
C	

Imagine a beautiful sun-filled tennis stadium, a shaded grandstand next to a fantastically immaculate velvet-green grassy tennis court. Outward from this court for miles in all directions past the horizon are gorgeous lawns, flowers, trees, and shrubbery. Think of it as a gigantic Garden of Eden, bountiful and beautiful; if you could walk through it, you would feel at peace. But we are concerned with the happenings on the tennis court; there the world's two greatest players are engaged in a titanic epic match without end. There are linesmen around the court and an umpire who oversees all. But these officials act like robots when making their calls, and their calls are always correct and quick. While the ball is in play, they sit in silence: motionless. They are as human as the net. Most peculiarly, five officials, the service-line judges and the net judge, never have to utter a word, for the players always put the first serve in play without strain. And this is also necessary, for there is only one ball, which never wears out or gets dirty. The players themselves are remarkable physical specimens—quick, agile, alert, strong, and paragons of stamina.

Some words about the play—the ball is at times hit harder or softer, with or without spin, with more accuracy on the volley than in any match in the history of the game. Whatever the situation calls for, whatever the strategy of the moment should be, the players are equal to the occasion and make the shot. Their strokes are fluid, their style is superb. In spite of their incredible offensive skills, their defensive genius guarantees long—interminably long—rallies as each player is able to scamper after apparent winners and send the ball back over the net sufficiently strongly or well enough placed to prevent the opponent from scoring a quick point. Drop shots that barely ease over the net, lobs that fall within an inch of the baseline, crackling serves and furiously hit service returns, incredible angle shots—these become the usual style of this evolving, continuous collision of tennis might. On those occasions when a point is scored, the player closest to the ball retrieves it and play resumes. The match has been going on for an age, and all estimates of the time required to finish it are too low. There is no sense in considering that aspect at all.

Curiously, for such a skillful match there are only two spectators sitting in the grandstand. They never get excited about what they are watching, never root for one player in preference to the other, and never applaud when a point is scored. These interested disinterested onlookers are strangers to each other, but a conversation begins to flow between them, sporadically at first.

"Fantastic, isn't it?"

The second spectator looks warily at the first and then responds, "Yes, it is fantastic."

The first looks at the second and smiles. "Fine day for playing. Pity we can't find a court for ourselves. I assume you play."

The smile is reassuring. "Yes, it's a lovely day. I play a little bit—but not very well."

"That's always the problem. I've watched them before and tried to imitate them, but I've never been able to get satisfaction from my game. Oh, once in a while I stroke a few balls properly but never for a match, not even a set—only a

lucky game once in a while. Allow me to introduce myself—
my name is Fault."

"That's a rather odd name," and then, alarmed that the
statement isn't very tactful, "but a very forceful one, becoming to a man."

FAULT: Why, thank you. I must confess that I agree with you
when you say it's odd. I rather like it, actually. It's unique
and has been carried by a member of my family for genera-
tions. The story is that it's given to the child most likely to be
the strongest individualist. [*Spoken with a wink*] And whom
do I have the pleasure of addressing?

Bubbling with girlish giggles, as if a presentation is about
to be made, she answers: "Oh . . . Double-Fault . . . ha."

FAULT: Ahh, what a pretty name to go with such a pretty
damsel.

DOUBLE-FAULT: You like it? [*Said with a ring in her voice
and a smile on her face*]

FAULT: Oh indeed, it has such a pleasant chime to it.

DOUBLE-FAULT: I think so, too, but it might sound a bit im-
modest to say so.

FAULT: Well, a fact is a fact.

The conversation then takes a usual turn about their respective styles, and why they like the game. Double-Fault
hasn't played very much but she thinks tennis invigorating.
Fault nods in agreement. They enjoy talking to each other.
Eventually Fault becomes silent, and although from a distance he looks as if he is intently watching the match, Double-
Fault senses that he is thinking about other matters.

DOUBLE-FAULT: That was a nice shot, wasn't it?

5

FAULT: [*Rousing himself back to the present*] Oh, yes, very nice. [*A short silence and then Fault starts talking very rapidly because he doesn't want to be interrupted before he finishes what he has to say.*] Look, this appears to be a very long match—it's been going for an age and it doesn't look as if it could possibly finish in the foreseeable future. Both players are too strong. Do you mind if I tell you a very long story—it would be an unburdening for me and I am sure, quite sure, that at worst you'll find it interesting. I can assure you of that.

DOUBLE-FAULT: [*Already attuned to the agitation inside Fault*] That would be super. I love long stories—especially if they're interesting.

FAULT: I should say first that I'm not necessarily the best of storytellers and I hope that I don't become too tedious for you. But the story is the thing—not the description.

DOUBLE-FAULT: I don't see how you can separate one from the other.

FAULT: [*Wishing to avoid argument*] Let me put it this way—there are hundreds of thousands of words. The ones I use and the way I use them won't be the only possible way to describe my tale. But all methods and words will describe the same story.

DOUBLE-FAULT: I don't agree. The emphasis can be changed by a change in words. That's simply obvious.

FAULT: All right, all right. I take back what I said. I will tell my story brilliantly. You've forced me to it. [*Shocked at what he has just uttered, Fault quickly regroups his wits.*] Interrupt me whenever you have a question or a comment or when something isn't clear. [*Listen, a brilliantly told story is clear.*]

DOUBLE-FAULT: Do begin, and I promise to be most attentive.

FAULT: Thank you. Let's see. [*Fault stares at the ground, obviously searching for a way to begin.*] A friend of mine—his name is "N"—

DOUBLE-FAULT: [*Slightly anguished*] I once knew someone with the same name.

FAULT: Well, it's not that rare. It's not common, either. Anyway, N's story—it is really all his story, I should add—began some time back. N was playing cards with some friends when J sat down at a piano in the next room. There were a few people around her, listening to some parodies she was singing. From N's vantage point he could barely hear her, but he became vividly aware of an instant interest in her. He excused himself from the game and walked over to the festivities. J was all smiles and laughs as she sang about the political difficulties of a then disgraced incumbent. Everyone thought it was clever, and compliments came thick and fast. Indeed, J was quite entertaining, which was not surprising, since she had been a professional cabaret performer. N said nothing, only observed, and wandered away. He knew that a big part of his life was about to begin. Some people have instincts about things like that, you know, and N felt his heart beat a little quicker, as the saying goes. He wanted to meet J and he wanted more than that. He wondered whether he was in luck or whether J had emotional entanglements that might prevent something serious from starting. He didn't exactly want to play a game, but he did want to work out the best possible strategy to follow for impressing J and getting to spend some time alone with her. In fact, N knew already that if J responded to him, he would want to marry her. Crazy that such a thought should come to him in such a short time. Love at first sight—absolutely ridiculous.

DOUBLE-FAULT: I should say so. You have to know people for long periods before you can be sure about marriage, and what does "love" mean anyway? The whole situation is positively ridiculous. I must say you seem to know quite a bit about the thoughts of this N person.

FAULT: I've spent many hours with him listening to him monologize about his life. I almost know it better than he does. Well, to continue. N's thoughts were racing, especially after J departed. He wanted to call her on the phone and invite her out for coffee, but logically he knew it was a poor idea. First she'd never remember seeing him in the group around the piano, so any physical attraction she might feel for him couldn't be brought into play over the telephone. Secondly, he didn't want to sound too anxious and if she refused him because he was a stranger or even for a more innocuous reason, such as the lateness of the hour, it might set a bad precedent for future invitations he might make to her. And thirdly, he knew that there was a party she might soon be going to and he thought it would be best if they met there accidentally.

DOUBLE-FAULT: Too much plotting, if you ask me.

FAULT: Love works different ways for different people. N was enraptured. He wanted action and that required analysis, which I suppose you could call plotting. But "plotting" sounds violent—N's intentions were just the opposite.

DOUBLE-FAULT: Well, I think it was plotting.

FAULT: N got very lucky the next day. J walked past him and he said "Hello." J walked right by, whereupon N said to J, "Don't you return a greeting?" "Oh, I am sorry," J said. "I didn't mean to ignore your 'Hello.' "

DOUBLE-FAULT: Wasn't he rude to speak to her in the first place and then more than rude to demand recognition?

FAULT: Not at all, for in this particular place all the people are strangers to begin with and he was quite correct to extend a cordial greeting to someone he passed. Not to have done so would have been rude.

DOUBLE-FAULT: I see. It's a local custom.

FAULT: Well, that's one way of defining it. They continued on their respective ways and N was jubilant. He had his "incident" and J would surely remember it and him for "causing" it. In fact, N was doubly lucky because, although he didn't know it at the time, rudeness was one of J's pet dislikes and she had been the rude one.

DOUBLE-FAULT: Not very rude, in my judgment.

FAULT: True. The night of the party arrived and N showed up early. A quick glance told him J wasn't there. He talked with his friends, danced a bit, but always keeping his physical eye on the door and his mind's eye on J. The guests began to arrive in numbers and finally—and N couldn't believe how lucky he was—J arrived *alone*. No one had asked her for a date, or if anyone had, she had refused the offer. If it was the latter, it could mean that she didn't want to be bound to one person for the evening, or since she was from another country—I don't think I mentioned that—it could also mean she was being faithful to a beau back home. N preferred to be optimistic and quickly put himself opposite J in the small circle of conversation that gravitated to her.

DOUBLE-FAULT: Sounds as if she was a very attractive personality.

FAULT: She was a *new* personality and people were curious. To add to the pleasure of their curiosity, J was attractive, talented, and had great ability in her academic discipline.

DOUBLE-FAULT: Well, even if you do emphasize "new," give her credit for being worth meeting. N surely thought so.

FAULT: By all means. I don't intend to slight her and will give her her due. That evening, N had what some people would term a "good night." He was funny without being vulgar or gauche, clever, full of wit and information that J found interesting. When they danced, she clung to him and he enjoyed it immensely. He had to control himself and he succeeded—partially, at least—in that respect. The tool does have its uses, but sometimes it can be an embarrassment.

DOUBLE-FAULT: I appreciate your choice of words, and I would also appreciate it if you could maintain that discrimination in further discourse.

FAULT: I will try to avoid lustful parlance as best I can. Around midnight, N asked J if she'd like to get some air and perhaps something to eat. J was quite agreeable to the suggestion; the party had been going on a long time and she had been on her feet continuously since she arrived. The two of them left and drove over to N's apartment where he scrambled some eggs and made some toast. Sometimes partying is hard work that stimulates the appetite.

DOUBLE-FAULT: Quite!

FAULT: The dishes were placed in the sink and forgotten as N and J went into the living room and sat on the couch. The conversation was pleasant chitchat interspersed with a few trivial questions. They were facing each other, and N studied that face from jaw to forehead, from ear to ear, and it pleased him. He did his studying discreetly, of course. J wasn't an object to be surveyed under a microscope.

DOUBLE-FAULT: I should hope not. Some men can be such boors.

FAULT: He looked at her and looked into her eyes and he desperately—a trite word, but exactly describing his inner feelings—wanted to kiss her. He slowly approached her on the couch, giving her every opportunity to put up a hand and refuse him, but she didn't. Their lips met, his weight was against her body, and they kissed. He enjoyed that kiss as he had enjoyed few kisses before it. To him, J's mouth was a paradise. The technique of this particular kiss was one of slowness, a chance for long, probing exploration, and N's thoughts went back in time to another woman he had loved who had kissed the same way. A gentle kiss from a gentle man to a genteel lady. They parted, and N remarked to J that he hadn't had a kiss like that for some time. He wasn't referring to its physical nature only but to his emotional satisfaction as well. His mind leaped ahead into the future.

DOUBLE-FAULT: Don't you think that's going a bit overboard on the basis of one kiss? I'll bet she wasn't thinking like that, simply enjoying the moment.

FAULT: Fair lady, what can I say? The man was overwhelmed by the feelings he genuinely had for J. Perhaps he was extrapolating too far into the future, but that's the way he thought. As for J, I am sure you're correct.

It was now very late, and J asked to be taken home. She needed her sleep because she had a lot of work planned for the next day. N obliged. He drove her to her residence and walked her to the stairs leading up to her room. She turned toward him and thanked him over and over and over again for a splendid evening. N couldn't believe how often, in the sweetest tones, she was thanking him. He said, of course, that it gave him great pleasure to have spent the evening as they did. He didn't add that he hoped they could get together again soon—he had decided that low pressure was needed to win her. She walked up the stairs and he watched her ascent. At the top, she stopped and waved good-bye to him and thanked him again. He waved, smiled, and thanked her, turned and left. To this day, the memory of that kiss and of J thanking him so profusely still haunt the reveries of his past. N was, to put it simply, ecstatic.

DOUBLE-FAULT: He was *that* taken by her. The manner of her farewell sounds so theatrical. Did it ever occur to him that J was putting on a "good night" performance?

FAULT: At the time, he thought she was sincere. He still thinks so.

It would be nice, if you're romantically inclined, to go on by saying that N and J dissolved into each other, realizing how happy they could make each other, and that their love grew and grew. But that would be a fairy tale. J liked N, of that there can be no doubt, but she wouldn't see him nearly as often as N wanted. She had her work to do and it was very important to her. In fact, one of the reasons she had left her own country was to get away from a man who wanted to marry her, while she wanted to concentrate on her career. She worked very hard, and was always using that as a reason —"excuse" would be too cruel a word—for not seeing N. N, to be sure, had his work to do also, but it seemed to him that they could meet a few minutes each day to talk and relax in each other's company. They went out once in a while and afterwards J would invite him up to her room for tea. N always accepted and, once in her room, would try to be as physical with her as she would let him be. She couldn't be counted on to be in the right mood. Once, however, they walked into her room and she quickly locked the door and took off her top clothes down to her bra and rushed to N's arms. He quickly turned out the light and pulled the shade and they worked their way to her bed and lay in each other's arms, kissing and fondling each other. She wouldn't permit N to have sexual intercourse with her—"No sense in starting an affair, it would only be a distraction"—and N was more or less content with the relationship as it stood. On another occasion, N was aroused and J said, "You can't go home like that," and she played with him until relief from nature's pressure was obtained. And yet there were times when she would

12

scold him when he became amorous. "You always want to be hot and bothered," she would say. This hurt him, for his physical desire for her was based on a love that had grown to full stature inside him. And what better way to express it?

DOUBLE-FAULT: Sex has its place, but one must be practical. Are you sure N wasn't overly sex-oriented? Always making demands?

FAULT: He was a man romantically in love. For that kind of feeling, there's no such thing as too much sex. And J liked him, liked his body, liked lying in his arms. She was always talking about how peaceful it was to lie with him. He would massage her neck and she would be at peace. She was the nervous sort, and these moments with N were very much appreciated by her. N could see this. But he couldn't fathom why she didn't reach out for him more often. Only in time would he discover the answer to this puzzle.

DOUBLE-FAULT: N thought it out and understood J's behavior, you intimate. I doubt it. He probably rationalized it from his own point of view.

FAULT: I am afraid you'll have to wait and see. I don't want to get ahead of my story. It was difficult for J during this period. She was much admired by many men and they were always calling her up. She would feel it was an imposition and that they were rude to bother her. Yet she wouldn't tell someone not to call again, and she always spoke pleasantly over the phone—and then would complain immediately after how she was hounded.

DOUBLE-FAULT: It's no laughing matter to be persecuted and harassed when you're trying to do your work. J was civil; you'd think the callers could take a hint.

FAULT: Perhaps. Or perhaps she expected to be understood too easily. The relationship between N and J reached a plateau—a very low one—and stopped growing. J's reluctance was not what N wanted. His desire was love—warm and deep. He was aware that other forces were influencing J but he didn't know how to overcome them. He believed very strongly —no, he even knew—that there was something about him in particular that J liked and thought special. He wasn't sure just what that something was, although J once told him she admired his mind. He felt it had to be more than that. N, of course, wanted to know what made J the way she was, and he would ask her questions about her past and listen to her talk about herself. He was particularly careful to pick his moments for these forays back in time, since resentment wells up easily against someone who is too prying and nosy. J had had some experiences, and to N she seemed like a giving person once she was in the mood. But giving wasn't always easy for her, not because she was shy or didn't enjoy the pleasure of an aroused man, but because she seemed to have some unfortunate notions about men and their assumed superiority over women. There was nothing N felt he could do but wait for a change in J. But he wasn't very hopeful.

DOUBLE-FAULT: Why didn't he forget her? That would have been the easiest way to handle the entire matter.

FAULT: I keep telling you—he loved J. Now, let's see—oh, yes—the year-end holidays arrived and J had made plans to visit some friends far from her present residence. I think they were acquaintances from her own country also staying in N's homeland. To make the trip, J put just about everything she had into a huge suitcase. It was far too heavy for her to manage alone, so she asked for N's help in getting it to the bus depot and he readily agreed to be of assistance. Before her departure from the bus terminal, N gave J a small box. "I bought you a going-away present. It isn't much but I hope you'll like it." J opened it, to see a small Scotty dog dressed as

14

a bagpiper, which could be pinned to a hat or a dress. N expressed the hope that the bonny dog would be a good-luck charm for her and he assumed she knew it was a token of his affection for her. J was quite pleased and happy to receive the gift. She gave N the address and telephone number where she would be staying, in case N had to reach her. He bade her farewell, stepped forward to kiss her good-bye and hear her softly say, "Good-bye." N would have preferred the two of them to go off somewhere together, but he had never broached the idea because J's plans had been made weeks before. Her baggage was put on the bus and J boarded the vehicle shortly thereafter. A few minutes later, passengers and luggage headed for holidays as the bus pulled out of the station. N saw it disappear down the street. Snow had fallen the night before and it was cold and snowy now. N left the bus station, his jacket wide open, already impatient for J's return.

DOUBLE-FAULT: Your description of N reminds me of a lovesick puppy. Perhaps that's why he gave her a little dog for going-away gift. Ha-ha.

FAULT: Let me patch up the disparity between what your impression of N is and what he's really like. I am sure the rest of the story will bring you to the same conclusions I have about him, but I guess it would be best to be explicit now. N was a man of strong feelings who was able—perhaps in defense of psyche—to completely hide his feelings from all who talked with him or were watching him. If he didn't tell you what was on his mind, you could only guess, because his face was unreadable. Do you understand?

DOUBLE-FAULT: You're saying that he could hide or mask his true feelings—that even if his thoughts were those of a lovesick puppy his behavior was normal.

FAULT: Precisely. He never tried to burden his friends with his problems because he felt it was a great inner strength to swallow one's own difficulties and chew them up until they were digested. In himself, he found his greatest strength, and the more weak-minded people he met, the more convinced he became that his way was best.

DOUBLE-FAULT: It *sounds* admirable, anyway. Go on with your story. I'll make up my mind about N when I've heard more about him.

FAULT: Well. J had bad luck. Her luggage, that great big suitcase, was removed from the bus at the wrong bus terminal, and all she had when she reached her destination was the clothes she was wearing. She was in a dither, and she called N to ask him to instigate some action at his end of the bus line. N quickly went to officials of the bus company to prod them into a faster search for the missing baggage. But it was the wrong time of year, people were traveling everywhere, and only cursory searches were attempted. The transport company simply needed its people for more important jobs than finding one missing suitcase. N called various terminals along the route, but to no avail. He called J back and told her she would have to get along without her wardrobe. She thanked N very sweetly for his labors, and he said it had been no trouble at all. He tried not to sound jocular when he told her to have a good time without her clothes and she said she would manage. About a week later, the suitcase turned up at its starting point. N picked it up at the bus depot, brought it back to his place, and called J to tell her it was safe. J was very relieved. It's a typical traveler syndrome when your baggage is misplaced: first you're furious you don't have it, then after a time you're happy it's not stolen even if you can't use it yourself. She said it was nice to hear N's voice. In fact, during this time N was dreaming about J constantly, for she had sent him a postcard and signed it, "Love, J." He focused on that word for the longest time. N could imagine anything out of a vacuum, but he didn't deceive himself into thinking the card had deep meaning, or any real meaning at all.

After two weeks, J returned, a smile on her face and a present in her hand for N—a fine leather belt. N was bubbling. They had dinner together the night she came back and laughed about some of the situations she had encountered on her "weightless" land voyage. In the late evening, N took J back to her room and there she told him that her work would require the deepest concentration now and she wouldn't be able to see him for some time. N tried to understand, but he was shattered. His expectations had plunged to zero.

DOUBLE-FAULT: Did J see how this affected him?

FAULT: Not from any outward sign, and she was too preoccupied with her own position. She felt she needed to be left alone. If she knew the effect of her statements on N, it didn't stop her—she had her priorities. As for N, he went about his day-to-day ritual outwardly composed, but inwardly in turmoil. He wanted to call J, but it was very difficult to guess when she wouldn't mind speaking on the phone. He would have hated to call and have her tell him she was terribly busy and couldn't speak. She had a self-admitted temper, a terrible temper, and it wasn't so much that N was afraid to shout her down as that he wanted their conversation to be sweet and soft. If she associated arguments with him, they could have no future.

DOUBLE-FAULT: I gather from that last comment that N was thinking of matrimony. But surely it seems so one-sided; he's the one in love, he's the one conjuring up heaven knows what out of nothing. What has J done to encourage such thoughts —sent him a postcard, of all things, with a signed "Love, J." He's being perfectly foolish, if you ask me.

FAULT: [*Staring at Double-Fault*] Sometimes one can't choose whom one loves, and hopefully love will always be more spontaneous than calculated. It's true N knew more what he wanted than J did, *perhaps*. But the point is, he never admitted he loved her and she never admitted she *didn't* love him. It was the worst of all possible stand-offs. As time passed, their relationship became no relationship at all. N felt compelled to do something. One night he went to J's living quarters, unannounced and unexpected. He heard her moving about inside and knocked on the door.

J: Who is it?

N: It's I, N.

Before she could open the door, he noticed that her transom was open. He decided to do something clever; he would chin himself like a monkey until his head could be seen in the transom—it would look comical, and when she opened the door she would be face to face with his knees. An amusing, harmless prank. As he pulled himself up, the toes of his shoes skidded against the door. It sounded scary. J screamed out, "Go away! Leave me alone. Just go away!" Her voice carried far more of a message than her words. She was angry and repelled. N dropped to the floor and ran. Words are insufficient to describe how bad he felt. He desperately wanted to apologize, but he realized that he would make her feel even worse if he called or went back. His legs carried him quickly down the stairs, out into the night, and in the back of his head a voice kept crying out, "Stupid, stupid, stupid—how could I have been so dumb as to play such a 'clever' stunt!"

DOUBLE-FAULT: Excuse me for interrupting you, but I can't believe what I just heard. Was N out of his mind—unexpected, unannounced, and behaving like an ape? The man is absurd.

FAULT: He made a mistake.

DOUBLE-FAULT: Mistake! Good heavens, that's no defense or excuse for his actions.

FAULT: It wasn't meant to be. It's a simple statement of fact. Let me go on, please. N knew now that J was lost to him for quite some time, perhaps forever. A very fatalistic thought. He vowed he would stay away from her, dodge out of her sight if he saw her first, get out of her life if that was what she wanted. And so he fell into despair, into a terrible day-to-day life with less and less hope that J would call him and forgive him. For weeks and months, he thought of her every hour—it was a waking nightmare. He plodded on in his work but would find himself daydreaming about her at the oddest times.

DOUBLE-FAULT: The poor fellow is obsessed.

FAULT: Yes, he was. Some two months after that horrendous night, N left his office in the early afternoon and headed for his apartment. His path took him down a flight of steps outside the building, across a bridge astride a beautiful gorge, and then down the sidewalk to his car. As he came down the steps, he felt the surge of the spring that was around him. He hit the pavement at the bottom of the steps, the joy of life lifting his feet. The familiar planks of the bridge came into focus. He looked through the cracks of the bridge to the flowing stream below. Spring thaw had turned winter ice into motion. He looked up, to make his way properly across the bridge. On the other end of the bridge, the figure of a girl coming toward him stirred up his thoughts of J. She was always just inside his forehead, so to speak, and any possibility of seeing her made his pulse rush and throb. The girl was as long-legged as J, and he quickly focused on her face. His mind became an anvil on which a hammer pounded out "J, J, J, J—it's J—J, J, J, J." His thoughts came in torrents. No, he would not stop her, nor would he look away, nor appear overanxious, nor would he look as if his heart were beating un-believably fast, nor would his face flush, nor would he look back after they passed. They approached each other, every step taking sufficient time for N to have all his thoughts all over again. He looked at her, she at him. They both said "Hello" and continued walking. She didn't stop. He wondered what she was thinking. He was sure his face was flushed because his heart was beating so rapidly. He looked back. J didn't. The bridge led onto a road, and N walked on and on. He rehashed and replayed in his mind all his thoughts and the sequence of events—that is, every step that had led them to each other. He felt terribly sad that his love for her was not wanted or appreciated. He had at least not forced her into a confrontation she may not have wanted. He wondered whether she would think about him that night. It was so long since she had seen him. Did she care? N thought not. She hadn't even looked back. But he knew J would not give in to an urge like that; she would have thought it somewhat vulgar or forward. That night he lay in bed wondering whether he would ever find peace. With J in his mind, apparently not.

DOUBLE-FAULT: My word, all that and all he did was walk past her. I still think he shouldn't let this happen to himself. He needs more control.

FAULT: Look, I am trying to tell you the story of a man tortured by his thoughts, thoughts evoked by an unquenchable love—that's "l-o-v-e"—for a woman, and you speak of control. Have you ever been in love?

DOUBLE-FAULT: That's none of your business and very impolite of you to ask.

FAULT: All right. Forgive me. I'll continue.

Weeks passed, and the jolt of that chance meeting had dissipated itself. N was even feeling merry; he walked with his head erect, almost with a smile on his face. Perhaps enough time had passed, he hoped, so that better feelings could emerge again. He decided to go to a certain place when he knew J would be there. He was going to conduct an experiment. It was his wish that she would see him and join him for a short talk. He arrived, looked around, saw that J was not there, and seated himself at a table by the door and waited. His heart was pounding. But he had to get this frustration settled, and the only avenue open to him was to talk things over with her. If only he could find something in her or about her to hate or despise. Many of his friends thought she was false, and conceited about her career. N believed his friends were more right than wrong, and yet, though he detested falseness, he could forgive J her bad moments. If it came to a choice between his friends and J, he would unhesitatingly pick J—and he liked his friends. Actually J wasn't as false as his friends believed. There was still a lot of little girl in her, and she acted the way she did because she saw herself playing a role. J's problem was that she didn't really know if she was up to the performance. To *act* superior and not *be* superior can make for a frenetic existence.

DOUBLE-FAULT: Wasn't she superior, really? She had traveled widely and was quite talented, according to your description, and her academic work was top quality—why shouldn't she think of herself as extraordinary?

FAULT: I don't think your question is as hard to answer as you perhaps think it is. I don't want to go into details now, because there is too much story still to go—we've barely started. But let me add this: someone once wrote that we are each three persons in one. We are what we think we are; we are what other people think we are; and we are what we *really* are. Suffice it to say, there seemed to be a difference of opinion about J.

DOUBLE-FAULT: Well, go on anyway, but you haven't answered my question.

FAULT: True—but I will. Where was I?

DOUBLE-FAULT: N was sitting at a table by some door, I think.

FAULT: Quite. Some people N knew—not friends really but people he saw from time to time—joined him at the table. He couldn't refuse them the right to sit down, and for him to get up and move to an empty table would have raised too many questions. He participated in the conversation, but once again he kept looking toward the door. Time passed—not a long time—and his feelings would peak and then ebb away as he wondered about J. He found it interesting to think of the possibilities of J coming through the door when he was either on a peak of feeling or in a trough. He felt distinctly aware that he was not interested in what he was talking about, but he had to be doing something, and talking was as easy as anything else.

It happened so quickly. J came through the door, head high, and in two steps she was half a step past N. He looked up and said "Hello" and she, realizing that someone had greeted her, turned to respond. An automatic "Hello" came forth, and then she recognized N. It was clear to N that his greeting had caught her by surprise; she had come into the room too quickly to see him and make up her mind whether to join him or not. J continued on, because to stand in one place and debate with herself would have been bad form. She got in line to get some food and then joined another group of people at a table across the room from N. She never looked at him. After a little while he left. He felt very flat—no confrontation, no talk, no anything.

DOUBLE-FAULT: All that effort and nothing to show for it again. Seems unreal, all this hocus-pocus. There must be better ways.

FAULT: N wished he knew them. The days passed lazily. N became engrossed in his work, but never to the point of forgetting J. She was locked in that mind of his like a bird in a cage without a door. The summer was upon them, and N realized he had seen J for a total of perhaps ten minutes in the previous five months. The thought was shocking. He didn't know whether J would be going away or not, whether her desire to leave the area was stronger than her connection with the work she had begun. J was unhappy here. Besides disliking the people who pestered her, she disliked the cold, wet weather of the region. The wind would go right through her thin frame no matter how many layers of clothes and sweaters she wore. N had heard that in midwinter, after his horrendous chinning exhibition, J had gone to the hospital just to recuperate from colds and the fatigue they caused her. And when N was seeing her fairly regularly she had been plagued with headaches. She babied herself with medications. Did I mention that her father was a doctor?

DOUBLE-FAULT: No. I don't recall hearing that.

FAULT: I suppose she wrote him for advice. She wasn't a hypochondriac and I hope I didn't give you that impression. But sickness—really just being under the weather—was an integral part of J's week-to-week life.

DOUBLE-FAULT: Some people can't avoid getting sick. It's not fair to criticize the poor girl just because she's not as healthy as some horses.

FAULT: Oh, I agree. I'm not criticizing her at all. Nor did N. And N was just the opposite—healthy as can be, and if he did get sick he didn't let it keep him from living his normal life. He never took pills and he never got headaches.

DOUBLE-FAULT: Lucky fellow.

FAULT: Do you think so? N heard that J would be staying the summer and that she had taken over an apartment about a block from where N lived. Again and again the thoughts of her stirred his innermost hopes. Perhaps you're right when you say N is lucky, for one day as he was driving back to work, he saw J walking in the opposite direction with a grocery bundle in one arm and some books in the other. He didn't think she saw him and he quickly maneuvered the car about and headed back along the street in J's direction. He pulled up alongside her and asked her if she could use a lift. Her packages really were manageable and she said she only had a short way to go. "Well, get in. The car will make it shorter," N said with a smile, and J laughed and accepted the offer. They exchanged the usual "How are you?" and "How are things going for you?" questions and the usual "Fine" answers, and in no time at all the car covered the route. J got out and thanked him for the lift. "Sorry it couldn't have been longer; you'll have to move further out," N proffered. J laughed again. Everything was pleasant, and if the pleasantries were a little forced it was probably due to the newness of their being together after such a long time apart. J thanked him again; he nodded, and said, "Good-bye." He drove off for work, but work was not easy to concentrate on. He was thinking about J, and he had in fact just gone through an emotional experience that required careful consideration. And yet it was intertwined with the most commonplace of occurrences—the offering of a lift. When he offered J the ride, he knew he was exposing himself to a possible curt dismissal. When she accepted, he had all he could do to prevent himself from bursting forth with a rush of questions like "Do you know I love you?" and "Do you love me?" and "How can you be so nice now without commenting on our past relationship?" and so on. That quarter-of-a-mile drive was a feeling-out process. Where was J's heart? He couldn't tell, of course, but now his hopes were not totally impossible any longer. When he got back to his office, he decided to call J. He knew the name of the man from whom she had subleased the apartment, since she had just volunteered the information. He looked up the phone number and wrote it down, and then stared at it. He knew he was going to call; it wasn't a question of finding the courage. What he was mulling over was the best, most appropriate, most propitious time to call. Now, he thought, was too soon. He would appear overanxious—which he was. He decided to call her later in the evening. Such fantastic energy spent in deciding such a question can only be accounted for by a person's being in love. It would probably have made no difference when he called, and if he called now he would be sure to find her home. But he waited. As I said, he didn't want to appear overanxious even though he knew that the moment J heard his voice on the other end of the line, she would know his thoughts and feelings exactly.

DOUBLE-FAULT: N gives her credit for being omniscient, as well as talented and the rest. Perhaps all he has to do is say "Hello" and J will tell him all he wants to know.

FAULT: [*Mockingly*] Possibly! Finally N calls.

J: Hello.

N: Hello, J, this is N. I hope I'm not disturbing you.

J: No, I'm not busy at the moment.

N starts talking at a slow-to-moderate speed. He asks J if she's free to join him this evening for coffee or perhaps frozen custard at one of those popular roadside stands. J says she would like to but she can't because she's very busy—but SHE SAYS IT SO POLITELY, as though she would accept the invitation if she weren't so tied up with work. Encouraged, N suggests a a date later in the week. J asks him to hold the line while she looks in her appointment book. When she gets back on the phone, she starts to explain, very politely, how her work schedule prevents her from making any social commitment

TILL WEDNESDAY, three days away. She is going to see him, HE KNEW IT. She keeps saying how awfully sorry she is that she can't go out sooner. N says Wednesday is fine and he can pick her up at any hour that's convenient for her. About seven-thirty, comes the reply. N repeats the time and says something like "Till Wednesday, seven-thirty. See you then."

> J: Right. Thanks for calling.
> N: My pleasure. Good night.
> J: 'Bye.

N hung up the phone. HE WAS FORGIVEN. He felt as if hope and life had been pumped back into him in one giant thrust. He jumped into the air and cavorted about. The days would pass with him counting the hours, but his patience would be superhuman. He didn't know what to expect, but he would see her again and talk with her. He hoped she would kiss him, but he couldn't be sure if she would. He had put so much emotional energy into the phone call that it left him spent. That night he couldn't sleep despite his tiredness. But he was happy.

DOUBLE-FAULT: It's almost sinister to think that one person can affect another one so. Look at all the months of unhappy thoughts N had wondering about J. If he had spent one tenth of that energy in finding another girl, he would have been much better off, I should think.
[*Fault looks at Double-Fault and wonders whether she'll ever understand.*]

FAULT: Wednesday night couldn't come too quickly for N, and seven-thirty in the evening felt further away from the sunrise than the ice age from creation. N had one bad habit that he tried to change but all attempts failed—he always showed up early for appointments or dates. This night was no exception. He had to force himself to arrive only two minutes early—a monumental feat judging by past performance. J looked—well, "nice" would be correct, but not really right. She looked sort of wonderful to him.

DOUBLE-FAULT: Punctuality isn't one of my fortes and a girl sometimes appreciates a man who's a little late. It gives her a little more time to prepare. A person like N should give that some consideration.

FAULT: Then why make appointments for specific times? Don't you think people should be ready when they say they will be?

DOUBLE-FAULT: Yes, but you can't always predict what will happen and be so precise in your scheduling. You can't be so hard and fast as to time.

FAULT: In other words, people make mistakes. They can't correctly manage their time.

DOUBLE-FAULT: I wouldn't say it was a mistake. It just happens.

FAULT: Like N trying to chin himself on the door?

DOUBLE-FAULT: That's not the same, and you can't trade off his behavior for some lateness for some appointment. That's sheer nonsense, it makes no sense at all.

FAULT: I see. O.K., let me get back to their reunion. They exchanged a few words of greeting and J showed him the apartment. It was a cozy place, which is a polite way of saying it was a bit cramped. The living room served as a study and bedroom, with a desk, and a couch that became a bed. There was a nice-sized kitchen and a small bathroom with a shower stall. It was all J really needed for her work and the length of time she would be there. They left very soon and drove down to one of those roadside stands for custard. N would look at J out of the corner of his eye to see if she was excited or happy. She seemed self-controlled and talked pleasantly, but N couldn't tell at all what thoughts were passing through her head. He drove mechanically—talked, but didn't try to force conversation or dominate it, for that matter. He wanted to say something funny so they could both laugh, but it had to be spontaneous, and nothing presented itself for pun or comedy. They arrived at their destination, had their treat, and went back to J's. It took less than three-quarters of an hour and the conversation never lagged.

When they pulled up to the curb in front of J's apartment, N came around to her side, opened the door for her, and extended his hand to make it easy for her to get out. I hate to bore you with all this trivia, but the point is that it made N feel good to do such simple things for J even if she didn't need his help. It was a way of communication, of two people being together; at least that's how N saw it. He followed J down the path to her door, where she fumbled with her keys—she had so many—before she found the right one. She invited him in and he went most willingly. As soon as he closed the door behind him, he asked himself a question. He was alone with the woman he loved, in a private place, late in the evening, and he wanted to kiss her, hold her, take her to bed if she'd let him. His question was "Should I make an advance or shouldn't I?" and he didn't know how to answer it.

DOUBLE-FAULT: It seems so stupid to have this obsession with sex that N apparently has. You would think that after five months of not seeing J there would be enough to talk about to last more than an hour.

FAULT: Well, it's true N enjoyed sex, but in addition he was aware that he could learn what a girl really thought of him by the way she reacted to his advances. Sexual behavior is a good mirror of a person's inner self. You're shaking your head, but that's what N believed. Well, while N was in this momentary quandary, J turned on the light, took a step over to the window, and pulled the shade down so neighbors couldn't see into the room. That decided N. He would try. He came close to her, turned her around to face him, pulled her close enough to kiss, and—well—he kissed her. If she had resisted at any time, he would have let her go. But she didn't. Nor did she try to embrace him. Perhaps she was afraid N would think she was "cheap" or "easy" if she cooperated or showed any passion. But passion was definitely building in N. He wanted to lie next to J and press his body into hers. He pulled her to the floor where they could lie side by side. He wanted to use the bed but thought that J might object—a bed is too explicitly where the action is, and N didn't want to jeopardize anything he had already achieved. Seems stupid to me but that's what he thought. Lying with her on the floor, N became convinced that J wasn't going to run away, and he got more amorous. Above them the ceiling light was illuminating everything, so N quickly got up, flipped the light switch, and got back down. J received him kindly with kisses and played with him until his passion was spent. It totally relaxed him, he could feel the tension that time had built up in him flow out with his seed. It was abundantly clear that he was not anathema to J—not in the least.

DOUBLE-FAULT: Do you think N was surprised by the way the evening was going?

FAULT: Yes and no. He certainly didn't expect to end up with J on the floor. But he knew that when she accepted his invitation it was because of some need she had. As I told you, J admired N's mind, and he had always given her good advice and tried to help her when she wanted help. She certainly felt something for N, but he couldn't judge the quality or depth of her feelings. He did guess one thing that J confirmed later, and that was that the former boyfriend who had wanted to marry her was no longer of interest to her.

DOUBLE-FAULT: How did he guess that?

FAULT: N had told J a long time before, that the next time she saw the man she would know how she felt about him. And N knew that J had seen him when he came to N's country in the spring on a short business trip. The fact that she accepted his, N's, invitation had to mean that she wasn't serious about the other man, and what followed was even more convincing. Anyway, N had this hunch and it proved to be correct. The evening, if I may get back to the story, both rekindled all the love N had for J and frustrated him. He wanted to tell J how much he loved her, but he knew that those were precisely the words J didn't want to hear. They would have required her to make a decision, and he knew that she felt marriage was wrong for her at her age. So, since marriage was his goal, N kept silent about his love. Let me be clear about N's intentions toward J. She was not an object to be won in a game; he loved her for many solid reasons, and he believed that they could have a great life together. But he was puzzled by the fact that she could now lay her head on his chest and fall asleep so easily and comfortably with him, while for months she had allowed their relationship to be interrupted. When he left, later in the evening —both he and J were very tired—they made plans to see each other the next day. "Good night, J, see you tomorrow." "Good night, N, sleep well." "Sleep well," he thought—exactly what she used to say to him in the days before their breakup. Just like a phonograph needle that's been taken off the record and then replaced—but five months later.

DOUBLE-FAULT: Are you implying that J's responses to situations are mechanical—that when she says "Sleep well" it's because she's some sort of robot that puts out that message whenever a boyfriend leaves her at night? Don't you think she has feelings, too?

FAULT: I'll let you decide. N and J began to see each other daily, or at least talk for a short time every day. Time was something neither of them had enough of, for they were both busily trying to complete their work. Still they would go sunbathing together. N would get tanned and J would get red. And at night, sometimes, they would go for coffee. While N drove, J would put her arm around his shoulders and play with his hair or gently tickle the nape of his neck.

Although they talked frankly with each other, N chose not to speak of marriage. He was waiting for J to give him some positive hint in that direction, and she never did. In fact, she would say things like "Marriage scares me," which would depress him. He had the patience to wait for her to change, but he wasn't optimistic; J's inner clock indicated it would take years for her to come round to home and family. Still he couldn't really be sure it would be like that, and as each day passed his hopes soared.

The moment J was to leave the country was fast approaching. She had tried unsuccessfully to get a permanent job, but government regulations made it impossible for her to stay. N knew all this very well, and time spent with J was very precious to him. One night they went for a drive around the countryside. She started singing to him some of the many songs she knew, and he, as unmusical as he was, sang for her two or three of his pet tunes as best he could. J got a kick out of them—I imagine his voice made them more comical than they actually were. The stars were out and the countryside was lovely. J suggested they go to her office, since there was a piano there and she would play for N. This appealed to him greatly—J was very talented and N had rarely heard her play. There was also a small clavichord in the office, and J had a merry time with it. "You must hit the keys gently or the strings won't last, it's all so delicate," she pointed out to N. He also became very aware of her bent pinky finger. "I had to practice very long and hard to get proper strength into that one," she said. N could imagine how she went about it, for she was an exhaustive researcher and was probably more demanding on herself in her drive to achieve more than respectability at the piano.

From the office, they went back to J's apartment and as soon as they were inside the door they held each other tight. In all the time they had been together, in spite of all the sex games they had played, they had never had sexual intercourse. Most unusual relationship, and I think N accepted such a state of affairs because he loved her so much and wouldn't force her to give herself to him. N started to undress J while simultaneously shedding his own clothes. They were kissing each other amorously and soon J lay stretched out on the bed, her nakedness staring up at N. He surveyed her with the greatest pleasure and his hardness was apparent. Yet he had to have her verbal consent.

N: Do you want me, J? Is it all right with you?

J was silent, looking away from him. N asked again, and still no answer. He decided her silence was one of assent, since if she were against it she would certainly have declared so.

N: Is it safe, J, or should I get a contraceptive?

J shrugged her shoulders a little. N decided to be on the safe side and quickly went to where his pants were on the floor, and from his wallet fetched the impregnable filter.

N: Do you want to put it on me, J?

Still silence. He quickly tears open the packet and clothes his rod in the finest garment possible. He is quickly back to J, who has now turned over onto her stomach. He lies alongside her, his chest flush against her back. He wants to be gentle, loving, but J is slow to move, completely neutral in cooperation. He finally rights her, mounts her so that his knees push her legs apart, and penetrates her. It is for him a supreme moment. As for J, it appears she wants him but still has a mental or emotional barrier. N tries to be gentle and robust at the

32

same time, to stimulate J. But he himself is much too excited; his orgasm is too soon, their technique is by any standard text poor-to-mediocre. N is disappointed for J, who is not fully enjoying what nature allows, but he thinks that things will get better. He is right. A few nights later, J is more cooperative, more a partner. N feels the muscles in J's legs reacting to the sensations she feels in her crotch. Her body starts to thrust up and down as her breath comes faster and faster. As she reaches her climax, she raises her head off the bed and grabs N about his torso, her head beside his.

J: Come with me, darling.

N wanted to, but nature had a different time schedule worked out for him that night, and his ecstasy followed J's a few moments later. N was overjoyed in his heart, in his mind, in his body. He wanted J to bear their children and being inside her held out to him the hope that one day, without some inorganic material separating them, she would. All his hopes seemed closer to fulfillment. He now had no doubt that in spite of the tempests he and J had shared, she had a deep feeling for him—if it wasn't love, it was close to it. Incredible how sexual intercourse can be so illuminating about a person and what barriers it can push aside.

DOUBLE-FAULT: I would have to agree with you now that N did stir up something inside J and wasn't just imagining it all. I was impressed by the fact that she never slept with him even though you say they played games. It would be interesting to know what decided her.

FAULT: It would be more interesting to know, after she decided in favor of it, why she didn't go at it with more zeal.

DOUBLE-FAULT: What do you mean?

FAULT: As N told it to me, she wasn't really an active partner. She would just sort of lie there. She wasn't very athletic.

33

DOUBLE-FAULT: But there are all kinds of techniques. Perhaps the one she used produced the best possible stimulation for her.

FAULT: Perhaps, but N fretted about it just the same. He loved her so much.

DOUBLE-FAULT: Well, maybe N didn't put the blame where it really belonged—on himself. It's conceivable that it was his fault.

FAULT: Other long stories I could tell you would erase that hypothesis. It was probably that they needed getting accustomed to each other. N hoped that was the reason, but his over-all satisfaction was so great that he didn't let his doubts bother him. Can't have everything. Let me continue with my story and I'll try not to embroider it too much. One night they were lying in each other's arms. In a few days, J would be gone and N desired—"needed" would be more appropriate—to talk about the future with her. He dreaded the thought of such a conversation because, as I've said, a decision would have to be made, and he didn't think J was ready to make the one he was hoping for. But ready or not, now was the time to talk. Surprisingly, it was J who started the conversation, and without uttering a word. As she lay there, she began to cry.

N: What's the matter, darling?

J: I'm going to be leaving soon. [*She is looking very unhappy.*]

N: Yes, I know. [*Softly said—he waits to listen to what J will say next.*]

J: I didn't think I would feel so emotional about it.

N is elated to hear that her feelings have overwhelmed her logic. She continues:

J: I didn't think it would be me.

The word "me" rings in N's ear; "She knows I love her," he thinks. "She is surprised she feels so strongly about me." N decides to make a small speech which starts out with a question. He is going to gamble—not big—but gamble nevertheless.

N: Do you love me, J? Do you feel for me?

J: Yes, darling.

N: Look, J. You have to leave. That's been planned and decided. I'm going to leave here shortly myself. There are things you have to do and something I have to prove to myself. We'll write to each other and I'll come see you as soon as I can. The future will wait for us. [*J responds with lots of "Yes, darlings."*]

N knew he would be able to fulfill a commitment that would last perhaps a year, a commitment to stay in love with J and nourish that love even though they would be apart. He was gambling on the hunch that J's love for him would grow. It was to be the test of time. Being close to her, in her arms, made it seem a good gamble, but past experience would not allow him peace of mind. J was fickle, unsure, cautious, and frightened of her emotions—not the kind of person you'd expect would see her way to a fixed objective involving strong emotional commitments.

After this exchange, they slept fitfully in the small bed. The next day, J packed and that night N took her out to a fine restaurant for their last meal together. J had a good time and was sweet and loving to N. They came home, that being the word N now used to describe J's apartment, but to N's disbelief J asked him to go home so that she could get a good night's sleep in preparation for her traveling the next day. N wanted to scream at her, "How can you ask me to leave on your last night here?" but he didn't. He bit his tongue and made some innocuous comment like "O.K., see you early in the morning." He didn't really want another night of sex with her; he wanted another night of love. It disturbed him to think she could afford the luxury of giving up their last night together. The next morning, N called for J and took her, as he had once before, to the bus depot. Her baggage was placed on board, and she turned around to hug and kiss him, and was about to utter some endearment when the driver started to close the bus door. She ran from N's arms the one step required to get the driver to stop, and boarded the bus. She turned and waved to N and he waved back. He went to the end of the platform and watched the bus leave, and then he ran through the bus terminal and down the street to catch a last glimpse of the bus crossing the city street to get to its highway route. It took all his will power to keep the welling water in his eyes from cascading down his cheeks. He wondered where the tears went, since he did not cry. She was gone. That was a fact. And I'll wager you can't imagine how long it was till they saw each other again.

DOUBLE-FAULT: That wasn't a very complimentary description of J as a woman parting from N. If it were true, how could he love her, and if it weren't true, why should she love someone who saw her that way?

FAULT: He loved her not for what she was, but for what she could be. And he believed that he, with his values, virtues, and faults, would be the proper catalyst to bring about in J the calmness, the sureness, the confidence in the future that he himself had.

With J gone, N finished up some business details for her and spoke to her on the phone every few days. She was staying with friends in the city from which she would be leaving for her homeland. N thought of her endlessly. He thought it might be nice to see her off from the airport, but he couldn't get away from his work.

J left on schedule and they corresponded. Her letters were anxiously awaited by N and he became a hawk about his mailbox, going back to it even after the mail had arrived to see if there were any special-delivery letters for him. When there was no mail, he would try to figure out why J hadn't written. She couldn't be expected to write every day, of course, but she did write regularly and they were letters that raised N's spirits. She would sign them "Love and kisses x x x, J," and he would brush the letter against his lips. Her letters were affectionate and newsy and he would read them many times over, especially lines like "The old haunts don't feel the same any more" and "My heart is back there with you." He even enjoyed her handwriting—it was a beautiful scrawl. Oh, life felt good to N. He had hoped he would be able to visit J over the year-end holidays, as his work was finally finished. However, his funds were insufficient, and he sorrowfully wrote and told her that. She took it well, at least judging by her letters, and he said he would have the money to come in six months' time, and she wrote that that was a nicer time to visit anyway.

So, instead of going abroad, N headed for his new job in a new locale. He went to Boresville. He was happy, he was in love, and he was receiving loving thoughts from J. It was almost the best of all possible worlds.

DOUBLE-FAULT: Boresville, where's that?

FAULT: Boresville is located in the heartland. Where else? His new environment was interesting in the beginning, possibly because it was different. He met some nice people and was anxious to start on his work and do it well. He had absolutely no interest in girls despite J's comment that "the girls will be crazy about you out there." Let them be—to him they weren't even a distraction. But once again it was nice to know that J was, if not jealous, concerned. He had a concern, too. He wondered if J's old flame would try to get in touch with her.

He never mentioned this in his letters—he didn't want to appear jealous or insecure, but he did think about the possibility.

Only a month after he arrived in Boresville, N started getting impatient. He couldn't contain himself any longer, and he decided to tell J of his love for her and ask her to commit herself to marriage. He telephoned her first and told her he was going to write her a very important letter but wanted to tell her first that it was coming. She seemed so happy to hear his voice and he loved—sorry if I overwork that word—the sound of hers. She threw him a kiss over the phone, along with a "Goodbye, darling" and N was exhilarated. He sat down and composed the letter of his life. He wrote her about the kind of life he expected to lead and the kind of children he thought they would have. He asked her to share his life, contribute to it, embellish it, take from it, and be more important to him than anything else. He sent it special delivery and waited for the reply. It was a time of exquisite agony, of hopefulness, and fantastic tension.

DOUBLE-FAULT: I've come round in my thinking and have become quite fond of N. I hope J accepts his proposal. He seems to be so kind to her, and helpful.

FAULT: You surprise me. But wait, now, listen to this.

Almost two weeks passed before a letter from J arrived. It wasn't clear to N why it should take so long to get an answer to such a serious question. When he got her letter at last, he went to a private, quiet place and sat down to find out what was to be. His heart was pounding so hard he could feel the pressure on his brain from the pulse of flowing blood in his temples.

DOUBLE-FAULT: I am sure she'll accept his proposal. I know it.

FAULT: She rejects him and asks him not to be angry with her for doing so. She tells him she loves him but can't bring herself to settle down in marriage. J leaves it up to N to decide whether to continue writing or not. She adores hearing from him, misses him, loves him—but no marriage.

DOUBLE-FAULT: What a pity.

FAULT: N is shattered. He writes J again to tell her he will always want to write her and he appreciates her honesty. He does, however, want to know how long she wants to be on her own with her work. He doesn't ask this question outright, but hopes the answer will become apparent to him in her future letters.

Their correspondence continues, and J makes it perfectly clear that she wants to pursue her career for at least a few years. But she tells him again and again that she looks forward to seeing him in the summer.

DOUBLE-FAULT: Her decision to further her career may be for the best and N shouldn't feel too bad.

FAULT: That sounds realistic enough. N was pleased she still wanted him to come visit. He clung to the hope that if they saw each other once more her emotions would overwhelm her logic and she wouldn't be able to bear their parting.

DOUBLE-FAULT: It's his only hope, isn't it?

FAULT: Yes, and he couldn't wait for the months to pass. With each letter J wrote, she told him how she simply longed for him to visit. His hopes kept soaring.

DOUBLE-FAULT: I shouldn't worry if I were he. With words like that—J will change her tune about marriage as spring affects her. Women are so romantic in spring.

FAULT: Perhaps you should be a weather forecaster. Because on the first of May, J wrote N that she didn't want N to visit her in the summer. Out of the clear blue romantic sky!

DOUBLE-FAULT: Why on earth did she do that?

FAULT: She thought, quite correctly, that the whole question of marriage would come up again, and she didn't want to be confronted with what that entails emotionally. J felt they were headed in different directions, and the path would become tortuous if they met at another crossroad. Again, she left the decision for continued correspondence up to N. And she signed the letter, "Love, J." N felt as if he'd been stabbed in the back. All the expectations, the promise of reunion, had become illusion. He wrote to J in the hope of convincing her to let him come to visit not as a lover but as a friend. He tried to change the basis for the trip. Her next letter was dated late May, a very long time since the previous letter.

DOUBLE-FAULT: She probably warded him off by telling him she had a busy schedule. And if she doesn't want to see him he should accept that.

FAULT: You're much better now than you were on weather predictions. She told him where she would be and what she would be doing, and she made it plain he wasn't wanted. But he wanted to go and he's stubborn. He wrote again but controlled his pen and made no mention of still wanting to go.

DOUBLE-FAULT: Good for N. Most mature.

FAULT: She replied—again it's a month between letters. This time she opened up the door for visiting—but in a negative way.

DOUBLE-FAULT: How so?

FAULT: She wrote that although she was sick and tired of dragging a deluge of visitors around sightseeing she hoped to be recovered "when (if) he arrived." Not a very positive statement. But he ignored the negativism so explicitly implicit. He wrote quickly—he would come in August. It suited his schedule beautifully. She wrote back immediately. She was explicitly explicit, I'm afraid to say. Her schedule was light-years behind and she was sick and tired, once again, of being "guide, counselor, and friend" to inundating visitors. "I have no time for you, N—is that clear?" And she signed the letter simply "J." The words "guide, counselor, and friend" sting N. He detests being thought of as a lovesick puppy in need of soothing words, as if he can't "solve" his own emotional affairs. The quickness of the reply burns him a little, too, and the fact that J didn't sign it "Love, J" infuriates him. Her previous letter talked about "when (if) he arrived." As for her schedule being miles behind—sheer unadulterated nonsense. That schedule does what she wants it to do. She implies she was nice to visitors who "inundated" her but she hasn't got time to be nice to N. Amazing. Absolutely amazing.

DOUBLE-FAULT: It's rather obvious she didn't want to see him in spite of all her declarations about how she likes writing and hearing from him. She was only being polite when she made reference to N's coming, and you notice she put in a parenthetical "if." He should have taken the hint, but it's clear he didn't want to. So she bludgeoned him to make him understand.

FAULT: I agree with all you've said and I am sure N thought that, too. But his love for her—what can I say?—he deliberately ignored all warnings, hoping for a miracle of sorts. Let me backtrack in time somewhat. When J originally wrote and said that marriage was not for her, N was, to put it mildly, disappointed, but he took it manfully, and wrote her that he wished her well and the best of all possible success in whatever she attempted. And in fact in one of her letters, a section I didn't speak of, she wrote that he was very understanding. So their relationship was still a good one, even if off course as far as N was concerned.

N started to devour himself with thoughts about J. Had he asked her to consider marriage too soon? Should he have waited until he actually visited with her in the summer? In other words, had his timing been smart or totally counter-productive? In retrospect, N decided that his timing had not been crucial, that there had been such long gaps between her letters it was clear that an unstoppable momentum was building up to shove J into a career. N recalled something that J had once said to him together with her "Marriage scares me" statement. "And besides," she had added, "too many people are counting on me." When he asked what she meant by that, she explained that she had spent so many years developing her skills that not to use them would be a big disappointment to her family. It suggested she felt that even if she loved someone she had to stay single in order to have a career, that she would not or could not let her love interfere. That thought frightened N—to know that someone whom he desperately loved loved him and wouldn't act positively on it.

Boresville became for N an impossible, intolerably dull place to live. His concentration on his work suffered, he was always thinking of J. His bedroom became a prison, it could not be a resting place. This day-in, day-out, all-night confrontation with his fading hopes made for the unhappiest period of his life. There was nothing but solitude and thoughts that could not be challenged, evaded, or turned away. It was worse than his self-exile when he and J were living near each other. Now his only link to her was her letters, which became less and less frequent and said what he had hoped he'd never read. He had known that someday she would write the first of May letter that started out "There's something I want to tell you and if it sounds a bit cruel . . ." That's when he had tried to be a contortionist, to change the basis of his intended visit. But J was equal to fending him off—her schedule, which could be amended, according to the earlier letters, now became a rigid structure insusceptible to change. What exhausted N was trying to guess the *reasons* behind her sudden resistance to the idea of his visit. In one letter he's expected, in the next he's not. What happened? Did anything happen? Was pressure applied by one of those people who were "counting on her"? N didn't know, and couldn't ask. J hated people who demanded chapter and verse about her, who harassed her.

DOUBLE-FAULT: This all sounds so very sad. Do you think J knew how N was taking this?

FAULT: It was absolutely impossible for her to appreciate his dilemma, and not because she didn't understand suffering. He hid his thoughts from her and how they drove him to distraction. He never wrote anything more than a "hope to hear from you soon" in his letters, which can mean almost anything from nothing to next-to-nothing. J could have no real evidence of the effect of her words on N, and if she had any inkling at all she thought that although it might hurt now, it was for the best in the long run. What else could she think?

DOUBLE-FAULT: Probably true. She couldn't have been as unhappy as N, do you think?

FAULT: Never. She never would have refused to see him if she felt anything for N near to what he felt for her. It was mostly a one-sided love, despite her wanting to hear from him. And when she said she felt a glow from reading his letters, one could only think that was a second-class emotion.

It's too awful to recount more of N's distress during this period but there is one bit worth telling. N decided to phone J in June, after he received the late May letter. That was the letter in which J said she had no time for him. It was a last straw for him, and he hoped that hearing his voice would revive memories in her that would impel her to say "Yes, N, please come." It was also conceivable to him that she would carry on like a termagant excoriating him for bothering her when she had already made her position quite clear.

They speak, and her voice sounds perfectly melodic to him, just as he remembered it from his previous call and from the

43

preceding summer. She is warm and sweet over the phone and concerned. He explains how he's been looking forward to seeing her, and even if she can't see her way to marriage he would still like to come. He talks calmly and surely. This is no time for begging or pleading. J listens and tells him that her schedule is complicated. He replies that she needn't guide him around, that he's not that keen on looking at old relics or buildings. She says it is still best that he not come and that they had better end the call before it becomes very expensive. It already is that, for it's gone on ten minutes. They both say good-bye, and perhaps it is electrical noise on the connection but it sounds as if J has blown him a kiss at the very end. The phone is replaced on its cradle and N goes out onto the sidewalk back to his office—back to work. The sun is bright, the temperature very hot, the sky the proverbial blue with puffs of white clouds—and he is depressed, the lowest he has ever felt in his life. The realization that he will never see J again comes to him as an absolute truth. His depression is beyond description—life is completely empty. He passes a friend whom he greets cheerfully and with a smile—he looks as bright and happy as everyone around him, but inside him a continuing nightmare is settling in.

DOUBLE-FAULT: N's unhappiness is easy to comprehend, but much of it was created by himself. Still, it would have been interesting and possibly helpful to him to understand what prompted J's vacillations.

FAULT: Do you think she vacillated?

DOUBLE-FAULT: It certainly appears so—first she was for his coming, then against it, and then she opened the door a little and slammed it shut again. If she had remained adamantly against it after changing her mind the first time, then it might not have been so bad for N as the interminable discussion of J's schedule and the possibility that he could somehow fit in it. What did N do after he finally accepted the final "no"?

FAULT: Life was hellish for him. Day after day of unremitting, heavy depression followed. No amount of logic or facing up to the situation mollified his inner unhappiness. Outwardly his appearance and manner remained calm and imperturbable. N mockingly thought of himself as one of the world's leading actors—a tragedian the equal of any who walked the stage. If anyone were to ask him for a synonym for melancholia, he could sardonically reply with some justification, "N." He did what he had to do—built a shell around himself and went to work to make it absolutely impenetrable. He would not be fit company for anyone until his J-sickness was cured, and he had to prevent the disease from spreading by isolating the region of greatest contagion. He would have to find in himself and by himself the medicine requisite for cure. He had done it before, he would do it again, and he knew it would be very, very difficult to accomplish.

I've never stressed this, but N was a tennis player of considerable competence—not great, but sufficiently adept to surprise better players once in a while. And in the hope of burning away the excess energy his mind generated, he began to play tennis like a maniac. He ran after impossible shots instead of conserving his energy. He rushed the net, ran for lobs, ran for wide shots, ran for short shots—just ran, ran, ran all over the court. When the sun went down and play had to stop, he would pray that he had tired himself sufficiently so that he could climb into bed and fall asleep. As I intimated, bed was an impossible place for him to be—a prison—for in bed there was no escaping the desire he had for J. Sleep required lying down quietly with no activity, and to put himself in a supine position with thoughts of J in his head was simply torture. Even with all his running, sleep never came easily, since N had boundless energy. He would sleep lightly, wake up, wonder about J, stay in bed till light of day came through the window, and then leave to play tennis. He would be tired all day, but to look at him chasing balls on the court, you couldn't guess it.

And each night again the same ritual. It was an impossible situation.

By August, the month he had hoped to visit J, he had reduced his agony to a point of mere depression. Or should I say he had raised his spirits to the point of sheer depression? N lived alone, as I've told you, and he discovered that if he allowed himself to stay alone for long periods of time, he became the inquisitor at his own inquisition. He would question himself for hours on end, give himself no peace. And yet he still chose to be by himself. It was the only way—being with people didn't stop his thinking about J, and so he preferred to be alone and not burden anyone else with his travail.

He went on a month's vacation in August—two weeks with his family and two weeks back to where he had met J. He still had many friends there, and when he was in their company he would sometimes surprise himself by not thinking of J for minutes on end. He was actually getting some peace, and an occasional moment of pleasure. But still J haunted him. N did something—or, rather, didn't do something—that caused him chagrin. He avoided driving by the house where he and J had spent such marvelous times together. Then, because he felt foolish about it, he deliberately drove by the place. Seeing it gave him a twinge of melancholy—started him thinking again of what might have been. He sent J a postcard.

DOUBLE-FAULT: Isn't it sad the way old haunts can keep coming back to you? Life might be so much easier if horrible recollections could be swallowed up by a monster that would "eat" things we wanted to forget.

FAULT: That would be some odd monster! But I couldn't think of him as really monstrous.

DOUBLE-FAULT: True. He would be so useful.

FAULT: But remember, if you had the power to rid yourself of all bad memories with the aid of this monster, then all you would have left would be good memories. And then you're in trouble, because things are only good relative to other things that are bad, and since you have no bad memories your good memories would cease being good.

DOUBLE-FAULT: Ha-ha—that kind of reasoning needs to be forgotten.

FAULT: Quick! Get the monster!

DOUBLE-FAULT: Better to go on with the story. I feel so peaceful and serene here listening to you.

FAULT: Well, N had reached the point where he had to do something he knew he wouldn't be happy about, but something that needed to be done. Sex. He hadn't had any in a long time and he was no monk.

DOUBLE-FAULT: I think N is perfectly right. Life can be so wearying without sex. But it's much better when you do love someone.

FAULT: So true. N is walking down a street and sees coming toward him an attractive young woman. He quickly discerns that she wears no wedding ring, and from her appearance and the neighborhood he guesses that she is just what he would like to meet—an unattached girl who is busy with her work and might like to have a good time with someone who won't be around long.

DOUBLE-FAULT: Where is this taking place?

FAULT: Sorry. It's still in the place where he and J first met. N acts quickly: he stops midway on the sidewalk and more or less prevents the girl from passing. She could get by if she wanted to, and I don't mean to suggest that N is acting malevolently toward her. Quite the contrary, he appears friendly and looks at her with a quizzical expression, as if he were wondering . . .

N: Excuse me. But haven't we met before? [*N is appalled at how obvious that must sound but he doesn't really care. If she's hoping to meet someone, it doesn't matter too much how he begins. He doesn't recognize her from anywhere and he has an excellent memory for faces.*]

THE GIRL: What? [*Taken aback that someone is speaking to her, she comes to a halt.*]

N: I said, "Excuse me. But haven't we met before?" I have an excellent memory for faces and I thought we had met before. I haven't been back here in a year and I'm here for only one more week. [*He volunteers this information to make her feel more comfortable and to set her thinking along the hoped-for lines.*] I thought we had met before. My name is N.
[*She shocks him.*]

THE GIRL: Yes, we've met before. It was at ————. Remember?
[*He doesn't remember, and then maybe he does. She looks different from the girl he recalls, but maybe not. Anyway, it doesn't matter to him.*]

N: I was there all right. Were you the one who served the cookies with the punch?

THE GIRL: I might have. I don't remember, but I did help out.

N: I'm afraid I don't recall your name.

THE GIRL: My name is T.G.

N: Well, it was nice meeting you.

T.G.: Nice to see you, too.

N leaves and goes back to where he is staying and looks up T.G.'s phone number in the directory. He feels it best if he calls and gives her the opportunity to accept or reject his invitation to go out. To have asked her on the street he feels would have been bad form.

DOUBLE-FAULT: I didn't think he cared too much about form, from the way he used that direct approach.

FAULT: N doesn't believe that rules and mores should frighten you away from doing things you want, as long as you respect other people's sensibilities. Some people are too sensitive about form, and others, I suppose, not enough. With N, if it didn't hurt other people or cause them grief, he saw no reason not to do what he wanted.

DOUBLE-FAULT: Still, I'll wager he ran afoul sometimes.

FAULT: To be sure. Like that night at J's door when he tried to chin his way into her heart. He had upset her and he suffered severely for it. He waited approximately ten minutes before calling T.G. This was all the time she would need to reach her destination, and N couldn't afford the luxury of waiting till evening to call. It might be too late by then or he might not find her home, et cetera, et cetera, et cetera.

N: Hello. May I speak to T.G., please? [*Polite*]

T.G.: This is she.

N: This is N.

T.G.: So soon! [*And she laughs.*]

N: I'm glad you find it amusing. [*He says it in good humor.*] Would you like to get together for dinner this evening?

T.G.: [*A short pause*] Yes, I would.

Let me rush through the evening. They go out, she likes him and finds him interesting. He likes her, she's a fine person—intelligent. She is good to look at and stirs him into discomfort when he sits opposite her at dinner. He's in a hurry. After dinner they go for a drive. Thoughts of J. He parks the car in a lonely spot. Thoughts of J. He excites her, and in spite of the fact that it's their first evening together she lets him dominate her and she plays with him. Thoughts of J. The next night he sleeps with her under the stars on a lawn. Thoughts of J. In a week, he realizes T.G. would love him and marry him if he were willing. Thoughts of J. He knows he doesn't love T.G. and probably never will. His heart is with J. He feels bad about T.G. He doesn't want her to go through the same great sorrow he did.

At the end of the week, without any future commitment, indeed with negative responses to T.G.'s obvious, even if unspoken, thoughts of the future, N leaves to go back to work in Boresville. His friends have lifted his spirits, and T.G. was what he needed physically even if he hates himself for the possible grief he may be causing her. The word "hate" is too strong. N doesn't hate himself. What he hates is that things have turned out the way they have.

Once back in Boresville, he throws himself into his work. At night, visions of T.G.'s body are intermixed with thoughts of J. In less than a month his spirits are down, he dislikes his work, and the place seems even more unattractive than before. Something else is brewing, too. Immediately on his arrival back in Boresville, he gets a letter from J. She acknowledges receipt of the card he had sent her and ends the letter with "Love, J." A far different ending from the simple "J" of her last letter. N writes back to J and receives no reply. He writes again and receives no reply. He is worried that she might have found a boyfriend. The weeks become months. He writes her again:

Dear J:

I think it's very discourteous of you not to have the decency to write me and ask me not to write any more if my letters bother you, especially in view of how many times you've told me how you like hearing my news and telling me yours. I also thought that you might be more considerate of me on the basis of what we once meant to each other.

If you are ill or in trouble or anything like that, I would do all I could to assist you and if that is the case, I apologize for the tone and content of the remarks made at the beginning of this letter.

Love, N.

N had upbraided J for her "form," her "manners," and he knew that was something she would react to, since she set so much store by those qualities. He got a reply. She wrote as usual about being extremely busy. She told him she'd been depressed, that she didn't want to see anybody. Hibernation, that's a good word to describe her wants. J was so profuse in her apologies to him about not writing and even went so far as to tell him how bad she felt—"extremely guilty for not having written sooner." She sent him love and kisses, and then added, "There is much I haven't said and much I can't write about. But I still love hearing from you."

DOUBLE-FAULT: She sounds as if she almost wants to talk to him. Must have been something rather important on her mind.

FAULT: Yes. It makes him believe he is still special to her. He accepts the apology, of course, and he tries to analyze the letter for its most microscopic meaning. He notices that J spends a lot of time saying nothing about what's causing her slight depression and then reminds him of it with her postscript. She reminisces a little—there are comments about how wonderful it was with N and how glorious the old times were. N feels as he always did when he reads those lines. There's something in him that she likes, admires, and needs. Why doesn't she want it always? He can't answer that question without knowing more about her relationship with her career and with those people who are "counting on her." He is both happy and unhappy with the letter. He interprets it as a reaffirmation of J's liking for him, but he has almost no clue as to what is bothering her or has caused her such grief. He notices that when J makes a mistake or is in the wrong she becomes sweetness and light to atone for it. He writes her but doesn't ask what made her so depressed. He wishes her well and says he hopes that she will be happy again soon.

He is very unhappy. His work doesn't stimulate him and everything is dull. He is sexually frustrated once more. He had written to T.G. and she had written back that she was surprised to hear from him. Apparently she hadn't become as involved with him as he thought she had. He is glad. They agree to meet for a week in a big city near Boresville over the year-end holiday. They do so, and in five days he has used her to relieve his sexual frustration, hurt her emotionally—he would never hurt a woman physically—by telling her he doesn't love her or want to marry her, and reminded himself how unhappy he is. They part on strained terms, she entreating him to tell her what's bothering him and he adamantly refusing to talk about his J-disease. She has been so nice, it's a shame for her to suffer because of J's emotional hold on N.

DOUBLE-FAULT: But that's not fair to J. She didn't feel she was holding N back, nor did she ask for that behavior from him.

FAULT: Very true, and I didn't mean to imply it was J's machinations that determined the state of affairs between T.G. and N. In fact, I haven't implied that, and N never would either.

Six months later, N leaves Boresville. These have been months of unending self-analysis, self-projection, self-denial, self-inflicted mental anguish. He has fought against himself,

52

he has fought for himself, he has struggled, and he has survived—as he knew he would. Time was his narcotic, his pain-deadener. And as spring came, N started to feel a renascence. And leaving Boresville proved to be another step in the right direction. He had a card from J just before his year-end holiday and had not heard from her since—over six months. He sent her his new address, but for the first time in the almost three years he had known J, he felt free of her.

DOUBLE-FAULT: That last part went a little too fast for me. What happened again? There's something I don't understand.

FAULT: Well, briefly, J stopped writing from December to June. N wrote her once—in February, I think—and then again when he left Boresville so she would have his new address. In that time, he grappled with himself almost constantly and finally managed to free himself from her.

DOUBLE-FAULT: Why didn't he write to her and demand some sort of answer as to why she wouldn't correspond?

FAULT: He felt he couldn't keep forcing himself on her. After all, from a practical point of view they were separated by thousands of miles and he had no emotional hold on her. And more to the point, he felt it was absolutely worthless to gain J's attention by demanding that she correspond with him. It would never lead to her loving him, and it was too bizarre a way of nourishing the relationship. So he left Boresville thinking it very possible he would never hear from J again.

DOUBLE-FAULT: You're joking. He had loved her so much, surely he still had some hope?

FAULT: Well—infinitesimal at most. Let me go on. N moved to Freedom, a very large city that offered much more than Boresville. Securely settled down in his new surroundings, N went about his way to fill his world with new acquaintances. Specifically, he hungered for a woman, particularly for sex.

53

Nestled amid the buildings in the area where he worked were to be found, as you might guess—

DOUBLE-FAULT: Tennis courts!

FAULT: Right! Half a dozen friendly, coercing, attracting tennis courts. And so, with the usual expectation that he would meet people who could introduce him to other people, N went over to this enclave of endearing labor and asked an un-partnered player who had come to the courts looking for a game if he would be interested in singles. The man was interested, and they began to play. Within an hour's time, N had outclassed him, beating him handily even though he was a fair player. While they were playing, the man's wife showed up and N had an idea. Why didn't the man and his wife and he and some other girl get together to play mixed doubles? That was a fine idea, they thought, and then N told them that he was new in the neighborhood and didn't have a partner. Would they bring someone? The wife quickly volunteered that she had a friend whom she would ask, and why not play tomorrow? "Why not?" says N, and the time of meeting was agreed upon.

The next day, the weather was more than favorable and N arrived with the hope that his partner would be pretty and after a fashion—if you follow his line of thought, and I'm sure you do—would be willing after a while. All three of his fellow players were already there—one of the few times in N's life when he came last to an appointment, although he was still on time. Introductions were made by the wife. "N, this is L-One, L-One—N." "Pleased to meet you," and all that nonsense followed.

DOUBLE-FAULT: Introductions *are* important and first impressions mean a lot. You never know whom you are meeting.

FAULT: Yes, yes. Let me tell you of N's first impression of L-One. Three things struck him right away. First, she was wearing a clean short-sleeved blue shirt whose sleeves were raggedy, and her shorts were not tennis shorts; second, she was cute, though slightly shorter than he would have liked; and third, L-One was a bit flat-chested.

DOUBLE-FAULT: My word! All he cared to do was size her up physically and criticize her. Some nerve!

FAULT: Well, it's very unusual for a girl not to be fashionably dressed for tennis. They dress well even if they can't play. And he wasn't criticizing, just observing. She was neatly attired and had nothing to be ashamed of, and he did say she was cute, very cute.

DOUBLE-FAULT: Well, all right. But most of it sounded like carping.

FAULT: Well, it wasn't meant to be. I'll go on. The game commenced, and as it progressed N became more and more the dominant figure. The others would hit the ball back and forth, but when N got his racket on it he hit it for a winner. He was polite, backed up L-One very well, didn't hog the shots. The more he watched L-One, the more fascinated he became with her smile. It was really a beautiful smile, and it made him feel good. And she had a wonderfully gentle, happy-sounding laugh. Not one of those booming guffaws, but a laugh that left you with the impression that something really funny had happened. When she made errors, she was very good-humored about it. N was surprised at the agility she brought to her play—she kept making shots N was sure she wouldn't be able to make. Alas, their opponents became sullen and rasping toward each other as their defeat became surer and surer. "Ahh—to be married," N thought. Some people expect to win all the time and have incredibly logical excuses when they don't. N and L-One endured a session of mutterings after the play was ended. Then a few last smiles and "Thank you"s and they all went on their respective ways.

55

DOUBLE-FAULT: You mean to tell me that N didn't date L-One?

FAULT: That's right. He didn't try. N thought about L-One and wondered what he should do, could do, wanted to do with her. She wasn't sexy enough for him, but then again a man who's been drinking at a dry well for over six months can't be choosy. Next day N showed up at the tennis courts alone, and there, sitting in the stands alongside the courts, was L-One. What luck!

N: Do you have a partner?

L-ONE: No.

N: Would you like to hit a few?

L-ONE: Yeah.

And so the two of them stepped out on the court again, this time on opposite sides of the net, and started to rally. N was good at hitting balls to women, let's give him credit—he had spent a lot of time at it. But L-One was different. First, she could run very well—most girls can't—and she had a fierce determination to get to every ball and hit it back; she never gave up. The game was new to her and she wanted to excel at it. The more N watched that little figure run, the more he observed her pretty smile, the more he saw that yellow pony-tail bouncing around, the more he wanted to take her to bed. It was that simple. She aroused him.

DOUBLE-FAULT: Is N easily aroused?

FAULT: No. He's very particular, but he has sometimes lowered his standards.

DOUBLE-FAULT: I think it's awful how callous men can be sometimes. Treat women like they were sacks of flour.

FAULT: Would you sleep with any man?

DOUBLE-FAULT: No, of course not.

FAULT: Then be quiet. This desire that was building up in N had another effect. For the first time, it made him feel free inside, not inhibited by J's memory, and it felt *good*.

When they had finished playing, N suggested to L-One that they go back to his place and that he would drive her home from there.

DOUBLE-FAULT: But he had other ideas, didn't he?

FAULT: Of course. She was agreeable to the suggestion. And so the two of them, with their tennis rackets sometimes cradled in N's arms, sometimes balanced on his shoulder, walked the short distance to the train station, making small talk. N was wondering whether L-One would sleep with him. He furtively sized her up and down, and the more he saw those lithe legs, the more aroused down below he became. It occurred to N how amusing it would be to walk down a street observing the distance of other men's pants from their bodies, thus gaining some insight into the state of mind of the wearers. He felt that if the public were to read *his* pants he would be labeled "pornographic." "Best to think about something else till we get to my place," N chided himself. They had a short wait at the train station before boarding; L-One sat by a window and N sat reasonably close to her. She had a nice habit of beginning a funny story by saying a few words and then laughing or giggling before continuing. It was infectious really, and as soon as she'd laugh N would smile along with her. She was so full of pep and energy—she bubbled over. The trip seemed even shorter than it really was, because they found each other so entertaining. They left the train at N's stop and two minutes later they were entering his door. He had a two-bedroom apartment with a living room, dinette, and kitchen, which was much more than he needed, but he liked space. He showed L-One around, saving his bedroom for last.

DOUBLE-FAULT: Does he always plot and scheme so?

FAULT: What should he have done? Should he have asked L-One, "Will you sleep with me?" when they were back on the tennis court? Plotting and scheming—L-One deserves some consideration. Some girls will refuse to sleep with a man even when they like the idea if he doesn't use some tact in getting them to a suitable place.

DOUBLE-FAULT: [*With some heat*] Well, there should be a better way.

FAULT: All right, you think of it while I go on. Where was I? Oh, yes—they're in the bedroom now; her back is to him and the bed is in front of her. He wants to succeed but he has to be gentle, too. One must always make it seem as if the girl could stop the sequence of events easily. N puts his hands on L-One's shoulders and slowly turns her around. So far so good. He wraps his arm around her body and pulls her tightly against him. So far so good. They kiss and L-One is not one to hang back. So far so good. N walks or stumbles or moves L-One with his body till they fall, he on top of her, onto the bed. He is hard and firm and she knows it. So far so good. He doesn't ask her and he doesn't talk. He unbuckles her belt and zips open her shorts and pulls them off. She either will or she won't, and so far so good. He hasn't bothered with her shirt for he isn't interested in that area at the moment, he just wants to be inside a woman. However, L-One takes off her shirt and is N surprised! She has beautiful, well-proportioned breasts that exquisitely match the rest of her figure. She is absolutely the ultimate in tawny, kittenish looks. So far so very good. L-One is aroused, has been aroused long before. He puts on a contraceptive that he always keeps within reach of the bed, gets back on top of her, and she accepts him.

DOUBLE-FAULT: Thank you for leaving out the four-letter words.

FAULT: I couldn't tell it any other way. N looked on this orgasm as the beginning of a new "era" and the ending of a monastic life. L-One had her orgasm almost immediately and kept having one after another. N thought she was remarkable, particularly since he was having his usual first-time difficulties.

After his emission, he lay in L-One enjoying their mutual smell, when suddenly L-One began to shake her head back and forth with a frenzied anguished look contorting her face, and then she started to beat N about his head and shoulders with her fists. N thought that perhaps she was having second thoughts about what had just happened, and he tried to soothe her and his conscience at the same time by saying softly to her such original lines as "Didn't you want this?" and "It's what you wanted, wasn't it?" and "I thought you wanted this, too." Really clever! He let her hit him some more, and she could hit—he decided she could easily get to be flyweight champion of the world. She didn't stop. He tried to protect himself by putting his head as close to her ear as possible, but that wasn't enough protection, so he grabbed her wrists and held them till she calmed down. L-One had tears in her eyes and N felt sorry for her, and although he was physically relieved after such a long drought he felt that perhaps he had been selfish. He tried to comfort L-One, to kiss her softly on the cheeks, to make her feel wanted and appreciated. After a while, she regained her composure. They talked briefly about her reaction, N hoping to hear that L-One didn't hate him, and she didn't. She said it had been a long time since she had last slept with anyone and it sort of threw her to do it again. N understood. Girls are sometimes like that. Later he drove her home and acted warmly and solicitously toward her.

DOUBLE-FAULT: It was nice of N not to be cold and unkind to L-One. In spite of his lust, you make him out to have some sort of conscience. That must have been a frightful experience for L-One. Things are always so difficult for women.

[*Fault raises his eyebrows at that last comment but doesn't wish to get involved in a male-female discussion that would surely lead to argument. He continues.*]

FAULT: I'm afraid I have to change the mood of the story abruptly, but this is important. The house where L-One lived was a beautiful one of stonemasonry surrounded by half an acre of luxuriant lawns, trees, and flowers. It was in a posh residential district outside of Freedom about—oh, I should say twenty minutes' drive from the tennis courts. The house, the courts, and N's apartment might have been the points of an equilateral triangle. That should give you some idea of the geography. L-One didn't save any time by going to N's place first and then having him drive her home, so she must have wanted to be in his company. But I digress. The house itself was big, roomy, solid—the kind of house a family could live and love in and feel that their lives were private from their neighbors. It had many large rooms and several small studies where one could sit and read and dream. N had always wanted a home like that, especially with those grounds. And yet he sensed that L-One rejected the whole lot. The image of L-One's raggedy tennis shirt didn't seem to jibe with N's sixth sense about the people who lived in that house. The place was too fastidiously kept. L-One had clean clothes—that fit; but they were ragamuffin clothes—and that didn't.

DOUBLE-FAULT: He's making far too much of L-One's clothes. I don't see how he could possibly jump to such conclusions.

[*Fault ignores Double-Fault's comment.*]

FAULT: L-One was living alone, because her father—who is a doctor, incidentally—was away at a conference, and her mother and two sisters were traveling around the country. The only real chore L-One had was to feed the dog. N stayed with L-One for about an hour and then told her he had to get some sleep because he was tired and had to start work early the next day. It turned out that L-One worked at the same place as N,

60

although not in the same building, and it was easy for them to arrange to play tennis again late the next afternoon. Which was fortunate, because N liked L-One—enjoyed her company and enjoyed seeing her on the opposite side of the net.

The next day, they met, played hard, enjoyed it immensely, and once again took the train back to N's place. As they sat next to each other on the train, they held hands and N knew his passion was beginning to boil and sensed the same in L-One. The train ride seemed interminable. When he opened the door to his apartment, L-One rushed through and headed straight for the bedroom, and N was right in back of her. He dropped the rackets just inside the door, and as L-One was throwing off her clothes she said, "You can have anything you want, do anything you want." In seconds, they were naked on the bed engaged in a private bacchanalia without the drink part. Just the orgy part. What a difference a day makes!

The next few days were nearly ideal—work, play, and hot physical passion with a partner N genuinely liked. L-One and N were like faucets—each could be turned on at the desire of the other. It was a time of discovery for both of them. Their talk was a kind of probing—definitely not prying, please— which ebbed and flowed but was never rushed. They talked of their pasts, their affairs, but N never mentioned J.

DOUBLE-FAULT: Why not? Was she still special to him?

FAULT: Oh, I suppose so. I guess J was exactly the kind of woman N wanted, and he felt it wouldn't be fair to L-One to let her know that she was competing against his ideal. N could very easily see loving L-One, and how often does any man meet his ideal? When it comes to marriage, most people settle for less, and if he and L-One were to get serious, having told her the story of J mightn't turn out to be a good idea.

N wasn't exactly shocked to hear L-One tell him that she

had had her first love affair when she was sixteen. It was during a summer vacation. N asked how she liked it—physical love at such an early age—and she looked at him as if he were peculiar and replied, "Fine." N laughed.

N: How old was the man?

L-ONE: He was an eighteen-year-old kid.

N: You were a sixteen-year-old kid. Remember? How did it end?

L-ONE: One day I told him I didn't want it from him any more.

N: Just like that.

L-ONE: Yeah.

N: What did he say or do?

L-ONE: He didn't say anything. He just cried.

N could believe it. L-One would really be something to lose, especially for a young stud.

DOUBLE-FAULT: Didn't this early promiscuity bother N? After all, sixteen is rather young.

FAULT: Oh, no. The past is the past. N was more interested in the future.

In one short week, N was coming around to feeling love and attachment for L-One. He was thinking marriage; he didn't say so but he was thinking it. And then came "The Observation" that turned N upside down and inside out. It came like a shot, and the impact of it will haunt N for the rest of his life. It occurred during one of their love-making festivals when N, his eyes focusing on L-One's arms, was shocked to realize that some marks he had vaguely noticed up and down the insides of her arms were actually a series of healed slashes. And in one or two places freshly formed scabs. He looked in disbelief. Surely they were knife slashes. N was galvanized; he had to know the origin and meaning of what he saw. Question after question followed answer after answer.

N: What's that?

L-One: What?

N: Those marks on your arms.

L-One: They're knife slashes.

N: Who did it?

L-One: I did it.

N: Why?

L-One: I just did it.

N: That's no answer. How long have you been doing that to yourself?

L-One: About three years.

N: Those scabs, they're fresh. When did you cut yourself last?

L-One: About four days ago.

N: The day after we were first together. When? After I left you at home?

L-One: Yes.

N: What's going on? Why? Come on, talk. Tell me.

L-One: It's a long story.

N: I want to hear it. Let's go—out with it. [*N is speaking softly here—not giving orders.*]

L-One: I don't know where to begin. [*Said with a small laugh*]

N: Try the beginning. [*He didn't say it facetiously.*]

L-One: About three years ago, I just felt like cutting my arm.

N: You've said that. Do your parents know about this? [*Of course they must, she wears short-sleeved shirts, but he wants to get her talking.*]

L-One: Yes. Sure they know. About three years ago, I wanted to destroy myself, so I started cutting my arm. Then one day I took a bunch of pills. This was when I was living in the sorority house near campus. Before I took the pills, I called up my house and told my folks what I was going to do.

N: What happened?

L-One: They called an ambulance and people came and pumped my stomach. I lived.

N: Then what happened? [*Getting L-One to talk was like pulling teeth, but she never held back once she was answering.*]

L-One: I dropped out of school and went into analysis with a psychiatrist.

N: What was that like?

L-One: I was an in-patient at the hospital, and I worked there, too. That was part of the treatment.

N: Did you continue to cut yourself while you were in the hospital?

L-One: Yeah.

N: What did the doctor do or say?

L-One: He said to stop or they'd throw me out of there.

N: What did you do?

L-One: I stopped cutting myself.

The conversation went on for hours and this is what N learned about L-One:

She was born during The War; her father was a doctor in the armed services and she didn't know him until The War was over and she was three years old. In her words, she had "rejected" him, but N had difficulty imagining a three-year-old staying cold to a loving man. L-One lived with her mother and grandmother during The War until the father came home. From then on, the father took jobs, each of fairly long duration and each an advancement over the previous one, until he now was department chairman at a renowned university where he taught medical students. Along the way, two sisters were born —Second and Third.

She disliked her father, thought her mother was a dolt, despised her older younger sister, but felt warmly toward the younger. At this time, remember, N hadn't met any of them.

L-One knew that her father hadn't wanted to come home after The War but wanted to stay overseas even if not in the armed services. She also knew that her parents had talked about getting a divorce when she was about thirteen years old. Second would have been nine and Third six at that time, so they might not have known what was going on.

When she was getting therapy, the psychiatrist insisted that her parents participate. That meant that all three of them had to talk and listen. L-One claimed that as a result of the therapy her folks started to get along better. As for her own problem, apparently her desire to destroy herself wasn't all-powerful; after all, she had called home when she took the pills, and the knife slashes obviously weren't fatal. The cuts were not deep—just deep enough to draw blood—and she was careful not to slash herself close to the wrist.

As for friends, she knew a fair number of people—"good kids" as she would call them—but of them all only a few were what you and I would call close friends. And of the close friends the only one she saw on a regular basis, mainly because they worked in the same place, was The Rose. N hadn't met her yet, either. Perhaps a little more came out in this conversation with L-One, but that's the gist of it. The whole conversation provoked a devastating, abrupt halt in N's thinking about L-One and the future. It was clear that there was a conflagration of animosity and tension, of love and hate burning inside L-One. N had a great deal of thinking to do; he needed reassurance that she was over her illness, and she herself had said to him that some people never get over such illnesses.

DOUBLE-FAULT: L-One seems to know quite a bit about her illness and yet she doesn't conquer it.

FAULT: That's how N felt—as though the patient controls the sickness. But actually he had more understanding of mental illness than that implies. He understood the meaning of the word "compulsion." But his understanding didn't make his problems disappear. And there was something else. After a hard day's work and an hour or so on the courts, N liked to come home and cook a steak and some vegetables, make a salad, and enjoy a good meal. But dinner with L-One was an ordeal. She didn't eat meat, which was fine with N. But she didn't eat anything else, either—except coleslaw. That she devoured. If he put vegetables on her plate, she would nibble a few and spread the rest out on the plate, presumably to give the impression that she had eaten. When N, who had a good appetite, finished his dinner, L-One would slump in her chair and say that SHE WAS FULL. Unbelievable. But later she'd be nibbling away at food left in the refrigerator and when N called to her, "What are you doing?" she would reply, "Nothing." He didn't give a damn about the food, he just wanted her to realize she couldn't deceive him and shouldn't deceive herself.

DOUBLE-FAULT: Didn't N stop to consider that L-One was looking after her figure? A woman knows when and what she should eat.

FAULT: Oh, come on. L-One did have a great figure and one has to watch one's diet and all that, but night after night she would eat coleslaw and nothing else. It worried N no end. A person must have food—that's . . . that's fundamental. My gosh!

DOUBLE-FAULT: There, there, calm down. Don't get so excited.

FAULT: Sorry. But you should have heard N lecture and plead and beg L-One to eat a square meal. "Just do it once, try it. It's so much more enjoyable to share the food than for me to eat and watch you push things around on your plate." It sounded selfish but it was for her sake—at least he hoped it was.

Something else L-One was in the habit of doing that gave N difficulty was her "ability" or need to fall asleep at the "wrong" times and not be able to sleep at the "right" times. For example, they would drive into the city, which was a relatively short ride. In no time at all, L-One would fall asleep as if she had passed out. Or they would go to a movie, one L-One wanted to see, and there she was asleep in her seat. It made N feel he was alone—reminded him of Boresville, and he preferred not to recall that, thank you. But it also brought home to N again and again that L-One couldn't control her life, couldn't shape it. After they made love, N would have liked it if L-One and he could have fallen asleep in each other's arms. But L-One would have to get up and out of bed—she would get peppy and have to move around. Not always, but often enough to bother N. And if he were lying in bed and he heard L-One walking around in the next room, he knew that sometime the next day she would fall asleep. Even worse was the feeling that came to him when he heard her go into the bathroom and then heard nothing. What if she was cutting herself with one of his razor blades or with a kitchen knife? He would get up and walk silently to the bathroom door, and if it was slightly open he would stick his head inside and ask quietly, smiling, "What's going on?" He always surprised her, and she would say, "Nothing." And that would be correct, since she wasn't washing her face or doing anything else. He thought perhaps she was looking at herself in the mirror.

DOUBLE-FAULT: I can appreciate his worry, but he should still knock first on the bathroom door. It's very rude not to.

FAULT: Didn't I say that? Sorry. He would knock and then stick his head inside.

The better he came to know L-One, the more baffled he found himself. He would cajole and entreat her to live more like a "square." He would say to her that he wasn't asking for conformity nor was he setting himself up as the ultimate in perfection, or pretending that only he knew what she should and should not do. He also pointed out to her that constant criticism from him would almost surely destroy their relationship. N told her specifically that by her acts and words she gave him the impression that she was inwardly unsettled and that it unnerved him to be intimately involved with a person who didn't feel secure in her own self. Would she please try to give him more confidence in her by changing herself?

L-ONE: Why can't you accept me the way I am?

This question led to a very long discussion on hangups and how people cope with reality. L-One asked N, who always acted assured and confident, whether he had any hangups.

N: No, I don't. None. Unless you call having no problems a hangup. I know what I want, and although I'm not sure I'll ever attain it, the success or failure of my attempt will not be the governing force in my life. It's that simple.

L-One wasn't like that and they both knew it. It wasn't, from N's point of view, that what she was like was intolerable. It was that what she was like was not anything she could continue being. N felt she had to change and he didn't know whether it would be for better or for worse. There was a song popular at that time called "I Am a Rock," and N used to tease L-One by saying perhaps she should sing, "I am a pebble —but one day I'll be a rock." And then, feeling he might have been too harsh, he'd put his arm around her shoulders and pull her tight against him and kiss her. She was so easy to love, and N wondered whether love would be enough for them.

DOUBLE-FAULT: I don't appreciate teasing. It is cruel and N is wrong to do it.

FAULT: Of course teasing can go too far, but N wasn't sadistic in his teasing.

DOUBLE-FAULT: Well, you can hurt people badly with words if you're insensitive to their sensibilities.

FAULT: Well spoken. Remember what you just said. N never knew when a blowup would occur. In this way L-One was a little like J. One day N had agreed to meet L-One at the tennis courts at a certain hour, but he showed up early. He saw two people he knew playing, and it was clear that not only were all the courts in use but there were people waiting. N's friends weren't interested in playing singles so they asked N to join them. He said he would like to, but that L-One would be coming shortly and he was waiting for her. "Well, when she comes we'll play mixed doubles and by the time that's over a court will be vacant for the two of you," one of the players suggested. "Besides, we're tired and need new blood. Come on, hit with us." N said that if L-One came and didn't want to play doubles, she and he would sit down. But meanwhile he went onto the court, took one side of the net, and rallied with his friends while he kept an eye out for L-One.

N spots her as she comes through the gate and with a wave of his racket gets her attention, and she makes her way to him. When she is a few feet from him, N is about to explain the situation to her and ask her what she prefers, to play mixed doubles or sit and wait for a vacant court, but before he gets a word out—now, listen to this—L-One, trembling, her face flushed, her mouth tense, says to him in a low voice crackling with fury, "Don't you double-cross me, N. Don't you dare double-cross me." Her knuckles are white from the grip with which she's clutching her racket. N understands exactly what L-One is going through. When she came through the gate and saw him on the courts hitting with others, she became jealous and afraid that perhaps N had abandoned the idea of their playing together. But in spite of his—shall we say—superior understanding of the situation, N was not going to let L-One hand out any nonsense, so he turned his back to his friends and now it was his turn to speak through clenched teeth.

> N: Don't you dare give me this garbage about double-cross. These people were nice enough to let me come on and hit with them. Don't hand me this double-cross nonsense. I won't tolerate it. [*Talking more naturally*] Now, it would be a courtesy for us to play mixed doubles with them; it'll be good practice for you, and we'll play singles later.
>
> L-ONE: You're sure we'll play singles later, N?
>
> N: Yes.
>
> L-ONE: O.K. [*Mollified*]

So N informed his friends, who must have been wondering what all the muttering was about, that they would play a set of doubles. L-One played well. In fact they played two sets, after which N's friends left and he and L-One rallied for a long time.

N: Was that so bad?

L-ONE: No.

N: Was it worth losing control?

L-ONE: No.

They went back to his place arm in arm. He apologized for speaking so forcefully and she apologized for blowing up. Back at his place, they played some more—but not tennis.

DOUBLE-FAULT: That must have been a terrible experience for N. It would scare me to be approached like that on a tennis court. He handled it very diplomatically.

FAULT: Does it make up for his teasing?

DOUBLE-FAULT: No.

FAULT: *C'est la vie.*

The summer was passing quickly enough, and in spite of their differences L-One and N gave each other a good deal of joy. Everyone remarked how much L-One's tennis game had improved, and she knew that it was the many hours of hitting with N that had done it. N enjoyed the tennis. And L-One gave N some beautiful moments off the court, too. Once, he had to wait on a street corner for L-One to meet him and she was a trifle late. He could see her about a block away but she hadn't seen him. She was running and skipping, her blondish hair in a ponytail bouncing up and down on her back. Her smile told the whole story—she looked so happy, that N was happy too. Call it transference, call it anything you wish, but N just felt it was good to be alive.

DOUBLE-FAULT: I've gotten mixed impressions about L-One. Sometimes she sounds rather juvenile to me, like this running-on-the-street business, but at other times I think of her as a sad woman buffeted about by other people. I'll take N's word for it that she's intelligent and all that, but I never think of her as a lady.

FAULT: You're judging her. Do you consider that buffeting L-One?

DOUBLE-FAULT: I have a right to judge her.

FAULT: I'm not questioning your right to judge her, I'm asking you for your interpretation of what it is you're doing. Are you buffeting her about?

DOUBLE-FAULT: Let's drop the whole subject; I'm sorry I brought it up. Go on with the story.

[Fault is tight-lipped but starts to talk again.]

FAULT: L-One's father came back from his conference and a few days later N met him. L-One's father was on his way out to get a tennis lesson from a pro. He was a short man, athletically built, with strong arms and legs. His hair was white and he had a lot of it, crew cut. They shook hands—his grip was firm—and then exchanged a few words. N's first impression of the man was a good one and didn't jibe with some of what L-One had told him. N's curiosity about the whole family had been whetted by L-One's derogatory stories, and he wanted to meet the ogres. Actually, N had taken some of her stories with a grain of salt but a couple of them had sounded plausible.

N was sure L-One's father and he would meet again and talk—especially about family matters.

DOUBLE-FAULT: One doesn't discuss family matters—it always ends in an argument. It's always like that, it's always been like that, and it will always be like that.

FAULT: Thank you for that conjugation. Just teasing. Which brings me back to my story. Near the end of August, N gets a letter from J. He recognizes it when he sees it lying in his mailbox even before he can focus on the handwriting. It's from J all right and it's a very long letter.

DOUBLE-FAULT: If it was a long letter, it must have been newsy. Tell me what she wrote.

FAULT: Delighted to do so. J wrote that a million things had kept her too busy to write for over eight months—her typical hyperbole. And N is to be completely understanding about this because her projects are so all-important that she couldn't interrupt them for even a short note. She will be delighted if he comes over for a visit—how often has he read that, he's lost count. But it still reads beautifully to him.

Let's see how this letter differs from the others. First, J reminisces about the many happy times she had spent with N. Second, she thanks him for his past efforts and the kindnesses he has done her. She sees them for what they were and is most appreciative. Third, the tone of the whole letter is one of nostalgia, suggesting that it might be nice to relive together some of those old times.

DOUBLE-FAULT: How marvelous.

FAULT: Thoughts of J now flood his mind. She sounds as if she will really let him come to see her. Maybe, he thinks, that's why she wrote—after all, she didn't have to. He feels elated, hopes are rekindled; his love for her wasn't dead, only dormant. He acts. He writes her a letter asking if October would be a good time to visit. J writes back within a week saying she and her sister will be too busy in October. She specifically writes: "I am not saying don't come—it's just a bad time." N accepts it and puts off the idea of his going to see her until the year-end holiday, the next time he will be free to travel.

The day after he writes his letter to J, he sees L-One.

N: I have something to say to you. There's a possibility that I may leave you at any time to take care of some unfinished business. I can't tell you what it is, or even if it will happen. I won't even discuss it. That's the way it has to be.

L-ONE: Can't you tell me?

N: No. I said I can't discuss it. No questions, please.

L-One is shocked, hurt, puzzled, and mortified—N senses whole oceans of thoughts making her feel insecure. He feels a strong attachment to L-One; he loves J more. He can only wonder if L-One will pay for his love for J.

DOUBLE-FAULT: Why did he say anything to L-One at all? He knew that his going to see J was not certain and that he would only be complicating matters.

FAULT: Call it a touch of honesty, but only a touch. Meanwhile L-One's mother and sisters came back from their travels and N met them also. The mother was a very pleasant woman who spent most of her time looking after her family and gave a few hours a week to community work. The girls were polite and the younger one was something of a comic. The whole family was in the process of learning to play tennis. The parents could be described as addicts they were so enthusiastic about the game, and the girls found it interesting, too. L-One, of course, as you've probably concluded, was already a fanatic.

The meetings between N and L-One's family were pleasant, and after a time—an initiation period, as it were—they started to bring up the kind of topics that reveal the way people think about life and the world they live in. Also N wanted to know more about L-One, especially from her parents' point of view.

DOUBLE-FAULT: Would you mind telling me the father's name? "L-One's father" sounds like the cart before the horse.

FAULT: The Good Old Doctor's name, if you must know, was G.O.D.

DOUBLE-FAULT: Thank you so much, that's quite irreverent. Please abridge that to "Good Doctor." Leave out the middle initial.

FAULT: Pleasure! When the fall term started, L-One moved into an apartment in downtown Freedom which wasn't far from school. It was a small world, L-One, N, and G.D. all working at the same place, but N never saw G.D. To N's knowledge, L-One never came by to see her father either.

Then the weather changed and tennis became impossible. The shorter days, the cold, and the rain all but eliminated the time they could spend on the courts. The relationship between L-One and N was also undergoing a metamorphosis. L-One seemed loath to stay overnight with him. When he would ask her what she was doing in the evening, she would say something about "ferreting out the interesting places" in downtown Freedom, or she would say, "I'm going bopping from bar to bar. You'd be surprised, N, how many interesting people you can meet in those places." This kind of statement would drain N of any hope of a permanent relationship between himself and L-One.

DOUBLE-FAULT: What about J? What was N's feeling toward her?

FAULT: His feelings are easy to describe—he still loved her, but he also felt he had to be practical. She wasn't writing to him, which destroyed his hope that perhaps she missed him or at least wanted to see him again. Let's say he had hopes for J, but L-One was nearer at hand. He was trying to burn the candle at both ends, but one wick had trouble being lit and the other wick had trouble staying lit. N would imagine that L-One's talk about going "bopping in the bars" was just to irritate him or shock him or show him up for being too square. N could, if he insisted, prevail on L-One to come to his place. Once she was in his apartment, there never was any

75

difficulty. They would make love at night and once again in the morning. If she left early for work, they would kiss good-bye and she'd call him her "god-damn stud." He was sure he meant a great deal to her.

DOUBLE-FAULT: Sounds as though they're both sex maniacs. My word, they're worse than rabbits.

FAULT: I trust that's jealousy and ignore your outburst. Trouble was still brewing for our two "rabbits," however. Ever since N was half-candid with L-One, you recall, about his leaving at some unspecified time, she had started to let herself go. Her eating habits were as bad as ever—quantity and quality. She never combed her hair; it was always hanging in front of her face.

DOUBLE-FAULT: Always?

FAULT: Well, you know what I mean. If she combed it in the morning, that was the last time she paid attention to it. She would push it out of her way with her hand, but really the hair had no travel restrictions—it could wander anywhere about her head—and she looked a fright. And N told her so. He lectured her a lot.

N was no fool. It occurred to him she might deliberately be making herself look forlorn in order to draw sympathy to herself, to keep his attention.

DOUBLE-FAULT: But not his respect.

FAULT: Right. But when the weekends came, things would get peculiar. N would call L-One, and a typical Friday-night conversation sounded something like this:

N: Hello, L-One.

L-ONE: Yeah?

N: This is N. What would you like to do tonight? There are some good movies playing.

L-ONE: I've made plans.

N: What do you mean, you've made plans?

L-ONE: I'm going to a party.

N: How could you possibly make plans without consulting me first?

L-ONE: I don't know. You never said anything.

N: But you know we're going to get together.

L-ONE: How do I know, N? You never say anything.

N: Well, it's obvious. Next time don't make any plans. Did you plan anything for tomorrow night, pray tell?

L-ONE: Yeah.

N: I won't ask. O.K., see you Sunday. Is that all right with you?

L-ONE: Yeah.

N: Good-bye.

In truth, even if he sounded annoyed, N was pleased when L-One made arrangements that excluded him. It gave him time to see his less traumatic friends—go out to dinner or see a good movie and afterward spend the evening in pleasant conversation.

DOUBLE-FAULT: Were these friends sometimes girls?

FAULT: Yes, but no affairs, if you please. When he would see L-One on Sunday, he would ask her how her weekend had gone. "Fine, just fine," she would say. Things were always "fine." Finally N told L-One that it was stupid for him to have to call her and that she should expect to be with him every weekend. If there was any change in plans, he would let her know in plenty of time. When the weekend came and he'd ask her what she'd like to do, she would always suggest something N was sure to reject outright—like "Let's go boppin' around the bars. You've never done that. You'd be surprised how much fun you can have." N would look anguished and say, "*No*. We're not doing *that*." Their being together on weekends wasn't working out. But what was really driving N up the wall were fresh cuts on her arms.

> N: Why are you trying to destroy yourself? Would you please stop for my sake? It unnerves me to discover fresh scabs.

He lectured her too much and he knew it. He would tell her how valuable she was and how great she was and how much greater she could be. But he would still inspect her arms almost as a matter of course whenever they made love. Afterward N would lie on the bed and conjure up pictures of what it would be like married to L-One. He could see himself coming home from work and stepping through the front door of his house to discover their children dead on the floor—slashed through the throat and arms. Sometimes, in his hazy vision, L-One had also slashed herself; other times she just stood there, her hair covering her face, but her eyes were visible, looking like glass marbles. He was afraid that, away from home, he would always be thinking the next phone call would bring him news of a domestic tragedy.

DOUBLE-FAULT: This N person really has a too imaginative and meandering mind. He should arrest himself for mental cruelty. But I think it's mostly his fabrication. People aren't so easily disposed to doing away with themselves.

[*Fault is extraordinarily quiet and contemplative. Then he lashes out.*]

FAULT: Your analysis is brilliant. Too bad it's wrong. If you don't mind I'll continue.

Often N would call the laboratory where L-One worked and many times he would get a chance to speak to The Rose. The

Rose was quite a character—good-natured, outgoing, and level-headed about most things. She carried her hurts well and could roll with life's punches.

N: Hiya, Rosie. How be ye?

THE ROSE: Fine. Want to speak to L-One?

N: Yes—in a minute. Can you talk?

THE ROSE: For you, N, I've always got the time.

N: Ha-ha. Listen—it's L-One—I'm worried about her. What's up?

THE ROSE: I'm worried, too. She's depressed all the time, really moody. You're bugging the hell out of her and she doesn't know how to handle you.

N: Yeah, I know. She's on my mind, too. It's a real dilemma.

THE ROSE: But there's a new complication.

N: What now?

THE ROSE: I think some of her so-called friends are inviting her around to smoke pot. And she shouldn't be trying that stuff now. She'll get whacked out on it. I've told her to take up drinking—hell, alcohol will make her pass out in no time. That's better for her.

N: What's your considered opinion?

THE ROSE: Gotta keep on our toes and watch her. Listen, N, you're a good influence on her. Don't desert her. It'll crack her up.

N: I don't intend to desert her, but I'm not so sure how potent my influence is. I've tried talking with her so much that even I can't stand myself for being such a pedant. Well, we'll keep trying. Thanks for the information.

THE ROSE: Right. Nice talking to you. You want L-One?

N: Yes, please. [*He waits a moment.*]

L-ONE: Hi. What were you and The Rose talking about?

N: Not what but who.

L-ONE: Oh.

N: Yep. We can't stop talking about you. How are things going?

L-ONE: Fine. Can you come over for dinner tomorrow night?

N: Tomorrow? Sure.

L-ONE: O.K. I'm cooking dinner for you and The Rose.

N: Should I bring anything?

L-ONE: Uh-uh, I've got all the stuff. See you then.

N: O.K. 'Bye.

The next night, N comes over and L-One is a frazzled-looking mess, her hair as usual out of place. She looks as if she needs sleep. The Rose shows up with a bowl of fruit compote for their dessert. L-One is cooking with the aid of a cookbook. She's never tried the recipe before but thinks it's interesting. The Rose helps out as N provides commentary that keeps them laughing. He should have been a comedian. The meal is ready to be served. L-One puts on a dress, but is tired and needs help serving. She has cooked enough food for eight people. It's positively delicious. L-One hardly touches her food and in less than five minutes she falls asleep in her chair. N and The Rose eat and enjoy each other's banter, but N feels lonely every time he looks at L-One. The Rose tries to be cheerful. At meal's end they tell L-One, who is now awake, that the food was great. Shortly thereafter The Rose leaves to meet some friends and N and L-One sit together on a couch. She falls asleep again.

N: You'd better get to bed.

L-ONE: [*Her eyes half closed*] Uh-uh.

N: I'll call you tomorrow.

L-ONE: 'Bye.

DOUBLE-FAULT: Maybe she needs watching after all. That drug business scares me, especially with L-One the way she is.

FAULT: Ahh. You're awake. It's getting close to year's-end holiday again. N solicits J's opinion as to whether he might visit her at this time.

DOUBLE-FAULT: J again?

FAULT: Yes, I'm afraid so. She writes back that she's leaving The City and won't be back till mid-January. Even if it is true, N laughs. Same old J. Their correspondence has taken on a pattern. When she writes, he answers, forgets about her for the most part, and waits till she writes again. It causes him not much discomfort, but still some. His feelings for her are too deep. He thinks it will always be that way.

Since he can't see J, N makes other arrangements—but not with L-One. They can't keep away from each other but they both need respite from their battles, N especially. So he doesn't suggest to L-One that they spend New Year's Eve together and instead asks her what she'll be doing that evening. L-One knows that whenever N asks her what she'll be doing instead of telling her that he wants her with him he's looking for an out.

L-ONE: I'm going to a party. What are you going to do?

N: I'm going to have a reunion with an old friend—just a friend. [*That didn't please L-One but she couldn't prevent it.*]

New Year's Eve came and N traveled the requisite hundred miles to join his companion of the evening. She was smartly dressed, her hair was well taken care of, her make-up was fastidiously applied, her fingernails polished—she looked as if she had stepped out of a picture in a woman's magazine. They reminisced, laughed, talked about the mundane and the inconsequential, caught up on their respective histories—N made no mention of J or L-One, of course—went out to dinner at a fine restaurant, went to a movie which finished shortly before midnight, walked the streets with the crowds of people who were about to ring the New Year in, did not kiss at the stroke of midnight, went back to her suite at the hotel, talked, and lastly N tried to seduce her, but she wasn't interested—for which N was silently grateful, because he really didn't want to sleep with her. Finally he left to go back to Freedom.

DOUBLE-FAULT: Well, that's certainly a mouthful. Are you sure N was grateful that this friend or companion or whatever she was didn't sleep with him, and it's not sour grapes?

FAULT: Absolutely sure. On the trip back to Freedom, he compared L-One with his rotogravure-looking friend, the combed *vs.* the uncombed, the cordial *vs.* the silent one, the gay chat *vs.* the argument. And he knew if he had to choose whom he wanted for the rest of his life, it was L-One an easy victor. No sweat.

He had been thinking before the reunion that perhaps it would be best if he and L-One stopped seeing each other. It wasn't that he was deserting a sinking ship but that the relationship wasn't going well.

DOUBLE-FAULT: Sounds sensible to me. He should have done that long before.

FAULT: Maybe. The day after he arrived back in Freedom, he called L-One and said he would like very much for them to get together for a quiet talk. It probably sounded ominous to L-One, and when she asked what about, N said he'd explain it when they were facing each other, not over the phone. Once again she bowed to his wishes. He picked her up and they drove to a roadside diner, found a table far removed from the few other people in the place, sat down, and ordered toast and coffee. L-One looked very anxious and N started the conversation in low tones.

> N: Our relationship isn't going the way it should and I'm probably more at fault than you. I've criticized you too much and verbally boxed your ears with too many harangues about your changing—I refuse to be part of a relationship that makes me act like that. I like you, I admire your abilities, I've enjoyed your company and felt happy to be with you. [*As he is talking, N realizes he will not be able to say they should stop seeing each other.* HE DOESN'T WANT THAT. *So he changes the end of his speech.*] I think it would be best [*L-One holds her breath —she is very nervous and her face is pale*] if I stop criticizing you and we see each other only whenever it's mutually convenient or desired. [*L-One breaks out into a smile and a nervous laugh.*] Is that O.K. with you?

> L-ONE: Yeah. It wasn't as bad as I thought. [*She is starting to smile; she is obviously relieved.*]

N hasn't seen L-One in three days, and while sitting across the table from her he gets the desire to have her under him. He suggests they drive back to his place, and once they get there he becomes amorous. L-One resents his advances and yells at him, "I won't be used," and storms out of his apartment. N waits a minute to see if she'll come back and then realizes she's headstrong and won't. He races after her and catches up to her on the street. He knows she has no money with her and she lives miles away—an impossible distance to walk, and he doesn't want her hitchhiking.

> N: Look, come back and I'll drive you home. If you don't want to sleep with me, you don't have to. Whatever

you say. Come on. I'm not using you, I like you too much for that.

They go back to his place. He asks her, "Shall we stay or go?"

L-ONE: Sleep with me.

N: You won't think I'm using you?

L-ONE: No.

DOUBLE-FAULT: All these declarations of intent to the contrary, was he using her?

FAULT: He had sexual desires that he wanted satisfied. He did indeed like L-One. He felt a little guilty about the possibility that he was using her, but it's not true that he kept the relationship going *strictly* because of sex. He genuinely and sincerely had more than affection for L-One.

The new era of their relationship didn't prosper very well. L-One was getting high on drugs—not hard drugs but marijuana and pep pills. She had some "lovely" friends—her "good kids" were having smoking parties and she always wanted to be one of the gang. N asked her if she ever considered that they were using her to do their thing. Like cattle at a watering hole —all of them feeling secure because all of them are there.

N had heard so many stories from L-One about her being an "outlaw" kid. If it was forbidden, she'd try it—that's how you get recognition, acceptance, and respect. But from whom? Talk did no good and N didn't push it. He had promised her he wouldn't criticize her and he used considerable restraint. But the situation was bad.

DOUBLE-FAULT: Things are never as bad as they seem. Don't exaggerate.

FAULT: Is that so? Let's see. Oh, yes. One night N picks up L-One at her apartment—it's about ten o'clock and he starts to drive her back to his place. It's a lovely drive at night, part of the way going through a beautiful park on a road that bends its way along a river. N is feeling warm and loving that evening, and he reaches across to L-One to squeeze her hand. Suddenly she starts to react oddly. N is startled to see her squirming from side to side and he asks her if she's all right. He can see she isn't, but she can't or won't talk. She acts as if she doesn't hear him. He suddenly realizes that she must be undergoing the effect of a bad marijuana experience; she must have smoked when she was depressed and it had increased her depression. He grabs her forcefully by the arm and commands her to hang on, they'll be in his place soon. She starts to scream.

> L-ONE: I don't want to die. I don't want to die. I don't want to die. I don't want to die. I don't want to die.

> N: Hang on. YOU WON'T DIE. Just hang on. Everything's going to be all right.

He pulls her close to his chest and drives with one hand—a stick-shift car at that. He pulls into his parking space and races around to the other side of the car to help L-One out. He half carries her upstairs to his place—fumbles with his keys ("DAMN KEYS") and takes her inside. N carries her into the bedroom and lays her down on the bed. Her head and eyes are still rolling from side to side and she's a picture of torment and anxiety. He climbs on top of her; the weight of his body makes her immobile, and he clutches her arms by the wrists and holds them steady. He whispers softly to her, "There, there, everything's O.K. Don't worry. You're safe here. Relax now." She quiets down and finally gets control of herself. They talk for a while. No lecture from N. She looks at him and asks him to make love to her. He does and it's a good deal like old times.

N has been encouraged lately because L-One had stopped cutting herself. But he saw the drugs as an equally great hazard. So you see things were not better but worse than they seemed.

DOUBLE-FAULT: Never a dull moment with L-One, don't you think? How can one person be so pathetic and keep getting her life so tangled up?

FAULT: Perhaps if N married her it would change her completely. But that would be a risk.

DOUBLE-FAULT: I don't think he should. You never know what to expect.

FAULT: Let me go on. Much happens and I want to cover most of it.

Soon thereafter, L-One tells N that she wants to move into his apartment and live with him. There's plenty of room for her. L-One can't stand living where she is now, and it seems a good move for her. But for him the request poses a real problem. N was, in a sense, living a dual life. He had friends whom he liked and often invited up to his place, and this couldn't go on if she moved in. Had he felt that he was eventually going to marry L-One, N wouldn't have hesitated one second before saying yes, and would probably have initiated the idea himself long since. But he wasn't at all sure that they would ever get married. Also, as he had often told L-One, he didn't want to live with someone who was dependent on him to so great an extent that she became a worry rather than a joy. She would have to give up drugs and bopping around in bars—drastically change her life style. Could she do this? She said, "Of course, that'll be easy." But it sounded like an assurance given too slickly. She also said that she wouldn't mind if he wanted to go out with other people sometimes. But, again, that was too facile, and anyway he didn't really like the idea that she could bear to "share" him—it went against his grain. He thought it would be better if she demonstrated that she could change *before* she moved in. But she hadn't been able to change so far. As N saw it, letting L-One move in would be gambling against his better judgment, even though he did believe that if only they were more alike, their living together would be fantastic.

What finally decided him was a conversation he had with his sister. "She'll be using you as a crutch. I know how you feel about her, but believe me, you have as much chance of 'saving' her as you have of turning back the ocean by talking to the waves. Furthermore, this drug syndrome of hers is a hard one to give up, and if she gets caught and the authorities find out she's living with you, you'll be the one who'll pay for it. Not her. Be careful and think it over. It's for you to decide."

N respected his sister, didn't agree exactly with the analogy, but finally decided that he would have to say no to L-One's request. He wasn't at all sure he was right and it saddened him to refuse her. He made the decision and unmade it a dozen times a day. He wanted her, but if she moved in and was hell to live with it would be worse for both of them later on. Cautious and indecisive—both things he hated to be.

DOUBLE-FAULT: I think N is quite right and very wise to turn her away until she stabilizes. There's no such thing as too much caution—one can't be too sure.

FAULT: N felt he was being a coward. Perhaps it would only take his presence, the knowledge in L-One's mind that at the end of every day she would be with him, to make her better. N would never know. He told her the answer was no, and added that he thought it best if she moved back with her family. In his considered opinion, L-One would not be able to find herself until the animosity she had for the rest of her family was broken down and analyzed away. He thought this because the other four members of her family got along splendidly among themselves, and N knew from observing them and talking with them over the months. L-One was the outcast, the pariah, and N didn't think it had to be that way. Sure, L-One was different from her folks and she was by far the most intelligent of the three girls, but she should be able to live with them without showing her fangs all the time.

L-One's reply to his advice was that she had decided to move in with another man—a friend who had a neat apartment they could share. N told her in a no-nonsense tone of voice:

> N: If you move in with another guy, you and I are completely and utterly finished. That's all there is to it.
>
> L-ONE: Why? [*An uncomprehending look appears on L-One's face, astounding N.*]
>
> N: Why? I'll spell it out for you. I will not call for you at a place where you are living with another man no matter how innocuous you claim the relationship is. I just won't accept that.
>
> L-ONE: But nothing will happen.
>
> N: You bet. Nothing will happen between you and me. If you move in with him, we're finished. Is that clear?

DOUBLE-FAULT: Why does N think he's a coward? He told L-One off in no uncertain terms and was very strong about it.

FAULT: Maybe he was only being vain. His pride might have been hurt.

DOUBLE-FAULT: I don't think so.

FAULT: Well, what do you know—you and N agree! N wasn't concerned about his pride. His attitude was the only one that might keep L-One from moving in with that guy. Which he knew would be a mistake, a big mistake, for her.

After that exchange, L-One stopped seeing N entirely. She would listen to him on the phone but wouldn't talk to him. N didn't know whether he had done the right thing or the wrong thing but he knew that L-One was sinking and that he had to do something. He had a talk with The Rose.

THE ROSE: She's crazy to move in with that guy. He's got more hangups than a telephone operator with bad breath. They'll both be leaning on each other so hard they'll fall flat on their faces. I'm trying to talk her out of it but I'm not getting anywhere.

N: Keep calm. I've got an idea—something I've been meaning to do for a long time and this is as good a time as any.

THE ROSE: What do you have cooking?

N: I'm going to keep it under my hat. Sorry but I think that's best. Hey, am I still invited to your party Saturday night?

THE ROSE: You bet, kiddo, and you better be there. L-One's going to be there, too.

DOUBLE-FAULT: What's N going to do? Isn't it enough of a mess already?

FAULT: I don't think, in spite of what I've told you, that you appreciate the depth of feeling N has for L-One. She's not merely a slab of flesh in his mind. She deserves the best, at least far better than what she's had to date. Everyone who knows her loves her, but she's her own worst enemy. Can't you see that?

DOUBLE-FAULT: All I see is someone who's very dizzy. That's all.

FAULT: N telephoned L-One's father and made an appointment to see him the next day. At the appointed hour, N shows up dressed in a suit, out of respect for the good doctor. He is welcomed by Good Doctor and they leave his office, because it isn't private enough, and go to a laboratory. This suits N nicely. They will be alone and undisturbed. The door is closed, Good

Doctor takes a seat, and N sits himself down on a stool and starts to talk in a slow and halting manner. The good doctor listens attentively—he never interrupts—which surprises N, because in all their previous conversations neither has been able to wait for the other to finish making a point.

> N: I haven't prepared a speech and I'll probably seem unclear at times and very probably jump around in time. What I've come to talk about is very important to both of us. A long time ago, I thought that I might one day be coming to you to say that L-One and I were in love and were going to be married and would like your blessing. Actually, I don't know whether you and your wife even love L-One, and that's one of the reasons why I'm here. Things aren't working out, they haven't been working out for some time, and the future looks bleak at the moment. When I first met L-One . . .

N tells the story of his time with L-One. He talks about the derogatory stories she tells about the good doctor, her eating habits, the drug story, and the "I don't want to die" night. He leaves out all of their sexual relationship—what's the sense of telling the good doctor he's been sleeping with his daughter these past eight months? He tells him about L-One's possible next move—out of her apartment and in with some guy. He concludes:

> N: I've told her I think it would be best if she moved back into the house with her family. Since then, she won't speak to me—but that's not important. What is important is whether you'll let her come back, or what you will do instead. What do you think?

The good doctor started talking and N became the listener.

> GOOD DOCTOR: Yes, by all means we should try to get her to come back to our house. Moving into the setup

you've described would definitely be a step backward for her. Twice in the past, other men have come to me and told me that L-One was saying things about me and the family that simply weren't true. L-One has been a big problem in our lives. Of course we love her. She's given us great joy at times and at other times big disappointments. Her eating peculiarities go back many years. She would secretly eat only one item, like breakfast cereal, and then her mother would reprimand her for using it all up so that other members of the family couldn't have it for breakfast. She bullied her sisters and always had to have her way, and the consequence was that they were glad to see her out of the house. You have to give in sometimes and give up something to be a harmonious member of the family. L-One never thought of the others.

I don't think she wants to die. She called us up before taking the pills and she didn't take many—far less than a fatal dosage. And I believe she knew it—she was faking it. Well, we—that is, my wife and I along with L-One—went to a psychiatrist. My wife and I had to tell the psychiatrist about ourselves and we did it willingly to help L-One. Did she ever tell you she wanted to be a doctor—to save people? She asked me what I thought about it, and I had to be candid. I told her a person has to have her own life under control before she can help others, and that it would take years of effort and study. I said I thought she had the ability, but that temperamentally and emotionally she wasn't suited for medicine. Her saying that she rejected me when I came back from The War reminds me of a cute encounter I had with her when she was three. She came into our room, my wife's and mine, and she saw my military boots—they had just been polished—and she tried to put them on. I was lying in bed watching her and I reacted in a very military manner, for a man's boots, especially shined ones, are off-limits to anybody, and I sat up in bed and issued an order: "You leave those directly alone." Well, she ran out of the room crying and looking for her mother, and when she found her she wailed, "Daddy won't let me play with his 'directly.' " She was such an adorable little girl. Lately she's been asking me for pills, but I can't give them to her without a prescription or a diagnosis of my own that warrants them. She won't let me examine her, and when I ask if anything's wrong, she says there's nothing. Perhaps her friends have put her up to it. In the past, she's always come to me or her mother when she's been in trouble. I can't tell you how many times her mother has sat on the edge of the bed and cried and cried, asking herself over and over again where we went wrong or what we could do to make things better. It was constant trauma, and then we sort of got used to living with it. But we had to consider her sisters. . . .

Good Doctor said a few more things. He verified that he and his wife had considered a divorce about ten years before, but he didn't say what their disagreement was about and N didn't ask. He and N agreed to keep this conversation a strict secret from everybody. N would try to get L-One to come back home, and the good doctor would discuss things with his wife that very night and they would extend a warm invitation to L-One to join the household. When N and the good doctor parted, they shook hands firmly.

DOUBLE-FAULT: What an interesting dialogue. But tell me, is N always so secretive?

FAULT: What do you want him to do? Put an ad in the newspaper?

N thought over what the good doctor had told him and found it difficult to weigh the importance of some of his remarks. N was surprised to hear that other men had spoken to Good Doctor about L-One. He wondered how old they were and how old L-One had been at the time. He should have asked. He was glad to hear that her parents loved L-One, and the good doctor had said it so naturally that N was sure it was true, especially the part about the mother crying. It was very interesting that when L-One was in trouble she always came back—or is it fell back?—to her parents. She might talk against them but she still had enough trust in them to seek them out when things got too rough for her. Good Doctor's opinion that her suicidal impulses were fake was comforting to hear, but to N the acts looked real, and he wasn't certain that she wouldn't yet succumb to the desire to succumb. Still, L-One always said that there could be havoc and disaster around her and she'd survive.

N couldn't wait for The Rose's party. For the first time in a long time, he felt on top of things.

DOUBLE-FAULT: Even on top of his endless correspondence with J?

FAULT: N hadn't heard a word from J in months, since December, and it was now March. He had a dream about her one night in which he, his mother, and J were riding on a subway train but none of them spoke to each other or sat next to each other. In the dream, N didn't want to introduce J to his mother, because he didn't think she deserved to meet her. He wrote J and told her the contents of the dream, omitting the part about not introducing her to his mother, but she didn't respond and N wasn't going to write again.

DOUBLE-FAULT: What happened in the subway train?

FAULT: Nothing. Everyone just stared out the window and the train kept going. N thought the whole dream was a metaphor for his involvement with J.

Now let's get to The Rose's party. N shows up first, at eight o'clock, maybe even a few minutes earlier. L-One arrives about half an hour later. She looks fresh out of a shower, her hair immaculate and tied up in a ponytail. She is wearing a red sweater and looks as cute as can be.

N and L-One retire to a corner of the room and lean against the wall, just talking about nothing in particular and nothing in general. But both are smiling and clearly are pleased to be standing opposite each other. When The Rose comes over and says to N that she'd like him to meet some friend on the other side of the room, L-One is quick to say, "Never mind; he's doing fine right here!" Then N asks L-One if he can meet her after the party for a talk; there's something he wants to say—there's always something—and she is in favor of hearing what he has to say. Then they separate and mix with the other guests.

Much later, N returns to L-One, who is talking with a nice-looking guy who is obviously more than interested. N motions to her and tells her it's time to go, and she turns quickly to her new acquaintance and says, "Excuse me, I have to go." N realizes he's still in control, and that she really wants to please him.

> N: What I have to say is private and needs a quiet place. Do you have any objections to going back to my apartment?
>
> L-ONE: No, that's O.K.

They drive there; N doesn't reach out to squeeze her hand or anything. He keeps his body to himself. At about midnight, they are both sitting in N's place, L-One at one end of a couch, N in a chair about fifteen feet from her. There's nothing physical going on here. This is not an intimate, cheek-to-cheek, emotion-filled tête-à-tête; it's more like a conversation between a fox and a rabbit.

N: I've been thinking over a great many things about us and I want to check them out with you to see if I've reached the right conclusions. For example, although I don't agree with your folks on many issues, I find it very difficult to believe the derogatory stories you've told me about them. I think you made them up. Am I right?

L-ONE: Yeah, I made them up.

N: I think you said a lot of things just to get sympathy and acceptance for yourself. And you did a lot of other things for the same reason—like only eating coleslaw—to make me worry about your health. Is that right?

L-ONE: Yeah, I guess so.

N: Why did you do it? Don't you have any confidence in yourself?

L-ONE: I don't know, I just did it. I thought you were pretty dumb to fall for it, too.

N: You made me believe your parents didn't love you. I don't believe that any more either. Your mother is a sweet person, even if you think she's an idiot. You and I think differently about the world from the way they do, but they aren't monsters. What do you say to that?

L-ONE: What can I say? I've been found out.

N kept talking with the cunning of a fox. He told L-One that she had so much to live for and so much to give, that she was a wonderful creature, and that he had been very happy with her. He told her she was at a crossroads, that if she moved in with this other guy, they would be using each other as crutches and would both end up getting dragged down. N didn't care about the other guy, only about L-One. For her own sake, he argued, the best thing she could do would be to move back home, get reacquainted with her family, and live like a square for a few months. "You don't have to accept their ideas or agree with them on everything. All you have to do is think about settling down inside yourself." L-One agreed and kept saying "Yeah" to everything N said. When he finished, he walked across the room to where she was sitting, bent down, and gave her a kiss on the cheek.

N: Come, I'll take you back to your place.

L-ONE: I want to stay with you.

N: Are you sure?

L-ONE: Yeah.

They made love that night and it seemed better, as it always does after a crisis has passed. They slept in each other's arms. Next day N drove L-One back to her apartment, and a few days later she moved back home. N was feeling good; he felt there was a chance. He kept in touch with the good doctor and was told things were going well. The other night, Good Doctor said, when the youngest daughter, Third, started going through her routines at the dinner table, L-One laughed. Third would look at L-One to see if she was being appreciated, and when she realized she was, she pulled out all stops. The harder L-One laughed at her antics, the harder Third tried to make her laugh some more. It was hilarious and everyone was pleased.

DOUBLE-FAULT: Peace is so wonderful, especially among members of a family. Ruckuses are more the order of the day, though, even if everyone involved is supposed to be mature.

FAULT: I couldn't have said that better myself.

One of the consequences of L-One's move home was that she stopped seeing N. A possible reason for this was that if she saw him, she would sleep with him, and she knew her parents wouldn't approve. Or maybe she felt that N would never reciprocate her feelings for him in the way she wanted.

And why bother to get tense and upset over a man who will ultimately break your heart? N could understand L-One's possible points of view and he didn't fault her for them. But his newly found celibacy was not what he wanted and it was discomforting him.

DOUBLE-FAULT: Ahh, sex. What would we do without it!

FAULT: Probably play a lot more tennis, those of us who are left. N decided to make a weekend trip back to the place where he first met J. It filled him with nostalgia, but not of the oppressive variety. He decided to call up T.G.—you remember her—the girl he had that week-long affair with. She was still in the same place. They went out to dinner and afterward back to her apartment. She said she had been able to forget him, but there must have been some residual feelings for him because he was able to seduce her. Actually there's no such thing as a seduction. She must have been for it—at least a little. N felt lousy afterward. Disgusted with himself for letting his physical desire overcome him, and for being unfaithful to L-One. He hadn't even enjoyed it and it certainly wasn't fair to T.G. to come and go as he did, so he made some sort of stupid excuse and left her shortly afterward, hoping that he hadn't opened up old emotional wounds for T.G.

DOUBLE-FAULT: N always seems to have a guilty conscience after he satisfies his desire. Perhaps he's not a rock but a pebble under a magnifying glass.

FAULT: Listen, it's a hard cruel world. He wanted sex. What T.G. wanted was not necessarily N's problem. If she was unhappy, that was a shame, but N hadn't misrepresented himself. He came to her with a liking for her but no love, and if she was hurt he was sorry it turned out that way, but she didn't have to see him at all and could have said so. And she knew it. N doesn't like to see people hurt, but he believes you can't live their lives for them and make their decisions. Per-

97

haps it's only a rationalization, but if you don't live that way, your responsibilities become mountainous when they needn't be.

DOUBLE-FAULT: I agree you can't always be your brother's keeper, but still, if he felt he was going to make her suffer, he should have stayed away.

FAULT: He didn't have twenty-twenty foresight. Sometimes maybe hindsight, but foresight is asking too much. Perhaps he had done just what T.G. wanted. Who knows? T.G., probably. But the effect on N was to restimulate his love for L-One.

DOUBLE-FAULT: That sounds as if he compares his women.

FAULT: Doesn't everybody, men and women, compare various members of the opposite sex? When he got back to Freedom, he called L-One up immediately. He said he wanted to come out and talk with her. He had something to ask her. She said he could come over. N had been driving all day but he was wide awake as he pulled into the driveway of the good doctor's house. He rang the bell and L-One came to the door. He suggested that since it was a lovely night out, they could go for a walk around the block. She said that would be fine and went to get a coat. N didn't even go inside the house.

It was a beautiful night—all the stars were out, the air was crisp, and the gardens they walked past were still gorgeous in the moonlight.

> N: I've been away this weekend and I did a lot of thinking. I miss you. We haven't been close for a long time. I'd like us to try to grow close again, and if it's possible and things work out well, then we could get married. [*The last phrase in that sentence gets stuck in N's throat.*] Would you like to try?

> L-ONE: That would be very nice. [*Said as sweetly as only L-One could say things*]

They hold hands like two teen-agers and walk back to the house. He kisses her good night and she steps inside the door and waves her hand at him. She looks unbelievably happy. N gets in his car and drives off.

N: My gosh, what have I done? Did I really want to say that?

Then he was alarmed at having second thoughts. They start seeing each other and the old L-One life-style begins reasserting itself. N becomes pessimistic about a future with L-One. He decides it would be valuable for him to speak to L-One's former psychiatrist but he doesn't know the doctor's name.

DOUBLE-FAULT: Shouldn't be too hard to get, really.

FAULT: I'm coming to that, if you please. N doesn't want L-One to know he wants to talk to her doctor, so he drops over to Good Doctor's office as if he's just come around to pass the time of day. The good doctor is even more of a pedant than N, and once he starts talking he supplies all the minutest details about the subject under discussion. Ask him a question and get an answer.

GOOD DOCTOR: . . . patients in the hospital . . .

N: Oh, incidentally, what was L-One's doctor's name?

GOOD DOCTOR: Ah—Dr. Reform—patients in the hospital have to be treated . . .

N thinks to himself that Good Doctor doesn't realize he's given N what he came for. N thinks it best not to tell him that he and L-One are thinking seriously of marriage—it might cause unnecessary and unwanted questions.

DOUBLE-FAULT: N is always so secretive.

FAULT: About some things, yes. Can't spread your business before the world. In half an hour's time, their conversation ends and N leaves. He figures that he will go to the hospital and ask to speak to Dr. Reform. He knows there's a strong possibility he may be refused an audience with the doctor because whatever passed between him and L-One is confidential. But N decides to try.

DOUBLE-FAULT: I think he's wasting his time.

FAULT: Listen and learn. Next day N goes to the hospital.

N: My name is N, and I would like to speak to Dr. Reform about some private matters.

RECEPTIONIST: What is the private matter about?

N: It's private but I guess I can say that I wish to talk to him about a former patient of his.

RECEPTIONIST: That's positively out of the question.

N: You're sure?

RECEPTIONIST: Yes.

N: I see. Thank you very much. [*N goes outside and walks back and forth through the gardens in front of the building. He sees that there is no way to get into the building without passing some official checkpoint. Therefore no chance of getting to the doctor's office. He leaves.*]

Later that night, he finds Dr. Reform's home number in the phone book, and calls it.

VOICE ON THE TELEPHONE: Hello.

N: Hello. I would like to speak to Dr. Reform.

DR. REFORM: This is he speaking.

N: Doctor, my name is N and I apologize for calling you at home, but I want to discuss a very private personal matter with you. I tried to come to your office today but I couldn't get by the receptionist.

DR. REFORM: What is it?

N: L-One was a former patient of yours, isn't that so?

D.R.: I am not at liberty to say.

N: Well, I know she was and she and I are seriously thinking about getting married. I wanted to ask you whether in your judgment she is cured, or well.

D.R.: I can't discuss that with you, but if you and she want to come to my office and talk things over that would be possible.

N: I can't ask that of her. She doesn't even know I'm calling you. It means a lot to me to know whether in your opinion her knife-slashing days are over.

D.R.: As I said, I can't discuss anything with you. But I don't think she's ready for marriage.
[*N thinks: "A leak in the dike."*]

N: Why not?

D.R.: I can't discuss this with you.

N: Judging from what I know, I think she's come a long way since last year.

D.R.: Your day-to-day association may be very meaningful and you may be in the best position to judge things for yourself. If you want, make an appointment for both of you to come see me. I can't discuss this any further.

N: Thank you, Doctor. I believe what you suggest is impossible. I also think L-One has come a long way from last year's life. Thank you for your time.

D.R.: Perhaps you're right.

[*N puts down the phone and realizes that he called to get the doctor's opinion, got it, and then argued with the doctor to tell him he was wrong. N smiles sardonically.*

"What the hell is the truth?" D.R.'s opinion no longer matters to N, but he's glad he has it and it doesn't bother him.]

DOUBLE-FAULT: All that for nothing.

FAULT: A little peace of mind is not nothing. Things at home began to get worse for L-One. It's hard to know how or why they started going badly but they did. For example, L-One wasn't allowed to drive the family car, but Second was. A conversation N had with L-One's mother probably gives an indication of what was happening.

N: Suppose L-One wanted to have a party here. Could she?

MOTHER: No. It's my house.

N: But she lives here, too. Where else could she have one?

MOTHER: She can't unless she finds someplace else.

N: But surely if she wanted to invite some friends over she wouldn't need your permission.

MOTHER: I don't like her friends. Wouldn't want them in my house.

It was too restrictive and confining for L-One there and she rebelled against the shackles. Perhaps it was all of them knowing each other too well, just waiting for things to go wrong again and then accentuating the family frictions that always exist. Whatever the cause, things did become worse.

DOUBLE-FAULT: Life seems to be a continuing melodrama with N.

FAULT: With time, N started to back away again from L-One, and she sometimes made it all too easy for him. Alone together in the house one day, L-One and N became involved once more with each other's bodies. When their exertions had ended, they lay in each other's arms and N started to stroke L-One's arm. Suddenly he sat bolt upright and grabbed the arm. He had felt—and now he saw—a fresh scab. He leapt from the bed and stood leaning against the dresser, his head in his hands, moaning, "Oh, no, not again, not again, L-One." L-One lay on the bed and sobbed, "I didn't mean it, this time I was sorry as soon as I did it." N was immobile and silent. He just stood there getting sadder and sadder.

    L-ONE: N—go to hell.

    N: I'm there already.

    L-ONE: This time I was sorry the moment I did it.

    N: I hope so, I really hope so.

After a few minutes he rejoined her on the bed. He didn't speak, nor did she, but her eyes were moving wildly.

DOUBLE-FAULT: She's hard to fathom, isn't she?

FAULT: Yes. But N believed her when she said she was sorry this time. Now be alert, for I have to report four or five things that were developing simultaneously as summer—and with it, good tennis weather—approached. First, L-One and N began to see each other less and less. N was numbed by the most recent cut on her arm and he wanted time to think. Secondly, he started to play tennis with a new group of people, and every time he went to the courts there would always be this fantastic-looking young woman playing with a man who was apparently her boyfriend. Thirdly, N had a new job lined up for September that would take him away from Freedom. Fourthly, he planned to move out of his place and live near his office until he could complete a rush project. Fifthly, he would be leaving the country for a two-week conference in July. Now for the significance of these items and their inter-relationship.

The less he saw of L-One, the more open he became to the idea of new dalliances. Marriage was almost definitely out and he began to accept that as a fact. Oh. I've skipped something—I haven't told you why N and L-One were avoiding each other.

DOUBLE-FAULT: Yes, you did. It was the new cut.

FAULT: Yes, that's true, but there's more and it's so important I wonder how it could have slipped my mind.

L-One became impatient with N and properly so. He had said that if things went well, et cetera, they'd get married. He was vacillating again, and more and more was a man trying to back out of an agreement. I told you he wanted time to think, but L-One thought he had already had enough time. Confrontations can happen so suddenly. They were driving along in heavy traffic near the shopping district adjacent to L-One's house. She said simply, "Are we going to get married? Decide now. No more prolonging the situation." He was driving the car perfectly well, *but his thoughts were on—J.* "My gosh, if I agree to this marriage I'll *never* see J again. J-J-J." He watched L-One out of the corner of his eye. She was sitting upright, her face alternating between pallor and flush—she looked straight ahead, unusually tense. He was still silent—searching for words—when L-One reached her hand out and patted his arm and said, "Poor N—can't decide, can you?" One of the most important moments of his life came without his realizing it and was over before he understood how important it was—all while driving through heavy traffic. Curious, don't you think?

DOUBLE-FAULT: Why did he get these thoughts of J? He hadn't heard from her in months. He seemed all wrapped in his devotion to L-One, or at least, if not devotion, his concern for her well-being.

FAULT: Some things can't be explained. He had no hope of marrying J, he didn't know whether he'd ever see her again, but still she came into his mind when he had to decide. It happened. So it wasn't only the cut that turned N's mind to virgin fields but also his failure to speak up and decide. Apparently, he had decided "NO." And I'll tell you something else: when he couldn't speak up, his heart went out to L-One as it rarely had before. He realized he loved her, as I guess he always had, but he couldn't marry her. He felt sorry for her. Life was being unkind to her, because he was all she wanted and, if you ask me, all she needed.

DOUBLE-FAULT: Then you think he could have saved her?

FAULT: Yes—I do. Now back to the points I enumerated. One day in mid-spring—I think it was early May—N shows up at the tennis courts and the good-looking woman is sitting all alone.

N: Do you want to hit some till your partner gets here?

MISS DALLIANCE: I don't think he's going to show up. And I've seen you play—you're too good.

N: Don't worry. Any two people can rally. Let's try.

M. D: Fine, but I warned you.

After rallying, N took her for a cold drink. They drive off in his car and start a conversation laced with questions from N. He gathers that she is a nurse; the guy she plays tennis with is her fiancé, but they're breaking up, and she tells him, without too much elaboration, the story of her life. Driving back to the courts, M. D has a lot to say.

N: Would you like to come over to my place for dinner—I cook quite a good steak.

She'd like to but she's busy working and she doesn't know when she can make it. She keeps talking. She's absolutely gorgeous and N is wildly aroused. He reaches over, pulls her head close to his, and starts to kiss and explore her mouth. She's something of an explorer herself. N knows that all he has to do to have an affair with her is to get her alone in his place. They make a date for her to come over for dinner. She comes, they eat, and then N leads her into the bedroom. No arguments, no coyness, she's with him all the way. Forgive me, I know you're a lady, but M. D has without question one of the greatest bodies any woman ever had. She is simply fantastically well proportioned, not sloppy like most heavily endowed women, and her legs are gorgeous, well-muscled but not muscular-looking, smooth-feeling pincers that lock him in.

M. D was uninhibited and N's body excited her. Physically they were a matched pair. But N began to feel guilty about these sessions, as if he were cheating L-One. He rationalized it by telling himself that he wasn't going to marry L-One, so what's the difference? However, N believed in having only one girl at a time. The end came in a bizarre way. He was in M. D's apartment and she was naked. N was sitting on the couch. He looked at her and he said, "I don't love you, and don't want you to be hurt later, as you might be if you start to feel too much for me. So I can't go on sleeping with you."

M. D.: I always knew there would be a first time. You're the only one who's ever refused me.

N: I can see why. [*He gets up.*] I'm sorry. Really I am. I think it would be best if I go.

She nodded, and when he reached the door he turned around and repeated, "I'm sorry." She looked downcast. Outside on the street, N began to feel both good inside and sorry for himself because of what he was missing. The girl he had left could have a proposition every day and a marriage every night. A short time later, N spoke with her again. She was going to marry some guy. Just like that.

DOUBLE-FAULT: This N is too cerebral. But I'll bet he felt much better for breaking off this liaison. You can have them all the time, but they don't satisfy.

FAULT: They satisfy and he was sorry he broke it off. Events had come full cycle. L-One was saying that the stupidest thing she ever did was to move back with her family and that she had been "nuts" to take N's advice. N was changing his mind about where L-One would be best off living. Home clearly was not the place—too much friction. So N decided to help L-One and at the same time make it easier for him to get to work. He moved out of his apartment to a place one block away from his office and gave his car to L-One. She needed mobility and she needed to get away from any dependence whatsoever on her family. N was warned however by both her parents that L-One was accident-prone, which was why they didn't let her drive the family car. He didn't care. The car was a material object—it could be replaced; L-One needed freedom. Perhaps he was assuaging his guilt feelings toward L-One. He also thought he would see L-One a little more often. Now that she had the car, she promised to drop in on him "all the time." But she came too infrequently to suit N. And then, of course, came his two-week trip out of the country.

DOUBLE-FAULT: Would he see J?

FAULT: I'm coming to that. He wrote J and told her where he would be. His schedule was too tight and he didn't expect to see her. The closest he came was flying over The City. He received a letter from J at the conference and a card when he got back to Freedom. On his last day abroad, he wrote J a letter in which he drew a little box and printed inside it the words "NEVER DOUBT THAT I AM YOUR FRIEND." I guess he wanted to tell her that in spite of his disappointment over the way their lives had gone, he still thought of her kindly. It was three years since he had last seeen her. Incredible.

DOUBLE-FAULT: Strange how one person will keep on loving or feeling for another without any encouragement.

FAULT: Yes, it is. As I said before, things were cool between L-One and N before he left, and they continued that way after he came back. Maybe L-One was preparing for the time when N would be leaving permanently. Even when she did come to see him, just being next to him for a while would make her want to sleep with him. After which she would leave. Emotionally, it was very difficult for L-One.

She had moved out of her family's home and was living with a friend. One night in early August, N was invited to dinner. L-One was all madness and meanness toward him. Once she took his hair in one hand and with her face screwed up in a contortion of intense—well, almost hatred, really— she put her fist up against his nose and said defiantly, biting off each word, "If you only knew, baby, if you only knew." N was sitting at the table while she was threatening him in this way, but he remained calm and in control.

> N: Only knew what? What don't I know? [*He said it unemotionally, but he had an idea what she was talking about.*]

Later when he asked her to come back to his place and stay the night, she refused.

> N: Well, I gave you the car to be free and it's your choice to come with me or not.

At the word "free," she began jumping up and down wildly, crazily, and shouting, "I'm free! I'm free! Yippee, I'm free!" She was acting as if she'd gone berserk. She almost fell down but N grabbed her. Then he left. L-One kept the car.

A few nights later, L-One showed up at N's place. N wanted to sleep with her because he was somewhat frustrated—now there's an understatement. Once they started, it was always what they did best, and while they were making love, tears came into L-One's eyes.

N: Why are you crying?

L-ONE: All this time we've been together, you've never told me you love me. And I love you.

N: Of course I love you. Do you think I would have gone through everything that's happened with you if I didn't? I've loved you from the first week we met.

L-ONE: Why didn't you say so? [*Tears flowing in rivulets*]

N: Because I didn't know what to do with you. You're the first girl I've loved and didn't want to marry. It's very sad.

They were getting close to their reward. L-One brightened; she started to pull him closer. "It's always so good, you great big stud!" It was hot, sweet, and relaxing, and they lay there, physically spent. L-One said how nice it was to know N loved her, she felt so glad. She continued to talk, tears still streaming from her eyes. It was a confession. The weekends she didn't spend with N she spent with other friends, her "good kids," and she slept with them. This is what N had guessed when L-One had said, "If you only knew, baby, if you only knew." L-One's eyes darted around the room. N had never seen any one's eyes move so rapidly, and her eyelids never closed. Eye motion is supposed to be related to the swiftness of new thoughts—L-One's thoughts were racing at an incredible speed. N heard the rest of her story. He felt no malice, no scorn. He held her close, and when she finished he said, "Listen," and he talked about his "infidelities." He didn't want her to feel inferior or think of him as an angel. He could have kept quiet, but she deserved to know. At least that's how N saw it.

DOUBLE-FAULT: This N is a funny bird.

FAULT: When the emotional conflagration died down, they got dressed. L-One looked happy, but she said she had to leave. With a smile on her face and tears still flowing, she departed and N felt as if a hurricane had blown itself out inside his head.

N's work in Freedom came to an end. His last three days L-One came to him each night to lie beside him. In fact, she said she couldn't sleep where she was living, that she had to be with him to relax. N had always made life difficult for L-One by his mere existence and her attachment to him. Yet, knowing she wouldn't have him in the future, she could have no peace of mind these last few days. It was just like that with N and J when they were together.

L-One drove N to the airport and at the departure gate he squeezed her to him. Tears came to his eyes; he couldn't hold them back.

N: I wish you were coming with me.

L-ONE: You would say that. [*And she spoke with wisdom and bitterness. Yet he hadn't said it as a mere formality, for if N could really have accepted L-One, his life would have been fuller and happier.*]

N got on the plane, L-One was out of sight, and he took his seat. The plane was delayed for forty minutes and he thought over his past year. He was crying.

A new place, new people, and new work were again to be the pattern of N's life. It was true and he would keep intact his ties with old friends and lovers, but by his own choosing

110

they were to be of minor importance. N was tired of affairs, tired of emotionalism that drained his energy, tired of the repetitious conflict, calmness, conflict that he had lived with back in Freedom. Still, one of his first acts was to write L-One a letter from his new location.

DOUBLE-FAULT: Where is he now? You'll think of a good name, won't you?

FAULT: I'll try. How about calling the place "Expectancy"? Yes, that will do the job. "Expectancy" it is. Here's his letter.

September 18

Dear L-One:

The plane had to wait forty minutes before taking off and I spent that time explaining to you in an imaginary conversation what I believe and want (need).

In summation, I do not wish to spend my life with a woman who needs from me, or expects from me, or manifests in me, or deserves from me constant criticism. The point I am trying to make is that criticism, when given by someone who loves you, is not meant to destroy. One can easily survive it. One does not have to accept it. But it is crucial to me that someone I want to live with be independent enough to make me confident that no criticism from me will be shattering. There are many things you do that I cannot appreciate. You have said to me that all I have to do is snap my fingers. You don't seem to appreciate my belief that a lover is not a puppet but a partner.

Skipping all the details, "logical arguments," etc., my conclusion is that I have spent far too many moments shedding tears for what could have been or might have been or should have been. Basically, I love you, but this feeling is so twisted by day-to-day living with you that it is not able to survive the stress.

111

I hope that, living alone, you will find for yourself what you want, and will understand what responsibilities it entails. If you feel that we are incompatible, then that will be the end of it. If the reverse . . . I make no guarantees.

Take care, work hard. Reflect.

Love, N.

DOUBLE-FAULT: And what was her reaction to that, I wonder.

FAULT: Ha-haaa. She read the letter, corrected his grammatical mistakes in red pencil, and made succinct comments where appropriate. N roared with laughter—he thought she was great. In a later letter, she wrote and told him how calm and non-neurotic she had been since the source and substance of her tension had left—namely, N. She wrote: "You were worse than a tease, you G.D.S."

DOUBLE-FAULT: What on earth does G.D.S. stand for?

FAULT: God-damned stud, Ma'am. N still had a very tangible link to L-One, since she was in possession of his car. Before he left Freedom, the good doctor purchased a second car for his wife to use, but L-One was still restricted from driving it. She hadn't shown enough responsibility was the reason given. How does one show responsibility?

Almost the worst that could happen to L-One happened. She had a car accident that nearly demolished the car. This pleased the "I told you so" people, but N didn't give a damn about the machine. L-One was unhurt, thus bolstering her belief that all around her might crack up but she would survive. The car was fixed and things returned to normal.

N's correspondence with J was still continuing. He had written her from Freedom telling her what his address would be in Expectancy. After he had been settled in about three weeks, he heard from her. In this letter N found food for

112

hope, for she wrote that she'd love to see him the next time he came her way, and she thought of him as being one of her great friends.

There was something else in that letter worth mentioning. J wrote: "Please don't think I want to be a (ugh!) 'STAR.' We don't have any publicity agent or manager or anything like that, and are interested mainly in the music. That's the only thing that makes the traveling on tour, the rehearsing, the grinning, etc., worth while." The "we" referred to J and her sister. An interesting comment!

DOUBLE-FAULT: Sounds to me as if she misses him. Do you suppose that's true? And her comment about her work indicates she prefers to be more the knowledgeable than the known.

FAULT: Exactly. N was heartened not only by what she actually said but also by the tone of the whole letter. And so he wrote her telling her when he could get away and what dates suited him best. He said he'd like best to come at year-end holiday time, since that was only two months away, and would have nostalgic overtones. It would be the third anniversary of the trip he hadn't been able to make for financial reasons.

J replied once again saying that year's end was no good because she would be busy but spring or next summer would be fine. Best to meet in a warm sunny clime, she suggested. Again N felt repulsed, but not harshly.

DOUBLE-FAULT: How many times exactly has he tried to visit her?

FAULT: I don't know, I've lost count. N decided on two courses of action, heading in exactly opposite directions. He loved J but felt she would always put him off no matter how sympathetic her letters were. He also felt lonely away from L-One. The thought of finding still another woman about whom he could feel strongly was abhorrent to him. And besides, he loved L-One. Maybe time had changed her and she was just what he was looking for.

DOUBLE-FAULT: Sounds to me like he's in the dumps raking up old romances.

FAULT: N decided to continue writing J in the hope that she would set a definite date to see him, and he simultaneously undertook an exchange of letters with L-One in the hope that he could find the courage to commit himself to marriage with her. "May the best of all possible outcomes take place," thought N.

DOUBLE-FAULT: That's duplicity. Outright duplicity!

FAULT: Yes, damn it, it is—of sorts. But he was not going to marry L-One and then discover that if he had waited just a little bit longer J would have opted for him. That would have been hell for N, and for L-One, and for J. This way there was a chance two out of three would be happy. Maybe. Maybe not. But that's the course he took. And duplicity is altogether common in love. Remember that N's infidelities were matched by L-One's infidelities.

DOUBLE-FAULT: True. But J is above that.

FAULT: Is she? We shall see what we shall see. N wrote to L-One and told her what he felt about life, what he wanted, and he asked her what she felt. Her reply came quickly, was nine pages long, and was beautiful, but far too long to quote.

DOUBLE-FAULT: I want to hear this letter, so don't hold back. Out with it.

FAULT: You didn't say "please," therefore only a short résumé shall be yours. Really, Double-Fault, it's too long. Be content with a synopsis.

[*She nods yes.*]

L-One said that she had no fear of any financial situation N and she might encounter. If there was money—good; if not—she could manage. The children would be showered with love and scrubbed with understanding. Regardless of how they looked, she would always think of them as beautiful and woe betide N if he ever thought otherwise. Whatever value system they adopted, they would have to live it, and there would be no "Do as I say but don't do as I do" statements made to the children. N is to have no qualms about her being able to meet her responsibilities, because that would automatically come through her love for N. Their home would be open to all. What else? Oh, yes. She tells him she has always felt he put her under a microscope and analyzed her too much. This put constraints on her and produced just the effects he was afraid to find in her. Since he left Freedom, she has survived nicely, but still misses him. She has no doubt he would be good for her. "Don't falter, N," she wrote, "because I am bursting with love for you. Quickly—make a decision for the most expendable commodity in all creation is a human being. I love you. L-One."

Double-Fault: And N was in full agreement?

Fault: Oh, no, by no means. L-One is a person who emotes and loves and wants to give, which is fine, but there are other considerations, too. From N's view, children need direction and instruction and guidance. He thought L-One was considering them too much as equals. In certain respects he did agree with her. He believed his home was not his private territory but belonged to the entire family, that a child is neither a guest nor a slave in his father's house.

There was one part of the letter that showed that in a certain way L-One misjudged N. And she couldn't have suspected her error, because N had never told her about J. N does not falter when he has a choice. Just the opposite. He considers his options and then acts. His vacillations with L-One were the result in part of her behavior but more the result of his J fixation. He had J on the brain and she was first choice and still a possibility, even if remote. L-One never knew about J, so it was, as N saw it, understandable that she thought he faltered.

DOUBLE-FAULT: Well, then, he faltered. He had the choice of marrying L-One, asking J to marry him, or forgetting each or both. He did none of those things. That's faltering, if you ask me.

FAULT: Well, you can call it faltering. N would say his options were still alive, and who defines the length of time necessary to make a choice anyway? It's your prerogative to think what you choose.

DOUBLE-FAULT: It most certainly is. He faltered—clearly faltered.

FAULT: Meanwhile, as I said, N had written to J trying to pin her down on a date. He had suggested next March, since he had been told the year-end holiday was out. J wrote him on December 22nd saying she couldn't be sure. But once again the tone of her letter was cordial. So since he couldn't get a firm date out of J, N invited L-One to come and see him over the year-end holiday, but she refused, which surprised him. He had answered her letter, raising a few questions. He wanted to start a dialogue by mail with her to try to iron out their major points of disagreement. He believed that when you have to explain yourself on paper you get clearer insight into yourself. And it suited him to play a waiting game with L-One until he found out what J really wanted.

DOUBLE-FAULT: Doesn't surprise me.

FAULT: The result was that L-One got impatient with N for dawdling and his old fears returned when she wouldn't come to see him. Also, the more he thought about J, the surer he became that he wanted to see her ONE MORE TIME. He was going to squirm away from L-One.

One day in mid-January L-One calls N. Things have gone badly for her—emotionally and materially. She has had another car accident and the death of an ex-boyfriend has shocked her. N writes his heart out to her and invites her to come live with him—something she has always wanted.

DOUBLE-FAULT: It's perfectly obvious she'll come.

FAULT: She refuses. She has had a fit of depression, a melancholia so deep that self-destruction seems a possibility once again. She wants to be alone and pull herself out of her despair. She has already started to climb out of it and N feels reassured because—from what she tells him—her progress appears real. "Let's wait till June," she says. "I still love you deeply."

DOUBLE-FAULT: What brought on such a tragic depression?

FAULT: The old boyfriend had committed suicide.

DOUBLE-FAULT: Oh, that's a shame.

FAULT: I once saw a bit of graffiti that made me laugh. It went, "Suicide is the sincerest form of self-destruction." But when it happens to a friend it's really sad.

DOUBLE-FAULT: Quite right.

FAULT: A few days later, N heard from J. "School plans are busy BUT COME IN APRIL." The reason—a "tiny factor," her "current boyfriend" was not going away for a long period until March.

DOUBLE-FAULT: It would be both embarrassing and unnerving for both of them to be around J. I didn't know she had a boyfriend.

117

FAULT: Neither did N. What were you saying about duplicity before, may I ask?

DOUBLE-FAULT: You don't know all the facts. Never mind for now. Go on.

FAULT: N knew J would be going out. My gosh, it was over three years, and he hoped the current boyfriend was one of a string of men whom she had known and dropped. He hoped things weren't serious, but when he thought about it, he realized they couldn't be. Otherwise she wouldn't let him visit. The real trouble was that April was impossible for him. He couldn't get away then. He writes and tells her so, but before his letter reaches her he gets another letter TELLING HIM HE CAN COME ANYTIME HE WANTS. N is gloriously happy and he prays that nothing will interfere. He writes J and tells her when he will arrive, for he makes his flight reservations the day he receives her letter. He is bubbling, ebullient, and every other word that describes immense inner pleasure. He is *alive!*

DOUBLE-FAULT: A complete turnaround and in so short a time! N always thought school plans were so inflexible— they're made months in advance.

FAULT: Don't be naïve. The current boyfriend would obviously be gone before March 1st. N didn't write to ask what caused the change in J's plans. Plenty of time for that. All he hoped was that there would be no letter from J canceling the invitation in this letter. The weeks went quickly. He heard from J in mid-February, and he received another letter three days before he was to fly to her. He opened that letter with trepidation, expecting nothing and everything all at once. In it she asks him to let her know what flight he is coming on and she will meet the plane. N is puzzled—he has already sent her that information. He is slightly worried but she obviously still expects him if she intends to meet his flight.

He decides to call her and make sure she has the information. It's the first time he's heard her voice in nearly three years. It hasn't changed. He gives her the time of arrival and adds, "See you on Saturday." "Super," says J.

N knows J uses hyperbole—"million things" as the excuse for not writing for eight months, and "tiny factor" in reference to "current boyfriend"—hyperbole in a reverse sense. The word "super" must be saved for special occasions—it's too expansive an expression. N feels thrilled and excited. His anticipation, already high, rises still further.

As for L-One, their relationship deteriorates rapidly. He had raised her hopes and dashed them again. "Human beings are expendable," she wrote, and he wishes he were two people. He would gladly give one of himselves to her.

DOUBLE-FAULT: Himselves?

FAULT: I just made up a word—so what?

N took care of last-minute details before he left on his maiden voyage—how's that for a play on words?

DOUBLE-FAULT: Horrid.

FAULT: Thought you'd like it.

The flight was a long overseas flight and before departure N picked up a gift for J at the airport—an Oriental shirt. He thought about getting a gift for J's sister but decided that might be too much. J's letters to him almost always contained some tidbit about her sister and J had once enclosed a picture of the two of them. The picture really punctured N's heart, it brought back so many memories. But N decided to wait and meet the sister before thinking about giving her even a small gift.

DOUBLE-FAULT: That was wise. There are few things worse than people wanting to buy your friendship with trinkets and nonsense. I'm glad N isn't like that.

119

FAULT: How do you know he isn't? Remember—duplicity. Maybe his gift for J is to buy him a "Thank you" from her.

DOUBLE-FAULT: It can't possibly work, for if she has no feelings for him she'll resent having to say "Thank you" and he would be worse off than before. As long as the gift isn't too expensive, it's just a nice thought.

FAULT: Agreed.

The plane landed in the early morning in The City and N came through customs. Taking a deep breath, walking erect with a confident stride, luggage in hand, his deepest thoughts hidden by a casual smile, he passed through the doors to face the dozens of people waiting for their friends and loved ones. N didn't see J, partly because he didn't know what she would be wearing and partly because he wasn't focusing on the crowd but was just taking in all the helter-skelter around him. But J sees him, and starts jumping up and down, waving her long arms as if they were antennae emitting broadcast signals directing him toward her. And he sees her and is pleased that she is so excited. With a radiant smile on his face he walks quickly toward her.

She doesn't look at all as he remembers her. He remembered her jet-black hair; he saw red hair, which turned out to be a wig. He remembered her pale complexion; now it was dark, and turned out to be make-up. As he reached her, she put an arm, one arm, around him and thrust her head forward to give him a kiss. He remained rigid and then responded with a peck at her cheek just as she was starting to move away from him. They must have looked extremely awkward. She led the way to the bus that was to take them into The City, and paid the fare. When they were settled in the bus, N turned to her and said, "Here, let me give you a better kiss than the one in the station," but this time it was she who was stiff and hesitant. Looking at her, N saw that actually she had changed very little. She did look older—a few more lines—and she seemed to him a little taller, but he knew that was impossible. Their talk was mostly about the scenery, but N was wondering what J was really thinking—he felt like asking her, "Tell me exactly what has just passed through your mind." J was looking straight ahead or to the side, and rarely at N. The thought that came to him after all these years of trying to get where he was now was this: would he be glad he had come? Incredible. He's not there fifteen minutes, after three and a half years of wanting and waiting, and already he's wondering whether he'd be glad he came.

N listened while J told him there was a nice room at The Flat for him, and that she had worked hard to clean it, and that her sister would be there when they arrived. Apart from what J had written about her, the only indirect contact N had had with J's sister was part of a letter she had written to J when J was working in N's country. He had admired her eloquence in that letter, especially as she was only sixteen at the time. In the course of J's correspondence with N, she often, as I said, would relate some milestone in her sister's life, and N felt that J's sister—C—was almost a member of his family whom he had never met. Never in his life had N wanted to like and be liked by someone as much as he did now in the case of J's sister. When they met, he would be especially polite, but not fawning, and above all he would be quiet and not a bombastic hail-fellow-well-met individual.

DOUBLE-FAULT: Are you saying that N was going to perpetrate a fraud of personality on J's sister?

FAULT: Not at all. Whether they would like and respect each other in the long stretch would not depend too much on their first meeting. But N knew—as you do, too, I'm sure—that you can't force yourself on someone and say, "Like me very much."

DOUBLE-FAULT: Change "like" to "love" and I'll still agree.

FAULT: "Love" is different. Let's not get deflected. N would give J's sister time to decide about him and not expect instant like or dislike on her part.

The bus ride ended at a terminal from which they took a taxi the rest of the way. When they reached their destination, they climbed a few stairs to reach the door of The Flat. J opened the door and N followed her inside—it seemed like another world.

Let me describe it for you. There was a long hall which zigzagged its way to the back. As you came through the front door, there was a small foyer from which this hall turned back at a right angle. The first door on the right that led into anything other than a closet was the entrance to the kitchen—a fairly large room with a small combination refrigerator-cooking appliance. The hall bent at right angles once again, away from the kitchen door, and directly opposite the kitchen door was the door to the bathroom. Again the hall bent at right angles—I told you it zigzagged—and led to a small bedroom, freshly clean for N's occupancy, and here, too, at the door to N's bedroom, the hall bent for the last time at right angles back toward the kitchen. There were two large rooms on the left side of the hallway here. One was the living room, the other J's sister's bedroom, and finally the hallway ended in the doorway to J's bedroom—a room slightly larger than N's but considerably smaller than her sister's. Well, have you been able to follow the geometry of the dwelling? No? It doesn't matter. But if you can picture this—you come in the front door, take two paces and turn right, walk eight paces to the kitchen door and turn left, walk three paces to the bathroom door and turn right, walk six paces, on your left will be N's bedroom door, then turn right and one pace ahead of you on your left now will be the living-room door, two paces more, still on your left, J's sister's bedroom door, and directly ahead at one-half pace, the door to J's bedroom. It's really rather simple.

DOUBLE-FAULT: Too bad you didn't state it simply.

FAULT: Ha-Ha—I'll ignore that. The rooms were high-ceilinged and N felt it was all very cozy. As they went down the hall, J called to her sister, who came out of her room to meet them.

J: N, this is my sister C.

N: Very pleased to meet you. [*Quietly said, with a nod of his head and a soft smile—whatever that is—on his face. He reached out his hand, and C did the same.*]

C: Happy to meet you, too. How was your trip?

N: Very comfortable, thank you.

N waited for J to direct him to his room, which she did while still chattering away to make him feel at home. Once there, he put down his bag, shed his topcoat and hung it over a chair, and pronounced the room to be a very cozy, comfortable place. And he meant it. J was pleased and told him how hard she had worked to get it in shape for him—and she recovering from a bout of flu. N was solicitous about her health. He remembered that she was prone to colds and he remarked that he hoped she hadn't exerted herself too much. J told him how dirty The Flat had been when the girls first moved in and how it had taken them three months of scraping, cleaning, scrubbing, and painting to get it in decent shape. She showed him around, and when they came to her bedroom she pointed to the curtain, for there, pinned to it, was the small Scotty dog playing bagpipes—the trinket he had given her when she went off on the trip on which her luggage was lost. N teased her by suggesting that she had just recently put it up, but she denied it. N said he was only joking, and they reminisced about that time. "So she kept it all this time," N thought. That reminded him:

N: Wait right here. I forgot—I brought you something.

And he went back to his room and brought out the gift-wrapped package he had picked up at the start of his travels. J started to open it, looking eager and pleased. It made N feel good to see her in such high spirits. And she liked it very much indeed.

DOUBLE-FAULT: You make her out to be some sort of vulture or something, attacking that package.

FAULT: No, no, no. She had the look most people have who are given a surprise gift. They're happy to get it and are curious about its contents. N decided that now he would get C something, too, because he had taken an instant liking to her. But first he would find out what suited her. C was as tall as J, a fine-looking woman who, N concluded, would turn many a man's head—but not his.

DOUBLE-FAULT: Sounds like she's turned it already.

FAULT: No, no, no. N only had thoughts for J.

N now unpacked. He had brought along some contraceptives, and as he removed them from his bag he wondered whether he would get to use them, then scolded himself for the thought. He would try to be alone with J. If she were in the kitchen, he would go there to sit and talk. But he had trouble controlling himself; he so much wanted to touch J that he kept going to her and putting his arm around her. He could see he was making her nervous, and once while they were passing in the hall he reached up almost naturally, put his fingers around the back of her neck, squeezed her as if he were massaging her neck, and said, "Relax, J." The look on her face was one of sheer nervousness. N decided that C's presence in the apartment was part of the reason for J's reaction but that his own behavior was the overwhelming reason for it. He concluded that he had some nerve to suppose he could just walk into The Flat and expect them to act toward each other just the way they had three years before. He was wrong to keep pestering her. If they were alone, she could tell him to stop, but with C present, even in another room, it would embarrass J to yell at him to behave. As far as N could make out, the current boyfriend wasn't current any more— he didn't see one picture of him in The Flat. Still it was presumptuous of him to believe that J would accept his advances. He decided to give J and himself a breather, and told her he was going to his room to do some reading while she did her chores. In his room he sat wondering what was going on in J's head.

Then luck started to favor N. C said she would be gone for the afternoon to do some work at the library. N said good-bye, as did J. N heard J go into her bedroom and he rose from his chair, went to his door, and looked down the hall to see J's door ajar. They were alone in The Flat—but N had no expectations. He knocked on her open door.

N: May I come in?

J: Yes. Of course.

N: I want to apologize to you for the way I've behaved since we came from the airport. At the airport I didn't know whether you'd want me to kiss you or if you wanted to kiss me hello, and I sort of stood away from you. Since we've come here, I've tried to make up for that cold greeting and I've tried to get too close. I'm sorry.

J: I didn't know what you'd expect, either.

N: It's been a long time—over three and a half years— since we last saw each other. The time ticked away. Were you watching the clock?

J: No. It just seemed to pass and we'd write each other our news.

As they continued talking, N began to feel like a lover again. J looked warm and receptive. He bent over her chair and started to massage her neck muscles as he used to do, his strong fingers kneading the knots out of her shoulders. He stopped, and slowly lifted her chin. They kissed—a warm, slow, sweet kiss. In a few more moments—for who watches the ticking clock now—the light was out and they were lying next to each other on the bed. N went about the pleasant task of undressing her, and she was—receptive is the best word, cooperative wouldn't be bad either, but would suggest that she actually helped, which wouldn't be quite right. When he asked her to move an arm or turn so he could undo a clasp, she did, but she wouldn't anticipate anything. Yet there was no doubt about the outcome. When N started to take the plunge, J spoke:

J: What are you doing?

N: I assume you take the pill.

J: No, I don't.

N: Wait a moment; I'll get a contraceptive.

He was down the hall and back in no time. He penetrated her and technically his love-making was lousy. He came too fast, because she excited him so much; just the thought of being in her started his fluids flowing.

N: Let's do it again when I'm ready.

J: Yes, of course, darling. Anything you wish.

It surprised N that she would be for it. He remembered her as cold. After all, she had sent him home their last night together, and one time when he had been inside her and had experienced some difficulty coming the second time, she had been impatient and complaining. But now when she said, "Yes, of course, darling," he wondered whether her previous boyfriend had changed her.

> N: I was worried that we wouldn't fit properly. The last time we made love, your "mound of Venus" just about gave me a bone bruise. We seem to fit better now. How do you feel?
>
> J: A little like an adulteress.
>
> N: Sorry. There's nothing I can do about that.

Apparently the last boyfriend was still an emotional hurdle for J. In less than an hour she leaped the hurdle again, and this time N was in complete control. They went back and forth, in and out, for more than twenty minutes—it was a technical masterpiece, for he collapsed on top of her very shortly after she collapsed in pleasure underneath him. And she had pulled him to her when she was at the height of her enjoyment.

Afterward, when they both had reclaimed their breath, N sat on the edge of the bed and J sat upright, her eyes staring off into space with the kind of look on her face that suggested an illumination.

> J: You still LOVE me. You STILL love me.

N looked at her and made up his mind to be positive and affirmative, for better or worse.

> N: Yes. I still love you, J. I've loved you all these years.

He said it matter-of-factly—after all, they were mature people.

DOUBLE-FAULT: She must have had some strong feelings left over about N, too.

FAULT: It's not clear at this point why she slept with N.

127

They reminded themselves where they were, and thought it best to get cleaned up. There would be time to talk, but now their worry was that C might be home early.

Close to six C arrived, and N invited her to join J and himself for dinner. She declined, because she had made previous plans with her boyfriend, and this didn't make N unhappy since he really preferred to be alone with J this first evening. So N and J went out to a nice restaurant nearby, walking there hand in hand. The place had atmosphere, the food was good, the conversation flowed, as did a little wine, and the more N looked at J, the more she resembled the girl he remembered. She also gave him the impression that she had become less excitable and more relaxed, by which N meant that the tone of her personality was calmer.

It was such a delightful evening—N enjoyed every moment of it. So did J. They walked leisurely back to The Flat after dinner, N's arm wrapped around J's waist. It was late when they arrived; by N's reckoning he had been up more than thirty hours and sleep would be appreciated. For J, too, it had been a long day.

J: Sleep well.

N: You, too.

They both went to bed.

She still used the same phrase to say good night. He liked it. As he lay in bed, two facts were obvious to N—J had feelings for him, but she also still had feelings for her "current boyfriend," who had been "current" for a year and a half, as her conversation had disclosed. That's a long time to be "current," N thought.

DOUBLE-FAULT: What does he mean, "a long time"? He had been pining for J for more than three years. A year and a half isn't that long.

128

FAULT: Try holding your breath for that length of time. Time. A very interesting word. We'll discuss it some time sometime.

N fell asleep wishing he were sleeping in the bed down the hall. In the morning he awoke to the first of four traumatic days. He knew that J's mind was in flux about whether she would accept him as her new but old boyfriend, or even whether she would want a boyfriend at all. Furthermore with C living in The Flat there was no privacy late at night when two people could get to know one another's thinking better, and lastly J's job gave her obligations in the daytime that made it necessary for N to accommodate himself to her schedule.

It was Sunday, and they got up late and went for a walk in a park. N didn't insist on holding hands. He thought it best to give J a chance to be herself, as she might have been the day before he arrived. Perhaps she would reach out and take his hand, which would have been better. She didn't, and N knew she was still tense about the previous day's love-making.

N: How do you feel?

J: A little bit like an adulteress. I knew you before, and that made it possible, but I still feel a little bit like an adulteress.

N dropped the subject. No sense in talking about something unpleasant. Things were still in the embryonic stage and confrontation on crucial questions was not to be looked for. After an hour they went back to The Flat; all three had dinner and shortly afterward J retired, since she had to get up early for work. It was agreed, however, that N would have morning coffee with J before she left The Flat.

On Monday, N had an incredibly bad start—dismal, in fact. His mind was active and he had had trouble sleeping. He was awake when the alarm went off in J's bedroom.

"Good," he thought, for he didn't start to feel alive until they were together. But there was no sound from J's room. As the minutes passed, N began to think that she had turned over and gone back to sleep, so he got up and tiptoed down the hall to J's door. Still silence. He pushed the door open and silently walked to the side of the bed. He touched the blanket where her shoulder was.

N: Hey, your alarm went off. Don't oversleep.

But she was half-awake and reacted soundlessly with violent fist-shaking, like a baby that can't be calmed. Then, "Get out," she said quietly, but she was furious. N left quickly, almost on a run. He had made a serious mistake while trying to be helpful. He knew how irksome it is to be roused from bed before one is ready to get up.

In his room, N sank beneath his covers. A few moments later he heard J get up, turn on the radio, and come flying down the hall with it on her way to the bathroom. N lay in bed telling himself he should never have meddled. On the other side of the wall he could just barely hear the radio over the sound of the water rushing into the tub. "Oh, well—to err is human," he thought, but it gave him no consolation.

J's morning ritual progresses. When the time comes, she sticks her head into his room and says, "Coffee's ready," and dashes off again down the hallway to the kitchen. N bounds out of bed and puts his robe on before joining her at the breakfast table. He doesn't want to say he's sorry about this morning's episode because he simply doesn't want it mentioned again.

J: You MUSTN'T do things like that.

N: Sorry. I heard the alarm go off and then silence. I thought you might have slept through it.

130

An excuse—ordinarily a good one. He didn't feel it was "ordinary" enough.

DOUBLE-FAULT: I don't blame her for being so annoyed. He must have frightened her half to death.

FAULT: Don't exaggerate. And if she had slept through the alarm she would have thanked him for rousing her.

N detested coffee but he could drink J's coffee by the quart. To him, coffee was one of the most overrated beverages there ever was—except when J made it. The day's plans were made at the breakfast table. He was to meet her across the street from where she worked at about 8 P.M., and they would go to dinner. Fine. The directions were given and he said he would find the place. It was well known and if he got lost he could ask anyone. J left for work and N went back to bed.

Later N had another breakfast with C, and then he left to wander around The City until the appointed hour for his rendezvous with J. He had no trouble passing the time and he marveled at how much he enjoyed himself just walking through the streets of The City. He even went into an art museum—something he hadn't done in years.

He arrived at the appointed place at 7 P.M.—an hour early. He thought it was wonderful—a small adventure—to stand on the sidewalk and watch the people go by. He had taken the time to buy J some flowers, and these he held behind his back as a surprise for her. She had told him to wait under a specific theatre marquee across the street and down the block from her building, and he found it with no difficulty. He walked up and down the street looking for her building, and when he came to it, it was dark—not a light on in the whole place. He couldn't believe it. There was no reason for J to make up a story. And yet he didn't quite trust her. His recollection of her was that she would do exactly what pleased her, but this made no sense. Why should she lie, or did the

131

place close early and had she gone back to The Flat? "Less than an hour to wait, N—don't panic," he thought. "Maybe I should call The Flat to see what's going on. No, better not. Wait the hour out and then act. It would be extremely stupid if I made an error somewhere along the way and my lack of faith in J became evident from a phone call." N stood under the marquee, his eyes wandering up and down the street but always resting on that dark building. Almost eight. There she was, coming up the street on the other side, from the other direction. He quickly crossed the street and he could hear her cooing "Hellooo." He was so relieved and overjoyed. He had been looking at the wrong building. Thank goodness he hadn't called. He stuck out the flowers and she gushed over them. He loved bringing her flowers; he loved making her happy.

J: Did you see me waving from my window over there?

N: No, I didn't. In fact, I kept looking at the wrong building.

J looked delighted—as if the morning's incident had never taken place. It was early evening now. They went to dinner at an exotic restaurant nearby. J was familiar with the menu and he followed her suggestions in ordering. The conversation drifted from the food to its preparation, and the waitress was very helpful in that respect, too. It turns out that the waitress is the wife of the chef. N enjoys the food and his pleasure is passed on back to the chef. The conversation abruptly changes to, of all topics, driving cars. N can, J can't, and the waitress tells a long story about rushing her husband to the hospital when he had a heart attack some time back. She goes on to say that her husband insisted she learn to drive when they first bought their car a long time ago.

WAITRESS: You'll never guess how long I've been driving.

132

N is quick with figures and assumes she started driving when she was twenty-one and thinks thirty to thirty-five years is a long time to drive. That's reasonable.

N: Thirty-five years.

WAITRESS: How old do you think I am?

N knows his guess is wrong by the way she asks that last question. She looks to him to be in her early forties but he adds twenty-one to thirty to get fifty-one, and he blurts out.

N: About fifty—fifty-five.

WAITRESS: I am forty-two.

J: [*To N*] How could you?

N: I'm sorry. They say flying from continent to continent makes you a little dumb-witted when it comes to numbers. I'm sorry.

J: [*Again to N*] How could you do that? That was terrible.

N: [*To J*] I said I was sorry. Twice.

WAITRESS: Well, I'll forgive you.

N: I'm sorry and I knew it was wrong when I said it, because you don't look anywhere near that age.

J: You really have to be more careful with your figures.

N had made a mistake and J would broadcast it until everyone knew it. His first apology would have ended the matter had it not been for J's second "How could you do that?"

Later, when they came back to The Flat, N told C how much he'd enjoyed the food and J repeated the story of how impolitic he'd been with the waitress. Once again the words "How could you do that?" came from J. N felt like asking her,

"How can you say 'How could you do that?' so often?" but he didn't. Later J kissed him good night before going to her bedroom. All in all, it had been a mixed day for N.

DOUBLE-FAULT: What should J have done when he was so impolitic, as he called it?

FAULT: She should have stayed mum and let him make his apology. Her loyalty should have been to N, not to the waitress. I hope you agree.

DOUBLE-FAULT: Well, maybe.

FAULT: On Tuesday, N went to meet J for lunch, only this time he went to the right building. She told him that C said he was the first person from his country she'd ever liked. N was exhilarated, for he had become fond of C. He wished she was a sister—in fact, a sister-in-law.

After lunch, N wandered off to see the sights while J went back to work. Later in the day, he met J again and they went back to The Flat, and on the way they picked up some groceries for dinner.

Dinner was always a cozy, looked-forward-to part of the day for N. The three of them would gather around the table to eat the fine meal that J had prepared. They were always hungry, J and C, and N had no trouble finishing a plate, either. As soon as dinner was over, J would turn to C and say something like, "Well, I cooked, you can wash." N would wince, C would make no comment, and the table would be cleared, all three carrying dishes to the sink.

It was already clear to N what the household ritual was. J considered herself the boss of The Flat, its mentor and chief custodian. She acted as if the running of the place were her responsibility. When decisions were to be made, J would ask, "What do you think, C," which always sounded to N as if J were throwing C a small bone. If the decision was an inconsequential one, J would let it go C's way, but in what J considered important matters she would give her view, and then ask C as an afterthought, "Don't you agree, C?" It was J who almost always determined when The Flat was to be cleaned, wrote the milkman notes if necessary, made the shopping lists, and, at night, checked to see that all lights and heaters were off. If she asked C "Did you turn the heater off in the living room?" and the answer was "Yes," J would check it anyway.

DOUBLE-FAULT: I see nothing wrong with that. Some people can't fall asleep if they know there's a possible danger to the house. Nothing wrong with checking, I would say.

FAULT: True. But often C would stay up later than J, and J would admonish her before going to bed to make sure that everything was turned off. C was being treated as a daughter by big sister. And when they went shopping, J holding on to the shopping list and C pushing the cart, J would pick the food. Or J would say to her, "C, you get that while I get this." Participatory democracy in full bloom. Why was C so compliant, why didn't she fight for equal weight? Because, very simply, it just wasn't worth the effort, and N knew it, and C knew it, but J would remark that C was a little slack in the management of The Flat and if she, J, didn't do things, no one would. People who think they do so much for others tend to believe that if they didn't, those others would shrivel up. C shrivel up? Ha—N would have given any odds against that.

But J saw it in a different light. She and N had talked the previous two days about their current lives and how they had changed since they'd last seen each other. J said that every year she felt she was a slightly better person than she'd been the year before. She said she was such a giving person. She gave to her mother by singing, she gave to C by living and working with her, she gave to her students. She was always giving, she said, and she didn't understand why some people made nasty comments about her. N knew why but he didn't have the heart to tell her. J wasn't a very humble person and sometimes she was extremely selfish. Her seeing herself in the role of a great giver was, on the basis of N's knowledge of her, ludicrous. N's mother, for instance, was a great giver, a sacrificer, and J had a long way to go to get into his mother's category. N was fairly sure J sang for the limelight and attention it brought her, in spite of her denying that she wanted to be thought of as a (ugh!) "star," even if it also gave her mother pleasure to see her perform.

DOUBLE-FAULT: Then she did "give" her mother quite a bit, didn't she?

FAULT: Yes—but you can't consider yourself a giver if you're doing something you want to do, no matter how much pleasure is derived from it by someone else. If it had suited J to quit singing she would have, no matter how much her mother wanted her to continue. That's what N thought at the time, anyway. It was true that J's mother made dresses for the girls and reveled in their talents and limited fame, but N didn't know at this time whether she actually demanded that her daughters continue their careers or whether she would have been just as content to see them do something else. In other words, perhaps anything J did would be "giving" to her mother.

As for C, she gave as much to J as J gave to C, and possibly more, for C's interests academically were definitely not in music, and to continue singing with J meant possibly holding up her own work. Also, for a teacher to feel that she gives so much to her students and to believe them lucky to have her for a teacher is rank egotism. Was she really a "giver?" N thought not.

J would always be the target for nasty comments because,

apart from people being jealous of those with talent and looks, people are contemptuous toward those who are haughty about themselves, even if they do have great ability.

J said something else that was interesting vis-à-vis the family relationships: "In Mummy's eyes, C is the one." N wondered why J was so sure of this.

Let me go on just a little bit longer before you comment. J had quite a figure in stretch pants or miniskirt with sheer stockings, but N knew that age was creeping up on her. Three years before, her legs had been firm and the skin tight. When they were naked, N saw that her thighs were fleshier and her veins more apparent. She was, to be sure, don't misunderstand, a very attractive woman—she was, is, and always would be so in N's eyes—but the point I am making is that one tends to have illusions about oneself. J saw herself as a great giver, but the observer saw very little "greatness" there. Probably J saw herself as a stunning woman but the observer saw that she was already a little on the downhill side. This dichotomy of belief—what J thought *vs.* what N thought—didn't for the slightest moment interfere with N's love for J. You may find it bewildering. Here we have a man who knows all a woman's faults, yet loves her with all the passion he possesses. If you know how to love, or what love is, you'll understand.

DOUBLE-FAULT: I understand perfectly well, thank you, but it's arrogant of N to presume he is the one in the right when he doesn't even know J's parents, for one thing, and has only known C for three days. Absolutely ludicrous.

FAULT: Ludicrous—it's ludicrous how that word gets bandied about. Let's forget for the moment—shall we?—N's and J's views of each other, and continue.

N could tell that J was glad to have him around. She would tell him how she liked fixing his morning coffee and shopping with him for groceries. Things were starting to settle in her

mind and it was the next evening—Wednesday evening—
that N started to breathe happily again. After a pleasant day
and another good dinner, C and J disappeared into their
rooms. C spent most of her time in her room anyway, and
usually she slammed the door loudly behind her. But J's door
was opened slightly, and as N came down the hall, he could
see her hunched over her desk, writing, perhaps a letter to
"current boyfriend," N thought. When she heard his step, she
stopped, peered over her shoulder, and became more guarded
about the letter. She was obviously trying to keep N from
knowing about it. N was no dolt. He realized a decision was
being made. He sidestepped into the living room. "If a decision is to be made," he thought, "let her do it now and in
peace." N paced back and forth on the rug. His mind was all
on the consequences of the missile being prepared for launch-
ing in J's room. Was she writing to say she missed the man or
to say he would be longer be missed? N felt by turns manly
and depressingly aware of how it would be if he lost J. He
could see his whole life with her, turbulent at times, but utterly
desirable.

In less than ten minutes, J came down the hall toward the
living room. N stood still in the middle of the room, his heart
pounding, his breath rushing in and out of his lungs, his eyes
fixed on the door, awaiting the first sign she would give when
she came in. And through that door she came with a faint
smile on her face, her hands held behind her back. She walked
directly toward him. HE'D WON!

They embraced and N held her close and squeezed her
closer as she put her long slender arms around his neck. They
kissed. N felt fantastic. Incredible how one woman can mean
so much to a man. They sat down on the rug, N leaning
against a chair, J's head resting on his chest, and they talked
softly to each other. They wanted to make love, but there was
no chance for that with C in the next room. However, C had

to leave early the next morning, and J's work didn't start until noon. She told N to come to her room as soon as C left. Of course N was all anticipation and couldn't wait for dawn to come and C to go.

DOUBLE-FAULT: So she decided for N, and he there only four days after three and a half years! He must be a remarkable fellow.

FAULT: Not really. He just happened to suit J.

Next morning, as soon as he heard C close the front door behind her, N bounded out of bed and made his way down the hall to J's room, praying that she remembered she had invited him to do so. He came through her door quietly with a soft "Good morning, darling." J sat up in bed as he approached, opened her arms wide, and, with a sleepy smile, gave him haven with her body. She felt so warm and tender and N held her close. The two of them lay in bed for a spell, their legs intertwined, J resting on his chest. And then, each feeling more and more the warmth of the other, slowly and pleasantly they found new positions. And as they became more awake and more stimulating to each other, they made that bed creak as if it were a sounding board to wake the world. It was indeed most musical, and the perfect way to start the day. And the days became better because their feelings were firmly established.

That night, N and J went to a movie. J was pleased to get out of The Flat. You could tell it by the happy way she dressed and did her hair up. They took a taxi to the theatre and J sat close to him, her head resting on his shoulder, making it easy to steal a kiss when the driver wasn't looking in the rear-view mirror. In the theatre, they held hands and J kept popping thin mints into his mouth. She loved candy and sweets and ate them constantly. She said she had a sugar deficiency in her blood and simply had to have a sweet from time to time. Even

139

though N was full from dinner, he accepted the mints from J's fingers when she pushed them against his lips.

In the darkness of the theatre, N started to get those feelings that make it uncomfortable to be in a public place. He wanted her, and he was afraid he would have an orgasm right there where he sat. To make things worse, J leaned over and gave him a beautiful, sweet, wet kiss on the cheek. N had to start concentrating on the movie. It was *Ulysses*. No luck there.

But that's how love grows—in those intimate moments that only occur in the passing of a mint. N was now sure that the years of waiting had been worth it. These moments with J were making him feel more alive than he had ever been before, and he knew there was more to come.

DOUBLE-FAULT: He sounds so happy. I hope it lasts for him.

FAULT: Do you really? Well, J disappointed him when they came home to The Flat after the movie. In the taxi on the way back, she told him how she loved to go places with him. That part was great, but when they entered The Flat, J was instantly aware that C's boyfriend was there. Perhaps C had told J she expected him, or perhaps J had a sixth sense about who was in The Flat. Anyway, J rushed ahead of N to get down the hall, and he walked quickly to stay close behind her. The hall coat closet was directly opposite the door to the living room. That door was closed, and it was obvious to N that C and her boyfriend were behind that door—talking or kissing or whatever. N started to hang up his coat and he and J made enough noise coming down the hall to warn anyone in the living room that they were back. N turned toward J to help her off with her coat, but she was standing at the living room poised to knock, which she did, didn't wait for a reply, and entered the room as C was saying, "Come in." Big smiles and hellos were exchanged between J and the two in the living room, who were sitting on the rug having tea and cake. N thought J was very rude for intruding—well, maybe not intruding, but entering so fast. Suppose they had needed time to rearrange their clothing? J should have waited, but she didn't. And it was clear to N she hadn't wanted to. N once asked J whether she thought C was a virgin.

J: Probably not.

N: Had an affair with her boyfriend, do you think?

J: I guess so.

N had been curious; he thought it was none of his business, but he had asked anyway. Shortly after J entered, N came in and introductions were made. Soon after, C's boyfriend left. N sensed that he hadn't wanted to be in the same room with J. As time went on, it struck N as odd that he rarely if ever came to The Flat, never had dinner with the girls, never picked C up—she always met him somewhere when they did get together—but he did call her every day. Sometimes those conversations were of the briefest. But N was sure C was fond of the man.

DOUBLE-FAULT: Do you suppose there was bad feeling between him and J?

FAULT: I don't know enough to answer that question.

The weekend was coming up and with it more luck, very good luck, for N. C had just finished some work and it would be the last chance she would have in a long time to go home to visit her parents. This meant she would leave Saturday morning and return possibly late Sunday night. Her going would make The Flat a deserted oasis for N and J. N couldn't ask for anything more—to do what they liked and to take their time doing it. Just the two of them, only the two of them, the two of them alone—all sweet phrases running around in N's mind. Apart from its physical aspects, this weekend turned out to be of utmost importance, because details and matters of the deepest significance were discussed. Before I launch into that, I want to digress at length about the relationships among C, J, Mummy, and Daddy, as N thought them to be at this time from what he had heard discussed by the girls.

DOUBLE-FAULT: That would be most appreciated. It will make it easier to judge their characters and comprehend their attitudes.

FAULT: Their father was a doctor, as you probably recall. Their mother, before she had married, had been some kind of performer or singer—connected with the theatre, at any rate. They were always so concerned with their economic status and with what they could provide for their children that they had limited themselves to two. J, born during The War, was the older by about six years. C happened along after The War, quite probably at a time when the parents had decided they could afford to have her. Daddy had served in The War, and his practice almost surely needed some time to grow after he became a civilian again. C and J felt that both of them being girls had been a blow to Daddy. As time passed, they came under the hegemony of their mother, and as they became more aware of their sex, they naturally gravitated toward her. And, as J tells it, Daddy often spent days away from home tending to medical duties, which left the girls and Mummy to their own devices. It seemed that the father was becoming the odd member of his family. As for any suggestion of infidelity associated with either Mummy or Daddy, the girls never mentioned it, perhaps because it didn't exist or perhaps because it did. Anyway, N had no opinion about that aspect of the parents' relationship.

From J's description of her early life, the guiding principle in the household was "wants *vs.* needs." If you wanted something, that was not sufficient reason to buy it. It had to be needed. Once, when J was a teen-ager, she wanted a bicycle, but she had no need for it that would satisfy her parents. So she joined a church choral group and, of course, in order to get to the church and back, she needed transportation. They bought her a bike. Another time, C was most anxious to buy a pair of shoes. She pleaded for them, even cried a little, but her father would not be budged. She needed them, she said. Daddy spoke up and requested her to go to her room and bring down to the living room all the pairs of shoes she had and line them up. The line of shoes stretched almost across the room. "Do you still maintain you need a new pair?" he asked. She gave up the idea. The girls were bright and good students, but C had a little trouble getting started because she had been somewhat silent as a very young child. Her mother was quick in her defense when a schoolteacher thought C was dumb in class and yelled at her to speak. To hear J tell it, Mummy nearly brained the teacher when they met. At home, C would have to command attention when she was little by raising her hand at the dinner table if she wanted anything. However, this phase fortunately didn't last long, and she sparkled once she started to talk.

Their parents demanded of them that they do their best, which was considerable, and to take pride in their efforts and in what they achieved. Good solid values—work and pride.

Daddy was a musician—a piano player of some skill. Both girls were taught music by Mummy from a very early age, with Daddy's blessing. J's pinky finger was slightly misshapen, and hours of practice under Mummy's watchful eye were able to erase the consequences of that physical disability. The point is that both girls were driven to do their best and to develop their latent talents; they wanted, and accepted as best for them, their parents' instructions. C could not only play the piano but she was also good at guitar. Both girls had fine voices. J was always pointing out to N that her voice was getting better—and they had, since they moved into The Flat, joined their talents to form a cabaret act. They sang songs in many languages, and danced a little. They were striking to look at. J had more experience than C, since she had had a singles act even before N met her. They didn't do much dancing—J, for all her musical skill and knowledge, didn't have the right feel for motion, although C had good dance rhythm. On a stage it didn't matter much, for their costumes alone would dazzle any observer. Which brings us back to the mother, who supplied their adornments, and both girls agreed she was living again in the glories of her children's work. She was a sort of "third member" of a duo. No opinion was expressed on what their father thought about the way their life was going.

In the past few years, an enormous amount of bickering had developed between the parents. Perhaps "bickering" is too mild a word. Shortly after J came back from N's country, a divorce seemed imminent, but the details are not known by N. Since then, the mother had periodically threatened to leave the household. Angry words would give way to the more mollifying kind and she would stay, although, as N heard it, she had actually left overnight on at least one occasion. Reasonable stability was the most that could be hoped for.

The financial arrangements were most perplexing. Both girls thought Daddy had a pile of money, but in daily life his "wants vs. needs" philosophy still prevailed. C was to be supported by the father until graduation, but her dependency was constantly held up to her by Daddy and indirectly by J, who would give C something for her weekly allowance. The source of that money was also Daddy, presumably. J had her job, of course, and she was very frugal. She had certain advantages going for her also—her clothes, as I said, were homemade and the rent for The Flat was paid by Daddy. N didn't think that J paid any part of the rent. Once, N accompanied her to her bank and he asked why it was so far from where she lived. Why not use a more conveniently located bank? She answered by telling him that this particular bank had a branch in Daddy's city and it was a better arrangement for all concerned. Whether J was financially independent was not clear, but she did have some money saved from her cabaret earnings, and was certainly better off financially than C.

In J's view, C was "THE ONE" most adored by Mummy, who had a never-ending supply of glowing stories to tell about her precocity. J had a protective, motherly attitude toward C, though at times that attitude was critical—"C hasn't been around as much as I have, and sometimes doesn't see things as they should be seen." On the other hand, she could remember C's childhood, the little silent girl waving her arm to get attention, and she felt that C should be made happy. How one can force someone else to be happy is not known as yet, but J talked as if it were her responsibility to find out for C's sake. She would be furious when Daddy treated C unkindly. "Every time she goes home, HE has something nasty to say to her—makes her cry all the time. You don't know how badly he treats her, he can be so caustic. It's just AWFUL. C dreads going home, and likes to leave as quickly as possible." But whenever J required medicine or medical advice, she was quick to call Daddy—"He can be so gentle with patients. I have so much trust in him." Any questions?

DOUBLE-FAULT: Just one. What was N's over-all view of the family?

FAULT: Over all? Despite the cabaret act that kept mother and daughters occupied in a common venture, N thought all of them were headed in different directions.

Before C left for the weekend, the girls received a phone call from Mummy, who was checking on when C could be expected. That information was transmitted, and then J introduced N to Mummy over the phone. J had forewarned him that Mummy could talk and talk. N listened politely until Mummy asked to speak to J again. At that point, J told Mummy, "Daddy had better be nice to C, or I'll have at him." Daddy never got on the phone, but it's not certain he was home. N thought a long time about J's admonition. Was it sound and fury signifying nothing, or was C really in for a bad time? In any case, J had really been outspoken about Daddy.

C left for home with her small suitcase and with an unhappy expression on her face. N felt she was making the trip out of duty. He was glad she would be gone and at the same time he knew he would miss her. Earlier in the week, while J was working and he was wandering around The City, he had found a gift for C that he thought most appropriate—a recording of the original sound track to the movie *Black Orpheus*. It was one of his favorites, but when he gave it to her and she played it, he was disappointed—it had only sketches from the movie and wasn't the record he had previously heard. He promised her that someday he would find the right one and send it to her. She thanked him warmly for the one he had given her and said he shouldn't have done it.

DOUBLE-FAULT: That was a nice gift. N chose wisely.

FAULT: Glad to hear you approve. On Saturday morning, after C left, N and J retired to J's bedroom and started on a two-person bacchanal. They slipped under the covers and their heat and desire were rapturous for both of them. N felt alive, peaceful, loving—he would rather be making love to J than doing anything else in the world, including playing tennis. And they made love, the most passionate love N had ever experienced—long intervals of plunging in and out of her, feeling her body's muscles and organs convulsively react-

146

ing inside her, completely spending himself, then resting for a while in her arms and going at it again. Take it from N, whoever said women don't feel a climax is an idiot. J wanted him so hard in her it was almost as if she hoped he'd split her in two. And N's control was perfect. He held off for the longest time to make sure she was pleasurably sated. She had some fantastic orgasms that completely exhausted her, so much so that all she could do was lie there under him while he reached his own climax. It was the kind of love-making that N had always wanted with J—to see her totally enervated and happy under him. With lots of "I love you"s from both of them—though, to be accurate, these were always initiated by N and merely echoed by J—they tried in one day to do away with three and a half years of N's frustration. Funny how J talked when she made love—she lisped, and to N it sounded cute and lovey-dovey.

DOUBLE-FAULT: Lovey-dovey! My word!

FAULT: They stopped in the late afternoon. N had reached a climax six times, almost as regularly as the tower clock struck its chimes—as if he were simultaneously coupling with the clock. J said it was marvelous he could inspire her so, that a woman likes to have a man want her to keep coming. And she knew that's what he wanted. But nature, being what she is, demanded after such a long, pleasant outing—or is it inning? —that they embark upon recuperation, especially upon the consumption of food and drink. N was famished. But first they would bathe.

DOUBLE-FAULT: I rather think they would need to after *that*.

FAULT: Quite. J drew herself a bath and N scrubbed her body with soap and massaged her back and around her neck while she sat in the hot water. Most appreciated and relaxing. After her bath, the tub was refilled and N settled beneath the hot water and J reciprocated. Life can be so idyllic, except that it goes on. After N stepped out of the tub, J tried to replace a clothesline the girls had installed for hanging up their stockings and underwear. It ran directly over the tub, and one end that fastened to a nail on the wall had to be rehung. J was having difficulty and N bent over the tub alongside her to take the end from her and do the job himself. J exploded, "Leave me alone to do it!" N recoiled. The tone and temper of J's words were like icicles driven into him. Life with J would have unexpected explosions. To be sure, all week N had tried to be as close to J as circumstances permitted, and he had been on guard not to give her that crowded feeling. Her words had been uttered out of frustration at his presence, at his trying to do too much for her. An "I can handle it, darling" would have been far nicer and more tactful than "Leave me alone." N fled the bathroom just as he had fled after chinning on her door. He remembered her shout that night, "Leave me alone." He went to his room and sat on the bed. He was out of her sight and that would calm her somewhat. "Why always explosions?" he asked himself. He started to get dressed, trying to understand how a conflagration could erupt so suddenly. Moments later, J came hurrying down the hall and burst into his room, her face a sheet of nervous anxiety. She was distraught—no doubt about it.

> J: There's nothing radically wrong, really. And I know I can make you happy. But you must give me room to breathe.
> [*N feels a little better already because she's come to him to make up.*]
>
> N: I know, I know. Sometimes I want to be so near you that I get in the way. It's been over three years since we've been close and it's fantastic for me to be near you. [*They are in each other's arms by this time and they fall on the bed, still embracing.*] We have so little time for

148

the two of us alone—sleeping down the hall from you is torture.

J: I know, darling, I know.

N: You'll have to be patient with me and I'll try not to corner you and stifle you.

After a few minutes of hugs and kisses, they get up and go to eat. All is well.

DOUBLE-FAULT: If you'd ever been hounded, you'd appreciate J's reaction.

FAULT: [*He stares at Double-Fault and doesn't ask the question "Can you appreciate N's position?"*] Later that night, they prepare for bed. They will both try to sleep in J's bed, which is small with a deep, wide, long indentation in the middle where J's body has carved out a hollow. J is tired, N has enough energy to make love once and would like to. They slowly get undressed—it's so good C is away—and J gets into bed first, taking some magazines with her. N can't believe what he sees—she actually wants to read at a time like this! This is one of the few times they will be fortunate enough to be able to make love without keeping an ear open for the front door. He fits himself in beside her and starts to be amorous.

> J: [*Amazed*] I can't just be mechanical.
> [*N can't comprehend why she isn't trying to satisfy his needs. And why be mechanical? Why isn't she dripping with anticipation? She should be like an eager bride. He halts his advances and brakes his desire. He turns the pages with her—it's a woman's fashion magazine. He's surprised that some of the pictures actually interest him, but when they are almost at the last page, he can't wait any longer. He takes the magazine from her and drops it on the floor.*]

N: Now, J. [*Said matter-of-factly, not as an order. He sees that she is receptive.*] How come you're ready now? [*His curiosity is sometimes a plague.*]

J: Because you're near me, darling. [*Said in a low voice and lisped.*]

You figure that out. They make love and sleep, but it's difficult on J's bed. N suggests they go down the hall and try his bed. It is almost three o'clock in the morning and both are awake. J has something on her mind, and the conversation turns to their three years apart.

J: I don't feel like an adulteress any more.

N: I'm glad to hear that. You wrote him on Wednesday, didn't you?

J: Yes. How did you know?

N: I saw you sitting hunched over your desk writing. You looked as if you were trying to keep it private. Who else could it have been?

J: How clever of you. I've known him for almost a year and a half. I was visiting his family when you went to that conference.

N: You wrote and said it was only friends you were going to see.

J: Well, yes. There was no point in telling you.

N: Sure.

J: He wanted me to marry him, but I'd have to go live in his part of the world. It's a different language, though that would have been no problem. But women are treated like dirt there—all they do is serve and service the men.

N: I see.

J: His family wanted him to go back and take over the family business. He asked me to go with him. I wouldn't;

he became unhappy. I told him I'd rather have him happy away from me than unhappy with me. He went back to his country. Then in January he came back here, and we went through the same ordeal all over again.

N: That was the reason for the sudden shift in your plans?

J: Yes. He came here again and left again. He didn't like the idea of my singing or traveling.

N: Didn't he? I think it's wonderful you can do all that. Do you remember a long time back when you wrote that you had to leave a lot unsaid? What did you mean?

J: When I came back to this country after leaving you, my old boyfriend started calling me again.

N: The one who came to visit for a weekend when you were living in my country? I thought he would call.

J: Yes. Well, I had no time for him. I didn't want to see him. He continued to call. Then toward late summer he called and said some old friends were going to get together and he wanted me to come. I accepted just to keep him from calling again.

N: Probably had the opposite effect. Sorry—go on.

J: Well, we went back to his place and then they all left. [*She starts to get tense.*]

N: You were alone with him. [*N senses what's to come.*]

J: Yes. He forced me into bed. [*Tears and trembling*]

N: Didn't you tell him you didn't want to? [*His anger is rising, his voice stays low, but he can't sit still on the bed. He is up on his knees now, looking directly at J.*]

J: Yes, but he wouldn't listen.

N: Couldn't you yell or fight?

J: Nobody was around and he was too big.

N: Did he hit you? [*N's teeth are clenched, his hand is a fist.*] Did he hit you?

J: Yes. He hit me.

[*Here I must interrupt the dialogue to give you N's thoughts. He feels that* perhaps *he has put words into J's mouth. And he is wondering whether she is adapting her story to his anger. He finds it unbelievable that she accepted the man even under duress. She is a big woman and all she would have to do is roll on her side.*]

N: That pig. Did he rape you?

J: Yes, yes—he raped me.

N: When I get my hands on that swine . . . What did your father do?

J: He doesn't know about it. I became pregnant. The man tried to get me to marry him by getting me pregnant.

N: That's the second time he tried that. I remember you telling me about your mother giving you some pills to take to have a period. Go on. What happened next?

J: I told him that I was pregnant.

N: Your wonderful boyfriend.

J: Yes, and he arranged an abortion when I insisted.

N: Where?

J: In my home city, in a hospital.

N: Why did he help you?

J: I told him I'd never marry him, and I threatened to tell what he'd done. After that I didn't want to see anybody—I just hibernated. Then in one of my classes this man—I knew he was a good man—asked me out. We started going together and it developed into a strong relationship that ended in January, I guess. [*N comforts J. He feels absolutely no animosity toward "current boyfriend," but he wants to choke the breath out of—what was his name? Oh, yes—A. Dick. He remembers it from some clipping from a newspaper J had once shown him. Two things still bother N, but he asks about neither. The first is J's ability to go back to a man who had raped her (that really bothers him) for help (that surprises him), and the fact that the man gave it. Secondly, he knows that J's home city, although sizable, is still too small for anonymity. Daddy might have found out all about it if the abortion were performed in a hospital. Does Daddy know? It bothers N. But despite these questions and doubts, N is raging inside. That pig—if N ever gets his hands on him, he'll tear his head off and enjoy doing it.*] I felt so miserable back then. I threw myself into my work and kept to myself.

N: Why didn't you write me for help?

J: It was a long time since I had last seen you, and we were heading in different directions. And you were so far away. I never thought of it. I couldn't ask you.

N: Yes, that's right. I was far away. [*N is still raging inside. He has formed a protective shield about J, holding her close to him and kissing the tears away from her eyes. That pig . . .*] I have a story to tell, too, and it's also sad. [*N tells her about his loneliness and how much he had missed her and loved her, and about L-One. He leaves out all the other girls. No sense to that—it would sound like bragging—but L-One has been a part of his life and he wants J to know it.*]

After his story, they are both emotionally spent and in need of sleep. J suggests that she go back to her own bed and he will stay where he is. He agrees. They kiss and she goes. N lies in bed. "That pig . . ." In the morning, he goes to J's room and gets under the covers with her, and they make love. By noon they are up and dressed, since C might return early. She does, and by the look on her face it's obvious that Daddy has yelled at her despite J's admonitions.

DOUBLE-FAULT: What a one-day binge of emotion that must have been. N is quite right to believe that people need time alone together to discover each other. But another day like that would be too much to go through, don't you think?

FAULT: No—I don't think. C was a little morose and sullen and went to her room to work. J was sympathetic. At dinnertime C began to perk up, and afterward N took them both to a movie. Then they came home and had some coffee and a sweet in the kitchen. And the conversation was about C's trip home. Not only had Daddy yelled at her, but he had said he would pay her way through medical school if she chose to go, but would provide no money for anything else. N didn't understand that man. Then— Oh, you wish to comment?

DOUBLE-FAULT: Yes, I do. I don't think it's fair to assume that C's father was in the wrong. There's probably something else to the story and we never get his side.

FAULT: You surprise me. I'll go along with you on that. It was decided that next morning N would go with C to her school and sit in on one of her classes, and that from there he would go to meet J at the school where she taught. Also of importance—if you care to keep track of such things—was the beginning of J's period after their morning romp, so that N could relax, in a manner of speaking, for the next few days. N was beginning to feel confidence in J's love for him, but he still wasn't certain of her. The next day, Monday, went just as planned, and N really enjoyed spending time with C. They had lunch together and talked—N wondered what would happen if C could read his mind. A great decision was going to be made that week and C would be making it. She would be graduating from college in June and she had two options, possibly three. She might take a year off to travel around the world, in which case J would go with her and perform with her to pay for the trip. She was already well-traveled, but only in a large local sense—not world-wide. Or she could go to graduate school in the fall and spend the summer touring with J. Or she could get married or do any number of other things that wouldn't involve J. N was perfectly willing to let J make the tour. He only hoped she wouldn't lose her love for him in the course of it. One more year before they started their life together didn't matter too much to him, if only it was certain that J would eventually come back to him. So they sat there eating—C and N—talking about the inconsequential while N waited for the consequential to happen. After leaving C, N went to meet J at the office in her school and found her talking with a fetching young woman her own age, perhaps slightly younger. N stood by patiently and silently till J saw him. Then she beckoned him over and introduced him.

J: L-Two, this is N.

N: Hello. How do you do?

L-Two: Hello. Oh, you're from another country. Nice meeting you.

J: Won't be a minute more.

N: I'll wait over here. Nice meeting you, L-Two.

And he bowed away from the conversation.

DOUBLE-FAULT: Going back to C's decision. Was she aware of the feelings that had developed between N and J?

FAULT: Good question. My, you are alert! The answer is, not yet, perhaps.

That night at The Flat, when dinner was over, J began her

usual "I cooked—you wash up" litany to C. J also said to C, as things were being cleared away and the dishes washed, that she wanted to invite a couple of her friends—both men, incidentally—over for dinner on Thursday, and she hoped C would oblige by helping her entertain. C was not receptive to the idea and answered, "They're your friends, you take care of them." But J concluded from the conversation that C would help out, while N's opinion was that C hadn't said yes but hadn't said no either. J invited the two men later that evening by phone, and let me say that N was not in the slightest jealous.

DOUBLE-FAULT: Are we in for a quarrel?

FAULT: Patience. The next day, a Tuesday, was a day off for J, and they decided to go to The Park and feed the ducks. It was a beautiful sunny day, the air was fresh, and The Park was lovely. They walked along the edge of a big pond tossing to the ducks the bits of old bread they had stuffed into their pockets before leaving The Flat. They had walked a fair distance when J turned to N and in a very nervous, shaky, emotional voice, barely audible, said:

J: I love you.

N: [*Bursting with excitement*] Is that true, J? Is it true?

J: [*Nodding her head and speaking faintly*] Yes.

N: Say it again.

J: I love you. [*Still speaking nervously and weakly*]

N took her hands in his and drew her close to kiss her on the lips.

N: I love you, J. I love you more than I can say.

They walked arm in arm around The Park and back toward The Flat. N was exhilarated—his hopes had grown with each day and now they were in full bloom. He would have liked J

156

to be more bold and affirmative—*zestful*—in her "I love you"s, but J was a nervous person who might never be able to.

DOUBLE-FAULT: When someone says it the way she said it, I would think it was for real.

FAULT: You would, would you? I suppose I would, too. That evening after dinner, C and N went into the living room while J cleared up a few things at her desk. N asked C to play some boogie-woogie on the piano for him. C tried, but it wasn't her specialty and she hadn't been practicing for a long time. Before supper she had played the guitar, and although she had been away from it for months, she played well. In fact, J had come in and the two girls had performed charmingly, singing, with C accompanying on the guitar and J on the piano. J loved to sing. She might complain about being sick, but when the music began she wanted to participate. After it was over, she remarked that it was so nice to sit and sing, and N agreed. He knew that "current boyfriend" disagreed, and he couldn't understand why. Anyway, let me get back to what's happening *after* dinner. C is playing rather loud, and the downstairs neighbors don't appreciate her efforts as much as N does. They start banging on their ceiling. Admittedly C hadn't been tickling the keys, but it was early—around nine— and she had just started playing. She stopped, and she and N drifted back to J's room to tell her what had happened.

C: The Birdwatchers [*that was the name of the people below*] were pounding on the ceiling again. [*To N*] They did it all the time J and I were practicing for our act.

J: [*Vehemently, at the top of her voice*] IT'S EARLY. GO BACK AND KEEP PLAYING.

C: Well, we were rather loud, actually.

J: IT'S TOO BAD IF THEY OBJECT. They're incredible, those people. When we were practicing, they'd keep

157

banging away on the ceiling. Nobody else complained. In fact, everybody liked our singing and playing so much they'd open their windows. They're rather odd, too—a mother, a daughter, and a son. He's always peeping out of his window or standing in front of his mirror admiring himself. [*To C*] You should go back and keep on playing. Don't let them stop you.

C demurred. She thought she might have been a little noisy. N could have predicted J's reaction.

DOUBLE-FAULT: J was in the right—it was early.

FAULT: There is no hour for noise. C was right to stop.
   Wednesday was a nice simple day until midafternoon. J and N were talking, and J sounded worried.

J: You don't think it's because our sex is so good that we love each other?

N: I'm sure it's not the sex. After all, I loved you while I was away from you for over three years and we didn't have any sexual relations then. [*The talk evolves.*]

J: You're so kind and considerate. You're a better person than I am.

N: Why should that trouble you, even if it is true? One of us has to be a better person. Our skills are different, too. But I think we complement each other. I don't think we'll ever be bored, and I think we'll have great children. Why do you worry so much?

J: I've always been cautious and I don't want to make a mistake we'll regret. Each year since we first met, I've felt I've become a better person.

N: I agree. And we're not very different there, either. [*What N really believed was that J could be as nice as*

158

he, though she wasn't nice as often. But he could never say that; she'd explode.]

J: But sometimes I sacrifice the people closest to me in order to do things I want to do. When Daddy was practicing medicine, he had to leave the family to go out on calls. Once, during an epidemic, he was scarcely in the house at all for days and nights on end. It was his job. But I feel I can always make it up to those closest to me later on if I put them second while I'm taking care of *my* job.

N: I've made it perfectly clear on several occasions that if we were married I wouldn't insist on your staying home. You could work as hard as you pleased and go as far as you liked in your work. And any time you wanted to take off and make a tour, that would be fine with me. You know that. Don't be so cautious, J. We really are a tremendous couple.

Let me elaborate on what N didn't say. He was just the opposite of J. His loved ones came first, and her idea that business was more important meant to him that there would always be a serious disagreement between them. However, he didn't care. All he wanted was to love and be loved by J. They had already discussed the type of parents they would be, and J's ideas were acceptable to N. She had stated that children should be taught and cared for by their parents, to make sure they were properly started off in life. N was in full agreement, and he believed very strongly that although J might be shrewish with him on occasion, she would never put her children second. The thought of leaving her children in order to work was abhorrent to her—at least that's what she implied. So N could accept her philosophy as long as she loved him. That's all he asked. And she already had told him in The Park that she did indeed love him.

DOUBLE-FAULT: You say that N thought J wouldn't leave the children. How could she go on working, then?

FAULT: J is a talented woman. Tours are not the only way to work in the entertainment field. There are other ways she could channel her abilities. It's really not that hard.

Anyway, later that evening a crisis erupted between C and J. J was reminding C that her friends would be coming the next night for dinner and telling C what she wanted her to do.

> C: I told you I had no intention of being home for that dinner. I've made plans to go out. So stop counting on me.

> J: [*Furious and pleading with C*] You did no such thing. You can't do this to me. You said you would help.

> C: You always include me in your plans without my say-so. I never said I'd help.

> J: You did, too, and I've been counting on you.

> C: Well, things can't always be the way you want them. [*C is agitated and gets up from her chair and leaves the room.*]

> N: It's all right, J. We'll handle it ourselves.

> J: No. I'll have to call one of them and set another date. We'll only entertain one. [*Said in a tone of despair, frustration, and hurt feelings*]

N thought about what had happened and concluded that J was more in the wrong than C. When she had first asked C to help, J had construed C's answer to mean what she wanted it to mean. C could have been more explicit, but J shouldn't have taken C for granted. If only J had asked C a sharper question. "Will you be able to help me on Thursday?" was all it would have taken.

During his stay, N had often observed the heat and stubbornness of C and J in their disagreements. I would say vehemence, but that's a little too strong—though just barely too strong. It was as if one of them—usually J, since C's nature was more docile—was trying to bend the other to her will, while the other adamantly refused to give up her independence of thought and action even if it meant defending positions she wouldn't ordinarily have taken. In this case, N was tempted to upbraid both of them—J for being so hard on C, and C for her inexplicit "No" given the other night, but he felt that he would be wise to stay out of their disagreements.

J called one of the invited guests to cancel the invitation, and over the phone you would never have known how belligerent she had been only a moment before. Or how frustrated. Then she left for bed, looking very unhappy. N went to his room, undressed, and sat on his bed waiting for J to come by for a good-night kiss. As I said, he was prepared to take up the cudgels in defense of C, but his determination melted when J stood before him. She was upset, near tears, nervous; her head was down, her arms were hanging lifelessly, and her shoulders were hunched. She looked as if she had had a fright or just narrowly escaped some disaster, and at the same time she looked like a child who had dropped her ice-cream cone.

N: There, there. She hurt you, didn't she? We'll handle it, don't worry. It will be all right.

He kissed her, but she wasn't capable of kissing and he patted her gently on the back. She turned around stiffly and marched down the hall to her bedroom—no cooing "good night" to C this evening.

N would have been stupid to argue with J at a time like that. But once again it was brought home to him that J was

161

incapable of keeping her other emotions from influencing the way she treated him. Oh, she needed to be patted on the back, but she had no interest in what it would be like for him. She didn't make any effort to make their kiss a pleasant one for N.

DOUBLE-FAULT: Well, she needed sympathy then; she shouldn't be thought less of because she failed to kiss him properly. She did come to him, after all.

FAULT: N has no quarrel with what you just said. But she had responsibilities—emotional responsibilities—to N. Besides, why such a violent reaction to a change in plans? The reason is, of course, that J displays her disappointments for all to see and share in. It's a technique for getting sympathy. The incident had been over an hour before she came to N's bedroom. She could have composed herself if she had wanted to.

DOUBLE-FAULT: That's unfair. She may be a person of very sensitive feelings who takes a long time to regain balance.

FAULT: Maybe. However, some people can be fragile on demand. Was J like that? N wondered.

The next day only one guest came for dinner. J had prepared a meal for six, but there were only the three of them. She couldn't relax and eat but kept jumping up and down to serve. It was as if she were being graded on the meal and its presentation. Actually it was a fine dinner, and N ate a lot and enjoyed it. The guest was an old school acquaintance whom J had identified as the boy with the harelip. His family was of lower-class origins and he had worked hard to become a doctor. That's right, a doctor. And now he was disappointed with the amount of money he was making and the working conditions. He was going to emigrate to another country where prospects were better. He gave the impression that he had become a doctor so that he could rise in class and get a little wealth. N judged that if he was interested in people, it was for the fee they paid him—which is not to say that he wasn't a competent doctor, only a slightly dehumanized one. The dinner was a success for J, if you can call having an old friend for dinner a success or a failure.

On Friday, J told N that C had decided to stay out of school for the coming year. N expected it. It's decided. The tour is on. Also, on Friday N asked J if she would go away with him for the weekend. He said they could tell C they would be visiting some friends of his in the country, and that they could then go to the seashore or anyplace else. J was not against the idea, but she objected to the seashore because she said it would make her feel like a secretary with her boss. J's putting herself in that category distressed N. She was talking about weekend affairs, while N and J were supposed to be in love. But N wasn't really keen on their traveling, and so what they finally agreed to was this: N would rent a room in a hotel across The City, and J would meet him in the room after he signed in at the desk. Everything would be in his name and there wouldn't be any "Mr. and Mrs." lying. N was pleased with the idea and made the reservation.

At dinner that night, they told C they were going away Saturday into the country and would possibly see some of N's friends. They would be back on Sunday—perhaps early. They would decide that on Sunday morning. N said he didn't know his friends' telephone number or address, and didn't even know if they were home. They were principally going to see the countryside. C asked no questions—N wondered whether C was all-knowing and indifferent or all-knowing and polite, or just plain indifferent.

DOUBLE-FAULT: She probably didn't suspect. She's not the devious kind, and wouldn't recognize a lie if she heard one.

FAULT: Alas, my friend, you do her wrong to treat her so discourteously.

Next day, N packed his valise with their clothes as if they were going on a trip. N would much rather have said to C, "J and I are going across town for the weekend—see you Sunday," but he couldn't very well interfere with J's image of C's image of J. So the sham was acted out. They said good-bye to C and went out to the street and hailed a cab.

> N: ——— Hotel, please. [*To J*] This is what we can do. I'll go in and register at the desk while you wait in the lobby. Then when I get my key and head for the elevator, you follow and get on and off when I do. How does that sound? [*When you're doing something secretive, you think all eyes are on you and all fingers are poised to point you out.*]
>
> J: All right, I guess.

But when they arrived at the hotel, J said she had to have some candy and told N to go in and register and get settled in the room, and she would come back, find out what room he was in, and come up. N knew it was senseless to argue, although he didn't like the idea of their separating. With a queasy fear of impending betrayal inside him, he went into the hotel, signed in, and went up to the room to wait. After a few minutes he became impatient, and after a few more minutes he went down to the lobby to look for J. He wondered whether he had taken the elevator down while she was going up, but he had taken care of that contingency by leaving a note on the door. His idea was to rush into the street, take a quick look around, and come back. It occurred to him that he could be going out one door while she was coming in another. He was in turmoil. They never should have separated.

He passed through the lobby—no J; out on the street—still no J. He became more and more anxious. Where was she? A bus pulled up to the stop and he bumped into one of the alighting passengers.

N: Excuse me, sorry— J! Where have you been?

J: The store nearby was closed. I had to walk a few blocks.

N: I was worried. I thought you were lost or not coming back.

J: I almost didn't. [*J complains of a headache.*]

N: Here's the key. You go up and I'll be there in five minutes. There's a note on the door—ignore it.

N was there in four minutes. J was a changed person. Her nervousness, so perceptible on the street, had disappeared, and she was smiling and breathing more easily. N relaxed. The room was small, but it was their private world. No one would knock, no one would call. There were only the two of them. They looked out the window at The City for a while, pointing out interesting places. "Shall we call C?" he teased. "Oh, no," she laughed. They turned to each other and embraced. Then they undressed and converted the couch into a bed.

DOUBLE-FAULT: Nice to be settled in and busy, isn't it? Especially when one is so active. It's nice that they can get their rest and accomplish their work at the same time.

FAULT: You surprise me again, Madam. I didn't know you had it in you. N loved J, really loved her, and he always marveled at the transfiguration or metamorphosis J went through before she would get into bed with him. She wore a wig, which she removed, and her own natural hair, far prettier than the wig, would hang below her shoulders; her make-up, which made her look as if she had a tan, would be wiped off, and her own pale complexion would shine through; and lastly, her false eyelashes would find their place on the dressing table. From a sophisticated, urbane, cosmopolitan woman would emerge a fresh, youthful, girlish creature whom N

165

adored. It was ironic to N that the plethora of make-up aids and cosmetics J used to hide the lines of age and to give her skin the proper moisture actually covered up and hid the very look she used them to create. And C was the same way. But of course N's relationship to C was altogether different.

The day passed while they made love, and at about six hunger drove them out of the room to a nearby restaurant. After dinner they came back, undressed, and lay in each other's arms watching television. All through the day, J would say, "How peaceful it is lying in your arms, darling." J was always remarking on the tranquillity she found beside him. She tells him that he's the first man she ever wanted to live with. He is amazed.

N: You mean you didn't want to live with "current boy-friend"?

J: No.

N: Come to my country and live with me. I'd love that.

J: [*A little frightened that she might not get the right answer to a question she is about to ask*] Where would I stay?

N: [*Positive, forceful, a little disbelieving that she did not know the answer*] Why, with me! Where else?

J: I thought you might not let me live with you.

N: Hell, if you stay anywhere except in my house and my bed, you can't come.

J: [*Relieved*] I want to cook for you, sew for you, and chase tennis balls for you. I love being with you.

This conversation makes N very happy. J can't see all the way into the future and sometimes it scares her—that's right, scares her—to try to, but N believes that if she comes and lives with him she'll never leave him.

At about 10 P.M., J leaves the bed to turn off the television. She comes back and stands beside the bed while N is lying there on his back, his eyes on J while he blows her a kiss. She is not looking at him, her face contorts, tears gush from her eyes, and she falls, literally falls, on his chest, sobbing over the fact that he will be leaving in two days. The thought is unbearable to her. Of course N is overjoyed that the thought of his departure can evoke such a response.

> N: There, there, darling. I know I'm going soon. I've been trying not to think about it. But I'll be coming back in two and a half short months. We'll write to each other and the time will pass quickly. I love you, J. I don't like to be away from you but I can bear it. Things will go quickly.
>
> J: Yes, darling, yes.

He soothes and comforts her. A moment later, a nervous, worried look appears on her face.

> J: Where would we be married?
>
> N: [*Relieved and overjoyed almost beyond words*] Why, anywhere you want! You say where and I'll be there. If you want to just go away—elope—that's fine, too.
>
> J: That sounds best. No fuss—better that way.

N is floating. In two weeks, just by being himself, he has brought her to the point of thinking of marriage and how it is to be accomplished. He prays she will hold on to these feelings and not be overcome by caution.

DOUBLE-FAULT: I must say his patience has been rewarded. He must be very confident, even though he's praying for her to stay the way he wants her.

FAULT: Quite the contrary. N sounded far more assured than he actually was. He remembered what had happened the last time they parted, and he wasn't at all sure that J, left to herself, would be able to sustain the loving emotions and thoughts she presumably had now. There was nothing he could do, however; he had to leave, and he was thankful that it was only for a brief time. He recalled the little speech he had made to her the last time they parted—he was always in the role of comforter, helper, or sympathizer to J, the masseur who soothes her recalcitrant back, the man who waits patiently for her to conclude her business, the errand boy who quickly dispatches himself to the grocery to pick up needed or forgotten items. N was always pleased to be of help, to do things for J to make her life lighter or easier. It didn't bother him at all to be asked to do the smallest task for her; all he wanted from J was her love. In the past, he hadn't brought up subjects like their future for discussion because he had been afraid of her answers. Now he didn't have to bring them up— she was thinking about them on her own. He knew he had logic on his side. What he needed now was luck.

So here they were again, locked in each other's arms on a small bed, with all the love and affection in the world flowing between them. They made love again, and when N tried to get her into a position on top of him she fled for the covers. She didn't like that way or had never tried it. Something to look forward to his next time here.

Every time he was exhausted by his efforts with J, he would be unable to sleep because her presence alone excited his thoughts. He liked to watch her get comfortable and then drowsy, and see her fall asleep with her head on his chest. At last he fell asleep, too, and they slept in each other's arms until morning. It was the first time J had ever been able to sleep continuously next to him; on all other occasions she had had to get up and find another bed.

J: Did you sleep well, darling?

N: Yes, very deeply. And you?

J: Oh, very well, and it's so nice to wake up in your arms.

Their sleep had refreshed them and soon they were making love again. It was good for them both, and afterward N asked J if he should try to keep the room from noon to six. She didn't object, but N was told that the room had to be vacated by noon, since new people would be coming in at three. N told J the bureaucracy had already decided their fate.

J: Oh, just as well. I'm anxious to get back to C and The Flat. I don't like leaving her alone.

N: [*Trying to hint that C was old enough to take care of herself*] Oh, she'll survive all right. Think of her as having gone camping in her bedroom. Let's get cleaned up and on our way. I love you, J.

J: I love you, too, darling.

Once J had announced that she wanted to get back to The Flat, it was like an edict or immutable law. Nothing could intervene—unless J changed her mind.

They showered and dressed and J put her make-up back on. N sat watching her prepare herself, seeing the girl he loved disappear into the girl he loved. He'd been doing it all week long. At first she didn't like him around at such times, and then she got used to it and then she looked forward to it. She even said she liked having him watch her as her nakedness disappeared beneath her clothes.

When she was ready, they took a taxi to The Flat. It was a little after noon.

DOUBLE-FAULT: That exchange between N and J about where to get married surprised me. I had started to think from the way she broke off with "current boyfriend" that she was too career-minded for marriage. Maybe N knows her best, after all. I'm really surprised.

169

FAULT: You shock me. Where did you ever get such wisdom? No offense intended.

As soon as the door to The Flat is opened, J makes her way down the hall toward her bedroom, N trailing behind. J coos "Hello" down the hall and C returns the greeting with a similar call.

> J: We decided to come back early. [*N laughs to himself.*]
>
> C: It was creepy here last night with no one about. The building has these creaking noises and it makes you think someone's down the hall. It was scary.
>
> N: All buildings have their shakes and shivers. [*The voice of knowledge speaks—positively brilliant.*]
>
> J: [*To N so C can't hear*] I don't like leaving her alone. It's good we came back early.

N nods his head in assent, but thinks that J is being over-protective. C doesn't ask any details about their trip and none are volunteered, not surprisingly.

They spent the afternoon reading the newspapers in The Flat, and when N asked what was interesting in the neighborhood—he wanted to get out for some fresh air—C or perhaps J, I'm not sure which, volunteered that there was an art exhibit close by that was open and worth having a look at. J suggested they go see it and N was in favor of that. But whom do I mean by "they"? It turns out I mean all three, and the decision that all three go was in retrospect somewhat comical. Whenever J and N went out, the question arose in their minds as to whether C should come, too. After all, "Two's company —three's a crowd" applies to lovers. But on this day, after her scary night, N was particularly solicitous of C. Furthermore, N and J would be going to a public place, and in any case his sexual potential was low at the moment and not likely to rise.

J: Should we ask C?

N: Yes, please. I think she should come. It would be nice.

J: C, do you want to come with us? [*Calls into C's room*]

C: Will I be intruding? [*Always considerate, that girl.*]

N: [*Quickly*] No, not at all. Please come.

C: Yes. I should like to go.

N: Great.

J: [*To N, very quietly*] You'd think she'd leave us alone at a time like this.

N was flabbergasted by J's remark, which, to be sure, C did not hear. What had happened to the mother-hen attitude that had driven them back to The Flat just a few hours ago? Didn't J remember her own words—"I don't like to leave her alone. It's good we came back early." Was she a hypocrite? Or, remembering C's words, "It can't always be the way you want"—was she just plain selfish?

DOUBLE-FAULT: Maybe she was feeling amorous and wanted to be alone with N.

FAULT: Then why didn't she say so? If that was it, N wouldn't have wanted C to come either. But J had given the impression of worrying about C and wanting her along.

All three go down to the gallery, and after an hour they wander away and walk along the river. Eventually they come to a beautiful cathedral. They decide to go in for a short tour, particularly because N has never been there. He enters first by pushing against the entrance door and then holding it for C. She in turn holds it for J, but J has lagged a step behind and C doesn't hold it long enough. The door swings shut on J, hitting her. She is not hurt, but she explodes at C.

171

J: What are you doing? YOU NEARLY HURT ME.

C says she's very sorry, that she didn't realize J had fallen behind. It is clearly an accident, but J continues to verbally box C's ears.

N: [*Solicitous, to J*] Are you all right?

J: Yes.

N: Good. Let's see what's here.

J continues her onslaught, but with less heat. She has the last word. N behaves like a nice, benign old man. He stays out of the argument, even though he wants to explode at J for being such a complainer.

In a short while, they have moved around the cathedral and are on their way out. They go home and eat supper. N wants to be near J and offers to give her a massage. J never refuses this offer from him, because he's good at it and she enjoys it. She lies on her stomach on her bed, and he pulls her shirt up so that he can massage her neck and back, touching her skin. In a very short time, his fingers have worked the temper out of her and she is as docile as a sleepy crocodile in the warm sun. He bends low over her back, kisses her shoulders and whispers in her ear that he loves her. She giggles.

DOUBLE-FAULT: I like massages, too. My back is as troublesome as J's. Any man who's good at massaging is a man who's good at massaging.

FAULT: Stop clowning and listen.

The next day, C leaves early, as usual, and N goes to J as soon as he hears the front door close. They make love as usual, get up, have breakfast, get dressed, and leave. N takes J to work and finds out what time he should meet her to take her back to The Flat. In the interim he goes to The Park where they fed the ducks, to the spot where she told him she

172

loved him. He stays there a long time and ponders the direction his life is taking. He is immensely happy at this moment and hopes he's going to be lucky as well.

As arranged, he picks up J. They do their last grocery shopping together, go to The Flat, and wait for C. They are in J's bedroom, where she seems preoccupied with removing and combing out her fall. When all her little cosmetic rituals are completed, she turns to N, smiles at him, and sits on the bed. He goes to her and starts to kiss her. N wants to be near her, to feel her body close to his, and she now seems ready to accept him. From down the hall comes the sound of the front door opening. C has returned, and N curses to himself because J took so long with her wig. They knew C would be home shortly; why didn't J hurry a little to give them some time? He jumps up and the hall resounds with their greetings.

DOUBLE-FAULT: Did N revert to an animal?

FAULT: No—just a lover. He wanted to touch J again. He was leaving the next day. But J takes her sweet time—as almost always.

The last meal is eaten amidst laughter and warm conversation. Later N packs for his long trip home, which begins in the morning. J is tired. She kisses N good night and says, "See you in the morning, darling." He holds her tightly, and kisses her. "Sleep well," he says.

After J is asleep, N knocks quietly on C's door.

C: Come in.

N: Didn't mean to disturb you.

C: It's no intrusion at all.

[*N walks over to the desk at which C is working.*]

N: A lot has happened since I came here, and right now J is seriously thinking about marriage. I love her and I'm hopeful that she'll decide in favor of it, but one never

173

knows. What I want to tell you is this—I like you very much. I more than like you very much, I've gotten incredibly fond of you—I wish you were my sister. I hope you'll be my sister-in-law. What I'm trying to say, and rather awkwardly, is that I'll miss you very much. [*And with that said, he bends over and kisses her on the cheek.*]

C: I'll miss you, too, N. Good luck.

N: Thanks. Take care. [*And he leaves.*]

In the hallway he recalls something J had said to him earlier in the week: "It would be wonderful if you and I were in your country together and C could come visit."

N came to persuade J to marry him. Now he wanted C for a sister-in-law, as well. "N—be lucky."

The next morning, C stuck her head into his bedroom on her way out to wish him a safe journey. He said he hoped to see her again soon. C left and he went to J's bedroom, where she welcomed him with open arms. Again they made love. Time was running against them now and they had to hurry to get N to the bus depot in time. J went with him by taxi. They held each other's hands, but N couldn't kiss her and spoil her make-up. She still had a day's work ahead of her. At the bus station, N gave her a last embrace and whispered to her:

N: Find us, J. It will be fantastic.

She nodded and got back into the taxi. N gave her money for her fare and she kissed his hands. A farewell kiss. N stepped back, closed the door, and told the driver where to take her. J and N both were near tears. The car pulled away, and N watched it as long as he could. He expected it to fade into the distance, but it made a complete turn and came back down the street toward him. He could see J now. She was waving to him and blowing kisses. It was an outburst of love and he was overwhelmed. He waved back and ran out into the street, jumping up and down, not caring if people thought he was crazy. In the cab, she had turned around and was now waving vigorously to him from the back window. He waved back, his arm high over his head. The car came to a corner and turned and then was out of sight. N's head sagged to his chest, tears streaming down his cheeks. HE ABSOLUTELY HATED TO LEAVE!

DOUBLE-FAULT: Who can blame him? But why did he tell J to "find them?" It seems, from her farewell, that she loved him terribly.

FAULT: Do you know what the word "simulacrum" means? No? Well, look it up. J's behavior at any given moment might be a genuine reflection of her feelings. However, the ability to sustain those feelings, and the conviction that gave birth to them were not guaranteed to carry over to the next day. It wasn't that J was deliberately deceitful; N knew that. He knew that right then, as he stood on the street waving good-bye, J's heart was crying out and she did love him. It was the next day and the day after and the day after that which would determine what he had participated in. Some people might say that "fickle" was the word to use about someone whose mind changes as much as J's. For she had run away, and always for "good" reasons, from every man she had said she loved, and in N's case this was the second time round. If she believed, as she said she did, that she and N were ideal together, but then decided that she couldn't see her way to marriage, she was either emotionally "dumb" or false or cautious beyond reason.

DOUBLE-FAULT: I just looked up that word, and it's not only very insulting to J but not true. No one could be described as she was in that cab and be perpetrating an emotional fraud. N must have been very dear to her. My heavens, only three nights before she had been worried about where they would hold the marriage ceremony.

FAULT: N agrees with you. He said that the test of time would give that episode its true meaning. Actually, J had already told N that if she had stayed on in his country they would have been married by now. But she hadn't stayed on. She would have married "current boyfriend" but for the fact that in his country women are treated like "dirt." She would have married A. Dick, that pig, a long time before, but at that time she was too young for marriage. He could see a pattern developing. Would a reason be manufactured for refusing every man who came along? On at least two occasions, J had teased N and herself with the prediction that she'd probably end up an "old maid, ha-ha." The little laugh was a basic part of the whole phrase. The idea of J's being single for the rest of her life nauseated N. He knew she was teasing, but it still made him feel queasy because he saw in it an element of truth. And then he would have the even more ghastly thought that one day she would marry someone else and *he* would end up an "old maid."

Let me just say this before you have a go. N thought their farewell was beautiful, fantastic, loving, tender, wonderful, et cetera, but he couldn't know whether he would always look back on it as the beginning of their union or as just another emotional episode to be made meaningless by some future turnabout. Now go ahead.

DOUBLE-FAULT: I think I can see N's point, but it sounds a little bitter. If J does love him but later turns him down, then he has no right to claim fraud and deception just because she appeared to be so close to accepting him. After all, he told C that "J was thinking about it and one never knows how it'll be decided," or something like that. I thought he was being realistic and practical about a very deep hope that he held.

FAULT: What you say makes sense, but the claim of fraud and deception could still prove valid, even if the proof requires an emotionally "dumb" J for consistency.

DOUBLE-FAULT: What do you mean?

FAULT: Simply this. Assume J is emotionally "dumb," that she doesn't know what's best for her—something she probably would never admit—and that she eventually decides against N. Then N could fairly claim that all her tears and agitation were a sham because she never understood the nature and quality of her actions—that she cried and she laughed, she shouted and she lisped loving words, not out of her own necessity, but for the effect it all produced on the other person.

DOUBLE-FAULT: You mean she was acting?

FAULT: Yes. Because she always knew deep down that she would never see her way through to marriage. It was too big a decision for her.

DOUBLE-FAULT: Well, does she marry N or does she turn him down?

FAULT: Patience, dear woman, patience.

The trip back to his country was a most discomforting one. He kept thinking he might lose her again simply because he wasn't there. What really worried him was if J refused to marry him on his next visit, would she be able to stay in love with him while she was away on tour for a year? N knew he would sustain his love for J; he wasn't sure of J reciprocating.

After N got home, he started writing J a daily letter. In fact, he couldn't get through the day without communicating with her and he would daydream about her all the time. At night, lying in bed, thinking of her, he found it terribly difficult to fall asleep, but he couldn't masturbate. N was violating one of his "observations on life" epigrams—namely, "Show me a man and I'll show you a masturbator." He just couldn't bring himself to play with himself. In public, he felt absolutely immune to the charms of provocatively miniskirted young girls who came into his view. Which gave him a great feeling of strength.

But there was also a great tension in his life, for whenever he thought back over his visit, Mr. A. Dick—that pig—would come to mind. He would rage against him—yet at other times he wanted to talk to him.

Dream Sequence Number One:

C, J, their parents, and N are coming out of a theatre in J's home city. It is night and the air is cold. J is wearing a long black coat and everyone else is dressed warmly except N, who wears only a suit jacket. Mr. A. Dick is leaving the theatre at the same time. J's face becomes ashen—N doesn't know why. They all go through the formalities of greeting each other. Even in her state of distress, J provides an introduction. N is smiling, happy to meet an acquaintance of the family. He steps forward in anticipation of the usual handshake.

J: N, this is A. Dick. [*Mr. A. Dick extends his hand. N's smile become in an instant a fierce grimace, his rate of breathing increases dramatically—the warrior ready for battle, the animal on the prowl facing its prey. His eyes stare at A. Dick's face. His teeth clench, his hands become fists, he advances. A. Dick realizes his peril. Mummy turns to Daddy and says something about "What's going on here?" that just barely filters through to N. J has stepped back, frightened and looking death-white. C keeps her hands in her pockets and seems curious about what's taking place.*]

N: [*In fury*] I don't shake hands with scum.

His arms start pumping at a fantastic rate, his fists driving home punch after punch to the scum's face. A. Dick falls to the ground, his face a bloody pulp, blood seeping from beneath his skin. The gore shocks the women, but no one speaks. Daddy smiles.

Dream Sequence Number Two:

N is back at The Flat. He tells C and J that he has to visit friends in the country and that he'll be back in a day or two.

Instead, he takes a train to J's home city and waits for night. He dresses himself in a leather jacket and a pair of dungarees, and heads for A. Dick's house, having already secured the address from the telephone directory. He puts a mask over his eyes and a handkerchief around his mouth, and walks up to the front door. No neighbor sees him—in fact, he and the house are the only two "objects" in view. Whatever family A. Dick has is away and he is alone in the house. N rings the doorbell and also taps the knocker against the door. A. Dick opens the door.

A. DICK: What is . . . [*N is very quick. Before A. Dick can focus on him, N has fired his fist into A. Dick's face and sent him reeling to the ground. N quickly steps inside, kicks the door, and gets a strangle hold on A. Dick with a leather rope he is carrying. Before A. Dick can regain his wits, he is tied to a chair. N stands before him menacingly. He has typewritten cards prepared so that he needn't speak. He holds the first card in front of A. Dick's terror-filled face.*]

FIRST CARD: You don't know me. I want information from you. I will show you questions which you will answer. I know the answer to some of the questions already. IF YOU LIE, YOU DIE. If you tell the truth, you live. I want the truth, NOT YOUR LIFE. Do you understand?

A. DICK: [*Weakly and with great trepidation*] Yes.

[*N proceeds to hold up cards with simple questions on them, such as "What is your name?" in order to make it easier for his hated captive to speak, and to relax him as much as possible.*]

CARD: Did you have affairs before you were married?

A.D.: Yes.

[*N avoids direct use of J's name.*]

CARD: Of those women you had affairs with, did any refuse to go to bed with you on occasion?

A.D.: Yes.

CARD: Did you force them to do your bidding?

A.D.: Some were more willing than others.

CARD: Did you ever strike or hit any of them to get your way?

[*A. Dick sits silent, his face suddenly expressionless. N produces the next card.*]

CARD: Did you ever RAPE anyone, A. DICK?

[*A. Dick continues to sit silent. N doesn't get his answer.*]

N wakes up. Has J been telling the truth? "DAMN NAGGING DOUBTS!" he cries.

DOUBLE-FAULT: Why should he have doubts? True, J is a big girl, but almost any man can overpower even the strongest woman.

FAULT: Agreed. But, look—she said that A. Dick beat her and that she didn't cooperate. Then how did he get her clothes off without tearing them? How did he hit her without inflicting bruises? Even if there were no torn clothes and no bruises, didn't anybody notice when she got home that something was wrong? Upset *always* shows on her face. Yet she had said no one guessed, not even her parents. Look, sure, it's possible she told the truth. But the story has loose ends. For instance, her going back to him to arrange the abortion. That needs more explaining. The possibilities are that either she had really threatened to expose him and he was afraid of the scandal, or she asked for his help and he had an attack of conscience over what he had done. Or—

DOUBLE-FAULT: Then you do think she was raped. . . .

FAULT: Maybe. But maybe she was getting tired of not having any sex and let him seduce her.

DOUBLE-FAULT: Did N believe that?

FAULT: He didn't believe it. He's cynical, but he hopes he's not that cynical. But he did *think* of it, even if he didn't believe it.

180

DOUBLE-FAULT: Well, if he can come up with a version like that, it means he doesn't trust her. Doesn't it?

FAULT: It's funny about N and J. She said she trusted him and loved to be with him, and she said to him, "I know I can make you happy." But N really *did* trust her and he *did* love to be with her. He knew he would make her happy and that there wouldn't necessarily be any vice versa about it. But though he felt she would make him miserable at times with her eruptions of temper, he was sure that nothing she did would ever shake his love for her.

DOUBLE-FAULT: Everything can't be a bed of roses, you know.

FAULT: Yes, but J promised lots of thorns. The letters N got from her were a prophecy of it. Are you ready for them?

DOUBLE-FAULT: I suppose so. But N had convinced me he was terribly in love with J, and I still don't see how he can have such thoughts about her.

FAULT: Try thinking about J for a while. Even I don't have the patience to recite the next two months' exchange of letters between J and N, or to relate their phone conversations. If they said "I love you" to each other once, they said it a thousand times. He sent her rose petals, she sent him rose petals. He dreamed of her, she dreamed of him. He longed for her, she longed for him. It would be monotonous—

DOUBLE-FAULT: Please, Fault—I said "please"—tell me more. I love to hear about love.

FAULT: How can I refuse you? J felt so lonely without N— she wrote him that her breasts were awaiting his return. She wanted to talk to him, put her head on his shoulder. J had lost all feeling for "current boyfriend"—he had become a man in her past. That pleased N. N—as you can imagine—wrote

J every day. It took him more than a week before he could touch his sex to loose his seed.

DOUBLE-FAULT: Really. Is that important?

FAULT: To some people it is. More important, J opened up to N her thoughts about children and married life—"I want to be a mother and I keep dreaming of what our children will be like." She wrote N how much she admired him for having the courage of his convictions to love her for so long from so far away. All her letters ended with "Kisses, more kisses, more love—J x x x x x." Really romantic scrawlings. Must I continue this?

DOUBLE-FAULT: Yes, please. Just a little more.

FAULT: Very well. The Flat was a desolate place without N. "I wander down to your room just to sit there." Can you imagine that—just to sit there. She wrote that all she wanted was to make him happy. And N felt that his years of waiting were worth it. But this was a period of exquisite misery for him. True, he was receiving love in massive doses from the woman he adored, but it was still a miserable situation because she was in The City and he was in Expectancy. He would be returning to her during the early part of June and this correspondence continued for two months—from March 25th to May 25th. Can I please stop now? You get the drift of it.

DOUBLE-FAULT: Oh, I do, Fault. And thank you for humoring me. You can go on now.

FAULT: Let me check with you. Do you think she loves him madly and passionately?

DOUBLE-FAULT: Definitely.

FAULT: Once, on the telephone, J told him that Mummy's palm had been read by a fortune-teller who predicted that one of her daughters would be getting married in the following year and a half.

J: What do you think of that?

N: [*Thinks to himself that with his luck it will probably be C.*] That's not such a spectacular prediction. Simple statistical consideration would suggest that two girls, good-looking, in your age bracket, are not long for the single life.

J: Oh. [*With a laugh*]

N: But I'll tell you what I'll do. I'll make the supreme sacrifice just to keep the prediction accurate and help the fortune-teller stay in business. I'll marry you.

J: Ha-ha.

N: What did Mummy say?

J: Oh, she just laughed.

J had marriage on the mind, don't you think?

DOUBLE-FAULT: Very definitely.

FAULT: Their letters were beautiful loving exchanges. Right?

DOUBLE-FAULT: Very definitely.

FAULT: It sounded as if J fully realized how good life could be for them if they married. Agreed?

DOUBLE-FAULT: Very definitely.

FAULT: He wrote to J once that he was happy their love wasn't one-sided, that they loved each other equally. Did you get that impression?

DOUBLE-FAULT: Definitely. That's the feeling I absorbed.

FAULT: Then absorb the following:

On May 25th, J writes N that she is so sick of dreaming how happy she'll be in the future that she can't enjoy the present. Marriage will simply have to be forgotten about, because thinking about it would interfere with her enjoyment of the singing tour. She still loves him, wants to see him, but can't avoid these sad truths. And she tells him it doesn't mean she wants to see "current boyfriend" again. She thinks that's all over.

After reading her letter, N calls J on the phone:

N: Hello—J?

J: Yes. I didn't expect you to call tonight.

N: Well, your letter arrived and it was a surprise.

J: I'm late to a party.

N: Sorry. [*He's peeved.*] What's behind this letter?

J: Well, I'm having too much fun. I just don't want to get engaged. Do you still love me—darling?

N: I still love you. We'll talk when I get there.

J: Good-bye.

N: Good-bye.

The conversation was short—phone calls are expensive and J, who worries so much about money, didn't even keep the conversation going through the time that was paid for. Her "having too much fun" statement, even if true, was made without any feeling about the hurt it carried. And as for being late to a party . . . Even if she was half an hour late, three minutes more wouldn't have mattered. She's a chronically unpunctual person anyway. Here she's been writing "I am so longing to talk to you," and then she's in a hurry to get off the phone! It really made N feel terrible. And then to ask if he loves her—incredible! And the letter itself—"I'm just sick of dreaming of the future so much that the present loses all meaning and value." What kind of person is it who expresses so much love and sees the future as so happy, and then wants to throw it all away for a few pleasant days? It's balmy. And most perplexing of all to N was her statement that she couldn't enjoy the tour knowing her career would soon be coming to an abrupt end. He had told her and told her that he wouldn't interfere with her work, and furthermore she had previously written that she now saw for the first time how each of them could help the other get more out of his work and life. And besides, the tour would end abruptly in any case, because C would be going back to school. So what was she talking about?

DOUBLE-FAULT: She didn't want to get married or engaged.

FAULT: [*Impatient*] That's obvious. But why was she backing away? After all the letters that had passed between them, all the loving words, all the hopes, this was such a contradiction. N's happiness turned to rage and despair. After coming so far, his hopes so high, he realized he was losing her. He got ready to fly back to The City.

DOUBLE-FAULT: He's being too harsh with himself and with J. Her feelings for him must be real.

FAULT: All right. How do you interpret this from J? "It doesn't mean either that I'm going to go back to 'current boyfriend'—I'm not. That's all over, I think." What the hell is the "I think" doing in there? She didn't foreclose the possibility at all, did she?

DOUBLE-FAULT: She did. Read it again.

FAULT: [*As if the discussion is hopeless*] Never mind. Let's go on.

DOUBLE-FAULT: No. Wait. Why should he feel that J is backing away or that he's losing her? The singing tour won't be over for more than a year anyway, and she's said she's looking forward to seeing him—she's said it often.

FAULT: Exactly. Precisely. Absolutely. Correct. First she says she's coming and then she says she can't stand to keep thinking about the future because it upsets her in the present. A long trip like the one she's written about so often requires a firm, hard, fast, secure emotional commitment. Not nebulous meanderings of now "I long for you" and then "I can't see ahead." Can't you get the feel of these letters in relation to the one she wrote after leaving his country? The same pattern. First loving and "longing for you" attitudes, then "we're going in different directions" pronouncements. Can't you see that?

DOUBLE-FAULT: No. I can't. I think this is different.

FAULT: We won't resolve this. Let's go on.

The plane ride back to The City was agonizing for N, but the closer the plane came to landing, the greater was his joy and the greater also his uncertainty as to how the next two weeks would be spent, for once again two weeks was all he could stay. One thing he was looking forward to, however, was the different sort of welcome J had promised him this time.

The arrangement was that since J couldn't meet him at the airport because of her job, he was to come into The City, go to the superintendent's office in the apartment building where The Flat was, and get a key—his key—to The Flat, along with any instructions J might leave for him in a letter. Then he was to wait for J, not at The Flat but at the hotel a few blocks away, in which J had booked him. Under no circumstances was he to go into The Flat, because C would be studying there in the afternoon for her exams. The reason J had given for not putting him up at once in The Flat was that he might interfere with C's preparations for her exams. Quiet was so important, J had written N, that even Mummy and Daddy weren't phoning without first writing to say when, and "even the birds pecking at her window are an irritation." N was not unhappy at the idea of living in a hotel for a week. That way J and he would have their own oasis any time they wanted to "drink."

DOUBLE-FAULT: The proper atmosphere for C is obviously of super importance. It appears it will lead to super sex, too. I can imagine how happy N is with the arrangement.

FAULT: When N lands, he makes his way to the apartment house and picks up her note. He reads it quickly. Dinner will be at eight o'clock and J's schedule is such that she won't get back to The Flat till six-thirty. If he's not at The Flat when she arrives, she'll phone him at his hotel. N studies these instructions. J writes that she hasn't really been able to communicate with him properly and is anxious to talk to him. He reads that part over again. Then a warning: "Don't interfere with C, as she is working very hard for her exams. I know you wouldn't do it intentionally—BUT DON'T DISTURB HER. Love and kisses—J."

The note tears at N. It's obvious that J is very nervous about something—at least it's obvious to N. He is worried about what she hasn't been able to communicate properly—that disturbs him. Also, he can't tell from the note whether she really wants him to meet her at The Flat or wait for her to call his hotel room. But of this there can be no doubt—stay away from C.

It was noon now and, according to the note, C wouldn't yet be upstairs. N went up to The Flat with his key—he had to drop off a package and he wanted to look around. The Flat was deserted and quiet. It was still so familiar to him—the light switches and all the other little things that one gets accustomed to and takes for granted in a place one has lived in. He went down the hall to J's room and stared into it. He called it "the niche"—her niche. The bed looked as inviting as ever, and memories of the fantastic loving they had done on it swept through his mind.

He left The Flat and made his way to the hotel. N wanted to be alone with J that night. If only he could talk to her now and straighten things out! Calling her at her office might upset her routine. The best thing to do was to fall asleep and wake up at six—the fastest way to pass time. And now N took a precaution that was to be the initial step in the direction of a hurricane. It seemed such an innocuous act. He didn't wear a watch and there was no alarm clock in the room, so he called down to the desk and asked them to call him at six—he was going to sleep. He didn't say that he shouldn't be disturbed, and it didn't occur to him that they might assume he didn't want to be. Then, once in bed, he couldn't sleep. His thoughts kept flashing ahead to the evening with J. He had kept a calendar of her periods and tonight was all right. In the distance, through the window, he noticed for the first time the clock tower of the bus station he had so often used. So he had a watch after all. The slowest way to pass time is to lie in bed thinking. Since it was useless to go on lying there, he got up, bathed, and dressed. It was about 3 P.M. At the desk he canceled his six-o'clock call and was told to his great distress that J had tried to call him but had been told that he had gone to sleep and that they would not wake him. Damn—why hadn't he thought that she would call? He knew why—he had underrated the possibility of any real consideration in J. She had said she'd call later, so he assumed she wouldn't or couldn't call earlier. "Damn—just damn," N thought. Mumbling to himself that he wasn't properly clairvoyant, he left the hotel. And suddenly he came alive with The City—the city he had fallen in love with on his last trip. Now was the time to do some gift shopping. N went to a nearby store, one of those all-purpose affairs. Luck was with him—he found perfume for J and lots of flowers. It was still fairly early, so he decided to go to The Flat and put the perfume on J's desk and the flowers in vases. N was sure that C wouldn't be there yet, but he was wrong. As he stepped into The Flat, he could

188

hear her in the kitchen. J was certain to be annoyed with him. He had violated an instruction.

DOUBLE-FAULT: Why didn't he wait as she told him to?

FAULT: He made a mistake in assuming that C wouldn't be there. He didn't think her exams would be over until four-thirty. He expected to be in and out with nobody there.

N greeted C warmly. She is still in an exam trance. She looks at the flowers he's carrying and he says they're for The Flat. C takes them from him and arranges them in vases. Luckily he hasn't interrupted her studies—she has just finished eating and has been cleaning up her dishes at the sink.

He is more than glad he didn't come while she was studying at her desk. After she relieves him of the flowers, N hurries down the hall to J's room to place the perfume right in the middle of her desk. She would even see it from the doorway. Now, his tasks accomplished, he is anxious to leave, but as he comes back down the hall C asks him:

C: Have you eaten?

N: [*He can't lie.*] No, I haven't, but I must go now and you have to study. J is going to be furious with me if I disturb you.

C: Nonsense. I'll make you a sandwich. It's no trouble. [*N is really hungry. He suddenly realizes he hasn't eaten since the day before, but he insists on leaving.*]

N: I really must go. I don't want you to bother.

C: It's no bother at all. [*Her persistence, plus N's belief that C knows what's best for C, changes his mind. In fact, she is so persistent that he feels it would be rude to spurn her offer.*]

N: All right. But ignore my presence.

189

She fixes the sandwich and talks to him for a while. "Maybe," he thinks, "she needs a small break from her studies." He asks how her exams are going and she replies that they're almost over and so far so good. Exactly what he expected her answer to be. He quickly finishes his sandwich and she clears up, despite his offer to do it.

C: You'll have to excuse me now. I have to study.

N: By all means.

She goes to her room and N, instead of leaving, goes to the living room and sits down. For one solid hour he stares at the objects in the room. His eyes keep returning to the piano and guitar that occupy one corner. How quiet they must be these days—and how much joy can be had from them. He barely hears C in the next room at her desk. The silence is awesome. Finally he can't sit there any longer and decides it's best if he meets J outside. He is sure she'll be very unhappy if she finds him in The Flat. N tells C through her door that he is going out to meet J, and he leaves.

Once on the street, N positions himself so that he can observe the only two ways J can get to The Flat. He watches the people coming home from work. His heart is beginning to pound. He waits and waits, wondering if perhaps she's gone to his hotel. After all, she did call, and he hadn't thought that she would. Maybe she wants to surprise him. It's getting near six o'clock. He decides to wait just a few minutes longer and if J doesn't appear, to head back to his room.

DOUBLE-FAULT: He seems not to know which way to turn.

FAULT: Yes. He's all excited about his reunion with her. And then he sees her. She is walking rather slowly, her fingers wrapped around the string of a net bag she uses to carry groceries. He watches her for a few moments, and then sprints to her side and reaches for the bag.

N: Give you some help with your bundle, Ma'am? [*He's smiling at her, and tries to kiss her. Her make-up has been running down her face in rivulets of sweat. Her thoughts are clearly elsewhere, and she doesn't react.*] I just couldn't wait to see you. [*Inside him a voice is telling him that he should suggest they go to his room, not The Flat—in fact, the voice is screaming at him to say that, but he doesn't.*]

And they keep walking toward The Flat. He tries to kiss her again but she is not in favor of it. Inside the building, they take the elevator up the two flights they normally walk. They are absolutely alone. Hoping that J hadn't kissed him on the street because of the public nature of the encounter, he tries to kiss her again. She stands back from him and hardly purses her lips. N stops trying. He is in agony. There's a bigger storm brewing and he knows it. Where is the waving girl who was so exuberant in greeting him on his first trip, the one who promised him a far better reception this time?

DOUBLE-FAULT: A woman needs time to prepare an emotional outpouring of love and affection. N surprised her and lost the greeting he sought.

FAULT: Emotional outpourings are not "be good and get rewarded" confrontations. They are spontaneous, damn it. Where was her spontaneity? Being manufactured?

Once in the apartment, J goes directly to hang up her coat while N goes to the kitchen to put away the groceries. He hears J enter her room down the hall and then the rapid advance of her footsteps toward the kitchen. By the fall of her footsteps, N knows that she is angry with him. She comes into the kitchen and stands with her back against the sink. She is furious, angry beyond words, shrewish. She attacks.

J: WHEN WERE YOU HERE?

191

N: I came this afternoon to drop off the perfume and the flowers.

J: I TOLD YOU NOT TO COME HERE. YOU'D DISTURB C.

N: When I came in, she was just finishing a sandwich. We hardly talked at all. [*N has told the truth but he has shaded the story.*]

J: IT DOESN'T DO ANY GOOD TO TELL YOU ANYTHING. YOU DON'T LISTEN.

N: J, there was nothing to it. [*He feels guilty that he hadn't spoken out directly about what happened, and tells more now.*] She offered to make me a sandwich, but I said I didn't want to disturb her. She insisted on making it.

J: SO THERE WAS NOTHING TO IT! OF COURSE SHE IN-SISTED. THAT'S THE WAY SHE IS. BUT SHE REALLY WANTED TO BE LEFT ALONE. [*J has now irritated N by this suggestion that C cannot express what she really feels or wants. He is preparing to argue.*]

N: C has a mind of her own, J.

J: YOU DON'T UNDERSTAND.

N: I sat in stony silence for one hour after I had that sandwich, and then I left. I DIDN'T DISTURB HER.

J: Shhh. You'll disturb C. WHY DIDN'T YOU LISTEN?

N: J, you're beating a dead horse.

J's anger is receding and she begins to look merely upset.

J: You think I'm being rude to you, don't you?

N: [*Firmly*] YES.

J runs out of the room. N stands there in despair. He thinks she has gone back to check on his story with C. This infuri-

192

ates him. He feels she is a hypocrite to drag C into their arguments at such a time. But he isn't sure that J is talking to C—perhaps she is trying to regain her composure. N waits in the kitchen. After a short time, J reappears, still agitated but apparently simmering down. She beckons him into the living room, and he feels that she will try to do something to atone for her vituperative assault on him. She starts talking about her work and produces some music. She sits down at the piano and N sits on the edge of the piano bench next to her.

> J: This is a little something I've written with C. How do you like it? [*She's bubbling now and she plays quite loudly and sings. N is absolutely appalled, flabbergasted. If the birds pecking at C's window make too much noise, this will positively drive her mad.*]

> N: It's nice. [*It wasn't, but this was no time for destructive criticism.*]

> J: It needs more work of course—ha-ha. [*Her little laugh, emitted whenever she feels she's being cute. N feels drained. J's behavior is such a contradiction.* UNBELIEVABLY, *the phone rings and it's Mummy. J is* SURPRISED!]

> J: C—the phone. It's Mummy!

C stops working and gets on the phone extension in her room. "So," N thinks, "during C's ordeal they write ahead of time to set up the proper moment to call, do they?" C concludes her part of the conversation, and J gets back on the phone. She makes no attempt to keep her voice low. The topic that excites both her and Mummy, for N can hear Mummy's voice even though he's five feet away from the phone, is the upcoming tour. The phone conversation finally ends, but not before N is handed the receiver so that he can greet Mummy. J and N then go back to the kitchen.

J: We may not get to go around the world, but we've been offered three months' work from September to December, with a month's break in the middle.

It seems that contracts have to be signed and that J needs C's signature to finalize the arrangements. She finds C a bit of a problem. C wants to go all over the world, nonstop, and not go back to places she's been before. J disagrees. It irks N again to hear J treat C as someone unable to discuss or understand her own affairs.

A moment later, J heads down the hall toward C's room. N follows. He wants to hear this. J knocks on the door.

C: Come in.

J: Hellooo. We have to discuss something.

J sits on the bed, N places himself a few feet away from C. He leans against the window sill and first looks to see if there are any birds outside. C has a number of books at her fingertips, and it's obvious she has been reviewing several years of work.

J: We have to make up our minds about signing the contracts. They want to know soon. They're offering us three months' work.

C: The purpose of this tour was to go around the world and not back where we've been.

[*N thinks to himself that here is C studying for the most important exams in her life and J is pestering to get what J wants. "DON'T DISTURB C" was J's admonition. He looks over at J—the woman he loves. She looks ugly to him just now. She sees him and smiles at him.*]

J: [*To N*] We often talk to each other at night like this. [*N nods his head but says nothing.*]

C: Tell them we prefer a long tour and see what happens.

J pushes on and gets a commitment from C to accept whatever is offered if they don't get what C wants. N and J leave C to study. Out in the hall:

J: This is best. She'll see.

Later in the evening, J makes dinner. She has calmed down and has thanked N for the flowers. The three of them eat together. N has offered to take J out, but she says she'll cook. She says it as if C's existence depends on it. N feels she's exaggerating, but agrees that C can't spend time cooking and cleaning now. The dinner is very good. J's cooking hasn't suffered from all her shouting. Afterward C goes back to study. She has been relieved of washing the dinner dishes. N helps J clean up, and it's quite late when they finish. N would like J to come with him now back to his room, and he suggests they tell C they are going for a walk. J vetoes the idea. She is tired.

J: Pick me up at work tomorrow at four. Then we'll go back to your place.

N is disappointed but in no position to change things. They kiss good night and N leaves. It's about ten. He walks back to his hotel. Today had started eight thousand miles away. This morning, he had read a loving note from the woman he loves. By six in the evening, she had screamed at him, and lied to him, and demonstrated her selfishness.

DOUBLE-FAULT: N doesn't really know that J lied to him about her parents writing to set up phone calls. Even if J sounded surprised, that doesn't mean the call wasn't prearranged. Or maybe she was surprised for the very reason that it wasn't prearranged.

FAULT: True enough, and when N asked her a non-question after the call, their exchange went something like this:

N: You sounded surprised to hear from Mummy.

J: It was nice to hear from her.

N: I thought you said they wrote to set up times for calling.

J: We got a letter the other day saying she would call.

But the way J said this, it sounded as if she were filling in details of an event that had never taken place. N felt like challenging her for proof that there *had* been a letter, he was so certain she was lying. But even if he could prove she was lying, it would only drive her away from him. So he dropped the subject.

DOUBLE-FAULT: So he really has *no* proof.

FAULT: Patience. The next day, N picks J up after work. He is impatient to get back to his place so he can hold her close. As she has done before, she stalls him by insisting on taking him shopping. They go to buy a few groceries and some sweets which J stuffs into her bag. Finally, they go to his hotel room. N is full of passion. This is the moment he has been dreaming about for two months, and J has been more than promising in her letters. And yet the only word that can describe what follows next is TRAGEDY. J is cold, unwilling to excite N. Her kisses have no feeling behind them. She is naked from the waist up and acts as if she's unwilling to be undressed further. When N tries to remove the rest of her clothes, she turns and rolls away from him. She has put her arms in front of her chest as if she were ashamed of her nakedness. N sits naked on one side of the bed. He has stopped trying to project enough passion for both of them. He looks at that long body stretched out, quivering, on her side of the bed. His thoughts disgust him, for he is thinking, "How the hell did A. DICK rape her?" All she has to do is roll over. Of course, he hasn't man-handled her and he's let her roll away. He gives her the benefit of the doubt—but the doubt is still there. He speaks to her softly.

N: What's troubling you, J?

J: [*Almost tearful*] I feel that there's a ball of ice inside me, knotting me up. I knew that when you came back you'd expect things of me like getting engaged or mar-ried, and I can't do it. [*Tears have started to form.*] Things look so remote now with the tour coming on.

N: I don't care about the tour. I would never ask you to do anything that would interfere with your work. What I say is that you can do everything. The Tour. Marriage. Do it all.

J: I felt so tense, like ice all over. I knew you'd be disappointed.

N: It's not as bad as all that. There doesn't have to be so much pressure. All I ask is that you don't close your mind to us. The tour will end. I'm sure there will always be a possible tour on the horizon, but that needn't inter-fere with us. You can always take the time to do them.

J: I can't see marriage at this time. I just can't see it. [*Sobs*]

J relaxes a little as N pulls back from forcing her to decide about their future. She has once again made herself out to be the hurt, hounded, and oppressed party in their relationship and N has to comfort her. She lets him undress her com-pletely, but he feels she's not really with him. They have coitus. It's horrible. N ejaculates in less than a minute; J has no re-action. He loves her, and although their skin is touching they are not close at all. It's as if J were a stranger to him. N lies

197

in bed staring at the ceiling. J is sobbing. N feels hollow. His love for her is still absolute, but she can't accept it and her rejection is calamitous for him.

N: I came too fast.

But that wasn't the problem. They lie in each other's arms for a while and then get dressed to go back to The Flat for dinner. Along the way, N buys flowers for J to cheer her up. He feels miserable but smiles as he gives them to her. At dinner he eats but he has no interest in the food.

DOUBLE-FAULT: He should have thought more about J's position instead of feeling sorry for himself.

FAULT: Listen, and get this through your thick skull—he ministered to her needs, not his. He kept all his disappointments to himself and tried to cheer her up. And all she did was turn her back to him and cry about how hard it was for her and how knotted up inside she was.

DOUBLE-FAULT: I beg your pardon! Please be careful how you address me.

FAULT: I apologize. Let's see. At dinner N is eating but his mind is elsewhere. Then C spreads her fingers and shows N a ring that Mummy had given her for her birthday.

C: How do you like it?

N: It's beautiful, C.

C: Guess what J said when she saw it.
[*N thinks to himself that J probably said she wanted one just like it.*]

N: I don't know.

C: She said it would fit her finger better than mine and Mummy should have given it to her.

198

J: C's finger is broader than mine and the band is too small. It looks better on my finger. [*Justification for selfishness, N thinks.*]

C: Can you imagine her saying that? [*The two girls start to talk, but not argumentatively.*]

N: Yes, I can. [*Said so softly that no one hears him.*]

After dinner N and J clean up again and C goes back to her studies. When it's time for N to leave, J escorts him to the door. They stand by the door and N bends over to kiss J and she kisses him warmly.

N: I didn't think the way I felt would interfere with how I made love to you. But I was wrong and it did.

J: Things were like ice inside me.

N: I love you, J, and it breaks my heart to see you unhappy. [*They are close to each other, J's body pressing against his body, her arms around his neck, while N leans against the wall. He can feel her full weight and it feels good.*]

J. Even yesterday when I yelled at you, I didn't stop loving you.

N: It was hard to tell.

[*They go on talking, tears in their eyes. Between sentences they kiss.*]

N: I don't know how we get into such disagreements. I love you so much. [*He squeezes her hard and she clings to him.*] I've always loved you.

J: I love you, too, darling. Last night after you left, I went into my room and I cried for me and I cried for you, and I just kept on crying. When I saw you on the street yesterday, I thought you didn't want to meet me at the hotel.

N: Oh, no. I didn't want to come up here. I wanted you. I wanted to go to my place and not up here. If only we had spoken over the phone yesterday.

[*N doesn't mention his thoughts about the argument in the kitchen and its aftermath.*]

They stand and talk like this for more than half an hour. They kiss and talk and talk and kiss. It gets late and N has to go. Before he goes, J tells him that tomorrow night will be different, and he knows that once she had decided it will be, it will be. J stands in the doorway and waves to him as he goes down the stairs and she waits until he's out of sight. They've made up, and for N life is glorious again.

DOUBLE-FAULT: My, things change rapidly from day to day for N and J.

FAULT: The next few days were filled with nostalgia for N. He loved walking through The Park, especially past the place where J had told him she loved him. One day J and N go to a different park and N rents a boat and rows J around a large pond. She likes sitting in the sun and he enjoys the exercise. Later they lie on the grass, J's head on his chest. She sings softly and gently to him while he watches two very high-flying kites dancing in the wind. It is late in the day and they decide to go to a restaurant for dinner. They order, and during the meal N wants a glass of water. He calls out to get the waiter's attention.

N: Sir!

[*J becomes very agitated and nearly jumps out of her seat.*]

J: Don't say, "Sir." It's bad manners and rude. [*She says this snappishly. J nearly yells at the waiter.*] Excuse me, please. [*The proper way to get his attention.*]

N never remembers how fast she can lose her calm.

200

J: You do things sometimes that make me want to run away from you.

N: What do I do?

J: You have faults, you know.

N: I'm sure I do. Everyone does. Please tell me what they are. [*He asks her politely, not sarcastically. He wants to improve himself, especially for her.*] Tell me what I do that's improper and I'll change. [*J is nearly in tears.*]

J: Don't change. [*Said pleadingly*]

It was winter and summer all in one day with J. First, lovely boat ride—then, lectures on his manners. N used to say that all the little things that caused them to bicker were only that—little things, unimportant and inconsequential. But J would retort that they were important to her. And when she said that, N would ask her to tell him which she felt were the important ones so that he could make them important to him, too. It really surprised him that she would make a fuss over these minutiae. Why look for trouble? She had written him in the past how greatly she admired his character and appreciated all he had done for her. It was a puzzle to him. She always wanted to have an advantage over you, and if she was on the weak side of an argument she would protest that you argued impolitely, thus changing the grounds of the argument from substance to technique.

J: It's very rude of you to talk that way to me.

N: Let's stick to the subject.

J: Not in that tone of voice.

N: I'm sorry.

You see, it works.

DOUBLE-FAULT: You've been very uncomplimentary toward J, and I, for one, don't like your tone of voice.

FAULT: Ha! Ha! While C was finishing up her exams, J was seeing to the business end of the forthcoming tour. Their agent would be coming over one evening with the contracts. There was a lengthy discussion between C and J as to what drinks they should offer him. C hardly drank at all and J would hold a glass and occasionally sip from it, but "form" is so important in these affairs. N was asked to stay in his hotel room, where J would call him after the contracts were signed so that he could come over for dinner. He waited patiently and, as the evening wore on, hungrily, for her call. They were meeting at five. At seven J called and told him to come over in an hour.

N: Anything wrong? What's taking so long?

J: We have to understand the contract and it's written in a foreign language which we're translating.

N arrives at eight and the papers have been signed. The bottle bought for the occasion is still nine-tenths full. N is introduced to the agent—a charming fellow. He leaves. They eat. J is cheery. They talk incessantly about the tour. C is glad the signing is over and goes back to her studying.

DOUBLE-FAULT: You keep making snide-sounding comments about these people. You insinuate that the way they conduct business is foolish.

FAULT: As you say. I beg your pardon.

Since J and N made up, their love-making has improved. Unfortunately J's period has started and she has never slept with anyone under those conditions. But she and N spend a whole day together and decide to go to a movie. It doesn't start till eight, and it's now six. They are close to N's hotel and decide to go up to his place to wait and talk. They undress and lie down next to each other. J wants him badly. It goes without saying that N wants J. She removes her cotton.

N: It's possible but it may be a little messy.

J: Women in a foreign country I know of sleep with their men during their periods.

N: Here, I'll lay this newspaper on the floor and you use the pillow for your head. Otherwise we'll make the bed-sheets look like a battlefield.

J: Go easy, it feels tender and a little sore.

N: How's this?

J: Fine.

N has entered her very slowly and moves very slowly in her. She has one of the best orgasms she has ever had. She lies beneath him and murmurs:

J: I can't move, I absolutely can't move.

N comes a few minutes later in a memorable burst that completely relaxes him. He gets off her. There's a little blood on the newspaper but not much. In half an hour he is hard again and re-enters J. This time the pace is faster. Again he comes after J, whose response is good but not up to her previous one. They take baths. N tells her that sleeping with him during her period is the second thing she has done or felt with him that she never could bring herself to do with any other man. The first was her desire to live with him. They dry off, get dressed, and go to the movies. J is very loving toward N the rest of the evening.

DOUBLE-FAULT: I have no comment to make about the preceding.

FAULT: Good.

C finishes her exams and C and J decide to give a party on

the weekend before N leaves. It's an all-purpose party to cele-brate C's graduation and birthday, N's visit and birthday, and J and C's forthcoming tour. For N's birthday J had a letter opener waiting for him, and after he arrived she bought him a belt.

N helps C and J put stamps on the invitations. Once he put a stamp on upside down, and J grabbed the letter away from him to set the stamp right side up.

> J: It's very rude to put stamps on the wrong way. It's an insult to the receiver of the letter and also to the person whose picture is on the stamp.

> N: Sorry. [*He thinks to himself that he's not even capable of putting stamps on letters. Better watch out; he'll be replaced by a machine. Now when N writes, he almost invariably puts the stamp on slightly cockeyed.*]

DOUBLE-FAULT: She was right.

FAULT: I suppose. But does she have to start every admonish-ment with "It's very rude . . ." Isn't there something else she can say? It's very rude to be like that.

It's his last night in the hotel before he moves back to The Flat. Since C has finished her exams, he has no reason for staying where he is. J comes over and they make love. He wants her to stay longer, but she says she has to get back to The Flat to make dinner.

> N: Let's call C and tell her we've decided to go out for dinner.

> J: I told her I would cook. [*Said matter-of-factly*]

> N: Well, let's tell her the plans have been changed.

> J: I said I would cook. [*Said stubbornly*]

> N: It's not unreasonable to alter plans sometimes. Let's stay.

> J: No.

N sits in the bed watching J get dressed. She comes over after a while to cheer him up. There is a smile on her face, a frown on N's.

J: We should go, darling. You shouldn't act like a lord.

N: I wasn't acting like a lord. We have so little time together alone. Why should we rush away from here? It would be nice to stay.

J: Yes, darling, it would, but we must go back. I told C I would cook. [*It was useless to try to change her mind. J had used C as an excuse and there was no getting around it.*]

They leave his hotel room, and as he closes the door he is sure it is the last time he will ever sleep with J. Later, when he returns to the hotel for the night, he looks out of his window and surveys the clock tower, its dial illuminated by bright blue lights. Each night in that room, he has checked the time on the clock before going to sleep, hoping that the morning would come quickly. He now has one week left and feels as if the clock were slowly guillotining him.

DOUBLE-FAULT: Why so pessimistic? Things sound good to me. She loves him.

FAULT: He has too long to wait before they meet again. But let's not get ahead of our story. Next day, he leaves the hotel for good and moves into The Flat. The coming Saturday night is the night of the party, and the two girls have been discussing arrangements for it. Their big problem has been the Bird-watchers, who are chronic complainers about noise. Remember the banging on the ceiling when C was playing boogie-woogie for N? They have decided it will be simpler to invite the Birdwatchers. A plan is set up to mitigate their presence, too. They are to be constantly engaged in conversation until it is very late, so that most people will have plenty of time to enjoy themselves. The party is planned with military precision

205

and J is general worrier over all details. On Tuesday, the day N moves in, the girls decide to paint the kitchen. It is an all-day project and is completed at midnight. Both girls work very hard. They are exhausted, and J takes particular care to focus attention on her aching muscles. N offers to massage her back. Offer gratefully accepted. J raves to C about how well N can give a massage. In no time at all, J is relaxed, almost asleep. Hurt muscles seem soothed. He is master of her back at least.

Next day is a historic? important? thought-provoking? day! J wants N to meet her parents. He is to take the train with her to J's home city. N likes the idea. Early in the morning—but not too early—N and J leave for the railroad station. On the train, J talks about Mummy and Daddy.

> J: Mummy tells you straight away what she thinks. She wants people to know how she feels. So don't be surprised if she talks incessantly.

> N: So I've gathered from talking—er, listening—to her on the phone. [*No meanness implied or intended. He is smiling as if Mummy's garrulity was merely the first characteristic he had happened to encounter in a personality he already knew he would be very fond of.*]

> J: Once C and I had to catch a train back to The Flat and Mummy was supposed to drive us to the station. We had lots of luggage, too. Well, we pulled up in front of the station and we needed Mummy's help to get everything out of the car and onto the train platform. And time was very short. So what does she do? She sees some total strangers who need help loading their car and she rushes off to give them a hand. We barely made our train. She should have helped us first. They could have waited if they needed her. She always does things like that. Can you imagine?

> N: Some people just have to help others.

But he's reminded of the way J puts loved ones second because she can make it up to them later. Maybe Mummy operates the same way. If so, it's ironic that J should criticize Mummy for it.

DOUBLE-FAULT: There goes N jumping to conclusions. He's never met the woman and he's spoken with her for only a few minutes on the phone, and yet he's analyzing her.

FAULT: Offspring are good reflectors of their parents, perhaps a bit tarnished, but reflectors nonetheless. But you're right. However, his conclusions were not rigid. He kept an open mind.

Once in J's home city, they take a bus to J's house. On the street N watches J just in case she sees A. DICK. N wants him and wants him badly. With her, in the streets of that city, he has lost all doubts. He clenches his fist in his pocket. But he makes an effort to relax as they get off the bus. J's house surprises him, since it looks nothing at all like the picture he had seen of it many years before when he first met J. They knock and enter, and Mummy meets them just inside the door. She is immediately talkative and cordial. Daddy is in the dining room watching television.

MUMMY: They're here. Come say hello.

Daddy comes out but clearly wants to hurry back to his sporting event. N understands even if the women don't.

N: Please don't let me disturb you.

After the introductions, N follows Daddy to the dining room and the television to see what's interesting him. Daddy doesn't exactly start a conversation with N—he works himself up into an angry monologue on the role of the doctor in society. It is obvious he is bitter. Another unhappy doctor. Age has frozen him into the place he now lives and works, and he can't go elsewhere to start a new practice. His malady is typical; the prognosis is more years of anger and bitterness, followed by retirement years in which to keep on complaining. Daddy turns back to the television, and N now moves across the hall to the room where Mummy and J are talking. N sees a picture of J taken when she was in her teens. She looks skinny but adorable. Soon Daddy joins them. He sits down at the piano and invites J to play a duet with him. J is a fine pianist but Daddy plays very fast. J can't keep up.

J: [*With a laugh*] Too fast, too fast, too fast.

Daddy smiles. Soon J can't go on. They stop. He leaves—back to the television. N follows him—he has an impulse to talk with him, about anything or nothing. They talk about what's on the screen. J joins them and asks N if he would like to see the house. He says, "Of course," and goes off with her.

When they come back downstairs, lunch is ready—good, simple, and appetizing. J has warned N that Daddy is always spilling things at the table—deliberately, in her opinion, to irritate Mummy. Daddy doesn't disappoint—he spills his glass of water as he reaches for it. After the meal, J's parents take N for a drive, Mummy at the wheel, Daddy next to her, N and J in back. They pass some tennis courts and a pond and arrive, at last, at their destination, the beach. N and Daddy walk down to the water's edge. The beach is very rocky, and N slips and slides. With the shoes he has on, it is difficult for him to maintain traction—the rocks are so smooth. Once he is about to fall, but Daddy reaches out and grabs his coat. They drive further along the shoreline and Mummy, Daddy, and N get out to climb a hill overlooking the ocean. They ask J to join them but it's too windy. She huddles in the back seat of the car and claims to be dizzy, putting on her best "hurt" look, and says, "Go on, I'll wait in the car." The three climb the hill. It is windy, very windy, and cold. J would have been uncomfortable. N remembers "wants *vs.* needs." She *wanted* to stay in the car, so she made it look as if she *needed* to. He knows her backward and forward.

The view is awesome—strong winds whipping up whitecaps on a great expanse of sea. N thinks to himself, "Life came from the sea. Maybe next time it comes, it will be smarter."

DOUBLE-FAULT: How often do I have to listen to you criticize J's actions? You're becoming tedious. She was upset, dizzy, or sick. There is absolutely nothing wrong with that.

FAULT: [*Ignoring Double-Fault's comment*] They head back to the house for tea, but along the way J says to Mummy that it might be nice to drop in at the local television station and say hello to friends. Mummy drives to the station, where she pulls the car into a parking space.

J: It's best you all wait here. I won't be more than a few minutes.

She gets out of the car, full of pep, and nearly sprints up the steps to the entrance door. Mummy tells N about the people at the television station and their connection with the girls' act. In five minutes, J is bounding back down the steps toward them. She mentions the names of everyone she met and repeats everything that was said. Mummy is all ears.

Within twenty minutes, they are back at the house and tea is served. Mummy starts to tell stories about C. C was a great child—N is certain of it. Daddy taught her to do magic tricks. They had an act when C was only five or six. Daddy must have loved her very much back then. Mummy is talking to N. She is telling him a story about a man who had some misfortune. She describes him as going comatose. Daddy overhears and knows the story. He interrupts Mummy:

DADDY: Not comatose, unconscious.

MUMMY: Comatose. [*Emphatically*]

DADDY: Unconscious. [*More emphatically*]

MUMMY: Comatose. [*Even more emphatically*]

She continues her story. She will not be overruled or corrected. Daddy says "unconscious" as she talks. There is electricity in the air.

Later J and N are driven to the train. Good-byes are said and Daddy goes to buy his newspaper. Mummy is still talking to J. Nobody kisses anybody.

DOUBLE-FAULT: You don't even have to say it—I know what N is thinking. He would probably describe Daddy as a man who concentrates on his own interests because his women drive him away or exclude him. And N sees Mummy as having a hold on J, since she's always talking to her.

FAULT: That's pretty good guessing, because I didn't describe to you J's attitude and actions around Mummy. J is quiet, obedient, a good listener, and never gets into a disagreement with her. N was astounded. J looks to Mummy for approval. At the dinner table she rarely spoke. Of course, no one spoke much except Mummy and N, who's a bit pedantic. But you're right—J is something of a puppet around Mummy.

DOUBLE-FAULT: My, you carry on so. As I was saying, N also probably interprets the "comatose" exchange between Mummy and Daddy as a preview of the way it might be for J and him. And, lastly, Mummy and Daddy are not happy together or they have settled into a fighting existence, a no-holds-barred style of living.

FAULT: Excellent. You've been most perceptive.

On the train going back, N tells J he enjoyed the day, the trip, the meal, and her parents. To pass the time, she tries to teach him how to sing.

J: If you can talk, you can sing.

N wonders why the world isn't filled with singers. He can't hold a note, as a rule, but once in a while he produces the right sound. He is encouraged. J gives him advice.

> J: The trick is to listen to the others singing. Listen to me.

She sings a note and he tries to reproduce it. When he's off, he hears the difference, but he can't seem to get to the right frequency. She slaps his hands when she wants him to stop and has very little patience with him. He wonders if that's how she teaches at school. He knows she doesn't. But from him she wants immediate perfection.

They arrive back at The Flat and tell C of the day's doings. They retire near midnight. J comes to be kissed as usual.

The next day is Thursday. J begins to devote her energies exclusively to making the party on Saturday night a success. It becomes the "reason for being." N has put out of his mind any hope that he and J will spend time alone together before he leaves. She can only concentrate on one "job" at a time.

DOUBLE-FAULT: I would say J was being practical. There's no chance for J and N to be alone and she, at least, realizes it. The party must be properly arranged and all the details must be attended to.

FAULT: If she wanted to, she'd find time to be alone with N. But let's not fight over that. N decided he wanted to finish a "job," too. He wanted to talk to C privately and time was running out. On Friday afternoon, after he took J to work, he went back to The Flat hoping that C hadn't gone out after lunch. He was in luck; she was just cleaning up the dishes.

He is going to dive into unexplored emotional territory and he must be careful. If his judgment is wrong, he will pay dearly for it. J hates secretiveness. He must trust C to keep the talk a secret between them. He has faith in her or he wouldn't try.

C has seated herself at the table and N stands, leaning against a kitchen cabinet. He begins, slowly and directly:

N: C, I've a few things on my mind that are troubling me. I need a new frame of reference, a new perspective. I'd like to discuss them with you and—well, there's no way around it—I'd have to ask a few questions and get a few answers. They involve matters of emotion and I really don't want to pry, but these things need asking and they may be hard going for you.

[*C is listening attentively and sympathetically, realizing that he has asked her for help.*]

C: Go ahead and ask what's on your mind, N, but I warn you that I shall probably cry. I always do. But don't let that stop you. [*What a fantastically giving girl. N is all admiration for her and will be furious with himself if he hurts her.*]

N: When I left here last time, the situation was this— J and I were in love and she was trying "to see herself" married. Also on the last trip J implied that we would be getting married if the tour hadn't been decided on. That's my interpretation. What I want to ask is this: was the idea of singing this year yours or J's?

C: Mostly mine. Last summer, when we finished working and came back here, we were both tired of singing and traveling. We needed a rest and to get away from each other. Then after a few months, when we'd had a chance to relax, I approached her about what we might do this year.

N: I see. That fits pretty well with what J told me. I hate to switch subjects so quickly, but I've got a few questions about Mummy and Daddy. Do you think they'll get a divorce? And does your Mummy live for the sake of seeing you two perform?

212

C: Yes, to the second question. Mummy can't do enough for us, and she'd be terribly unhappy if we stopped. It's like a second life for her. I don't think they'll get a divorce. They're always bickering and fighting, and Mummy has left Daddy on occasion, but she always comes back. I think that's their way. They've been like that for years.

N: And Daddy? What about his relationship to both of you?

C: Daddy, well, he sort of got misplaced or lost along the way. J and I both started to gravitate toward Mummy when we were in our teens. We made our own clothes and sewed and were always discussing things with Mummy. Daddy wasn't included, or didn't join in. It's probably my fault.
[N thinks about asking her if Daddy loves C and J, but decides against it. If the answer was no, it might upset C too much to think about it.]

N: The first day I came back here, I had a terrible row with J. She had told me that you weren't to be disturbed. Did I disturb you that day, incidentally?—that's not my question though.

C: You didn't disturb me.

N: Good. My question is this. J had said to me that Mummy and Daddy don't call you during exams without setting up a time to call first, by letter. Is that true? Because it seemed to me that J was surprised when Mummy called that evening.

C: It's definitely not true.

N: On that same day, J played the piano in the living room. And she had told me that even the birds pecking at your window disturbed you. Didn't her piano playing distract you?

C: It bothered me a little, but you get used to the noise of someone who's around all the time. It's different from noise *per se.*

N: I can see that. She's always here, so her movements are familiar to you. How do you two get on? [*He asked this question as innocuously as he could, for he knew that there might be an explosive answer. N believed that J had created a very comfortable setup for herself—she had her sister as a roommate and used her to justify doing whatever she wanted to do. He also believed that if C were to get married and move out—the possibility of which he hoped to investigate—J would no longer have a strong excuse for staying in The Flat. J was very cautious by nature, and perhaps a place where she felt secure would really have to crumble beneath her before she would leave it. In The Flat, J was a queen with an indentured servant.*]

C: All right, I suppose. We need each other for work. [*J had once told N that on tours C and she never argued, because you have to stick together if you are to survive. Typical J hyperbole? C continued.*] When we first moved here, J used to say mean things to me like, "The kitchen floor is dirty." She would say it as if it were my fault or as if I should clean it right away. And she'd yell at me when I did something she didn't like. I thought of moving out and leaving her, but in many respects it's really convenient being here together. Then I tried seeing things from J's point of view. If the kitchen floor was dirty, perhaps it was my job to clean it. But I got more and more quiet and hardly spoke to her at all. One time I

214

went out with my boyfriend and we stayed out very late, and do you know what J did? She called Mummy and Daddy.

N: SHE CALLED HOME! [*N walks back and forth shaking his head as if he should have expected that. C raises her hands to her face. The tension of telling the story has brought a gush of tears, but although she is crying, she goes on.*]

C: She scolded me for being late and wouldn't let me out of The Flat at night for a week.

N: Why did you let her get away with such nonsense? [*Another of N's beliefs was that C and J couldn't continue the relationship they now had. C would eventually "rebel" against her sister, which, in his view, would be better for C, worse for J for a time, and better for N. N didn't want to participate in the actual battle, but wanted to be around after it was over. I guess you could say he was willing to hold C's coat for her without J knowing it. As for J calling home, that was a rotten thing to do. There was absolutely nothing her folks could do to help —in fact, the only thing they could do was worry. Get this straight, C was over twenty and was out with a man she had been seeing for more than a year. Hardly any cause for alarm about her safety. If she was having an affair, that was strictly her business. She was old enough, and she knew her own mind.*]

C: After all that, J tried to be nicer to me, perhaps to make up for what she had done. I'm sorry I'm crying, but I warned you. Go on with your questions.

N: You've been seeing your boyfriend for some time. Are you thinking seriously about him?

C: I'm afraid I can't discuss that with you. My plans are my own and no affair of yours. [*She is crying harder than ever.*]

N: Sure. I'm sorry I asked.

C: My boyfriend has told me often that I have to be more assertive and independent around here. And I'm going to be. [*She is wiping her eyes and growing calmer.*]

N: C, please don't misunderstand, but if you'd like to be more independent and money is holding you back—say, you wanted to move out or anything—I'd be glad to give you the money to do it. [*It rankles him that C gets money from J—another "reason" or "excuse" for J to stay put.*]

C: Thank you for the offer, N, but it's not necessary.

The conversation comes to an end. N understands a little more now. He has great respect for C and he doesn't want to turn their talk into an interrogation. Also, it's almost time for him to meet J and pick up some things for the party.

DOUBLE-FAULT: It's interesting, this direct confrontation N had with C. Why did he feel he needed it?

FAULT: His instincts were telling him that he was losing J, despite the loving things she said to him. For instance, they were making love at the hotel and when he said he loved her, she said:

J: I love you when I cook for you.
I love you when you screw me.
I love you when we shop together.
I love you when you finger me.
I love you when you talk to me.
I love you when we lie in each other's arms.
I love you all the time.

216

Pretty potent speech! But his guess was that they were mere words. He felt he needed to get C's view of things. Let me go on.

He goes to meet J and she meets him with a smile. They go shopping and then back to The Flat. That evening after dinner, the party takes over everyone's attention. N pitches in; he scrubs and polishes the soup cauldron until it sparkles almost like new and passes J's inspection. The girls have started to get The Flat in order, furniture moved to the proper place and polished, rugs vacuumed, et cetera. In a few hours everything is ready except the food and the punch. They are scheduled for the next day. Then, early the next morning, the liquor and the rented glasses are delivered. The glasses are supposed to be clean but J wants them washed anyway. N groans—there are about two hundred glasses. He had hoped that sometime during the afternoon he and J could take off for an hour and go for a walk in The Park.

J: There's too much work to be done.

And so little chores take up all their time until it is time to get dressed for the party. N is sitting on J's bed reading the paper as J puts on her eyelashes. It is a delicate operation.

N: Hard to do, is it?

J: No talking now, N.

They are all ready by six-thirty. The girls look terrific. The first guests are expected in an hour. J is rushing around checking up on things in the kitchen. N sees J becoming more and more nervous. Several times during the day, he has said, "The party will be just fine. You're doing all that's necessary—providing food and drink and pleasant surroundings. People will enjoy themselves." Now he decides to leave her alone, because he's sure that anything he says will lead to an argument. N goes down the hall to the living room. C is playing the piano, just fooling around, really, as calm as can be.

N: You're not nervous, are you?

C: No.

N: What's with J? Is she always like this on tours?

C: Yes, she gets very nervous before a performance.

N: What do you do then?

C: Just stay away from her.

N: And you're always calm, cool, and collected?

C: I never get nervous, at least about performing.

N smiles to himself—C is really O.K.

At seven, a girl they have hired to help in the kitchen shows up. J starts explaining what she is to do and when she is to do it. N decides to chance the kitchen again; with a third person there, J wouldn't be rude enough to yell. Nothing like having a "stranger" around to insure proper treatment.

The first guest arrives at seven-forty. N had joked that it would be amazing if no one showed up. The girls were not amused. J now becomes a charming, smiling hostess. Her nervous energy can be directed at her guests. There is plenty of food and drink, and C's bedroom has been converted into a room for dancing. N hopes that at least once during the evening J will ask him to dance with her, but he sees her rushing about and doubts that she will. More guests arrive—some are C's friends from school, some are J's friends from work. C's boyfriend shows up, and when C sees him she goes up to him and says:

C: Well, here I am and all dressed up, too.

And finally—the moment of moments: The Birdwatchers arrive, Mother Hen and her brood of two. N had decided that he would make it his job to search out any guests who looked as if they weren't enjoying themselves and that, in particular, he would make the Birdwatchers his "problem." As they entered, N, J, and C quickly clustered around them. Mother Hen's first utterance was, "Where's ————?" (a titled neighbor who had sent regrets at the last moment). The Birdwatchers—in particular Mother Birdwatcher—were very class-conscious. After a while J and C left them, but N held to his post.

It was torture talking to these people, but it became a game. He would listen for a while, marveling at his own ability to take punishment. He wondered if any enemy could ever brainwash him. He devised tricks—like counting to sixty while giving the impression that he was listening avidly to what was being said. Whenever a sudden quiet developed in the conversation, N would say something like "So that store that sells everything sells everything, does it?" and they would repeat what they had said before. This went on for three hours, interrupted only once by fifteen minutes of cabaret by the girls. After the Birdwatchers left, J raved about the yeomanlike work N had done:

> J: You were fantastic. Wasn't he fantastic? You deserve a medal!

N saw J dancing with another guest. She wasn't enjoying it, but anything for a guest. N asked her to dance when the record was over, and they had one dance, and then the guests assembled again in the living room. They wanted more cabaret, and C and J obliged. And they were great. The audience sat on the living-room floor and the girls stood next to the piano, C with her guitar. After each song the party applauded, and J would smile and say, "Thank you." Only one person didn't applaud. You probably think it's N, but you're wrong. It was C's boyfriend.

Earlier, before the Birdwatchers, N had talked with the girls' agent. You remember that N had met him briefly after the contract-signing? Naturally, N was interested in knowing just how successful the girls could be with their act. J kept saying that her voice was getting better, but N had no way of judging whether she could make it big commercially. To his ear, she was better than some well-known people; maybe all she needed was exposure. The agent told N that they were an excellent act, but didn't work hard enough. C went to school and J taught. "You can't go very far with that kind of divided focus," he said. J had always maintained that this act was a hobby for her, and C was definitely more interested in her academic progress. When N told J in how much esteem the agent held their act, she said to C:

> J: It's always nice to hear that other people think so well of our work, isn't it, C?

As they sang in various languages, J would occasionally explain the origin of a song. She knew a great deal about her repertoire. And she could be a name-dropper as well. Earlier in the evening, L-Two had been looking at a certain piece of music, and J said that the arrangement had been given to her by a certain musician. "He's famous, as you know." J said it in the tone of someone who wants you to know she's at home with the most famous people in her field.

J left the room and C did a solo—the love song from *Black Orpheus*. She was great. She sang without the aid of the guitar, too—and accepted her applause humbly. While she sang, N made a special point of watching her boyfriend. The girls would be away next year and N wondered what he thought about that. The boyfriend didn't join in the applause.

J returned and the audience—excuse me, the guests— wanted C and J to continue. But J said she'd prefer it if another guest, a Mrs. ———, would sing. But Mrs. ——— said that J should go on.

J: I'm too tired.

MRS. ———: Why should you be tired, a young girl like yourself? ["*You tell her, Mrs. ———, you tell her,*" *N thought. He also thought it was admirable that J didn't want to hog the stage.*]

J: I'm much too tired.

This goes on for another minute and J prevails. Mrs. ——— will sing and J will accompany her on the piano without music. Before J hits the first note, she turns to the guests and with a laugh in her voice says:

J: I'm very good at arranging; this is my forte.

N cringes. Mrs. ——— sings, and unexpectedly, as far as N is concerned, she is quite good. When she stops, it is past two— late or early, take your pick. Guests start to leave.

Some of the guests are a group of C's friends who are interested in subleasing The Flat. The conversation drags a bit. J hurries them along.

J: All right, we'll see you next week, and we'll talk Flat. [*Sharply said*]

A few minutes later, J is standing in the doorway of the living room saying good-bye to a young man, also a friend of C's at school. He had played the piano earlier in the evening, commenting, while he played, on how badly he was doing it.

YOUNG MAN: Only you could have played for Mrs. ———.

J: Well, thank you.

YOUNG MAN: I couldn't have played for her. You were much better.

J: Well, thank you.

YOUNG MAN: It's hard to play without music for someone you haven't practiced with. You were really remarkable.

J: Well, thank you.

[*N wonders how long the young man will go on ingratiating himself. J, he feels, can take it forever; she makes no effort to hurry* him *along. She is all smiles.*]

YOUNG MAN: I can't say enough about how well you played.

J: Well, thank you.

Exit the young man.

N: [*Somewhat sarcastically*] You certainly can take his compliments.

J: He was drunk.

N: Even so, you might have been able to end the conversation sooner.

J: He was drunk. [*Getting heated*]

N: Well, he didn't look that drunk to me.

J: He was drunk. [*Heat achieved*]

N drops it and wishes someone else good night. At last, all are gone. The party is over. It has been a success.

My, I've talked uninterrupted for a long time. Any comments?

DOUBLE-FAULT: I wanted to hear all about it before I said anything. N is really troubled, isn't he? He sees himself going through another ordeal like the one three years before, doesn't he? And he doesn't know how to interpret J's sweet words and letters as opposed to her actions. I believe him now when he says he doesn't care how J acts or behaves as long as she loves him. He's admirable in a way. I hope he doesn't get hurt too badly.

FAULT: Most touching. You surprise me, dear lady—surprise me. Perspicacious of you, too—an acute analysis. I am really touched.

After everyone has gone, the place needs to be cleaned; it's simply a mess. However, they're all tired and they decide to do it next day when they wake up. It is agreed that the party was "super"—one of J's favorite words. Both girls toss more bouquets to N for his *tour de force* with the Birdwatchers before they retire for the night.

N of course woke up before the girls, and the girls, even after waking, both stayed in bed relaxing. N was impatient for J to get up. He was beginning to feel that there was almost no time left, and he wanted to share as many moments as possible with J. But J was still "recuperating" from last night's "work." N became restless and began pacing the living room. One glance at the room had told him that when J did get up she would insist that The Flat be spotless before she would agree to go out for a walk. So he announced that while they were getting their last rest he would start the cleaning.

J: [*Sweetly*] Don't start now, N.

N: It has to be done; I'm a bit restless. I might as well.

J: But I'll feel guilty. [*Always thinking of N!*]

N: Don't feel guilty. I might as well start. Get your rest.

J: Wait for us. I feel guilty staying in bed.

N: It's all right. Really it is.

N went to work in the living room collecting glasses, getting rid of cigarette ashes and butts, rearranging furniture. In an hour he had done about 99.9 percent of whatever cleaning the room needed, and the girls could eventually do their own rooms, so there shouldn't be much to keep J and him in the house. Meanwhile, J had got up and gone into C's room, so when N finished he headed there, too. The door was ajar, and both girls were on C's bed—C under the covers, J sitting on top—talking. N catches something J is saying to C:

J: . . . and you must talk more about your feelings if you want to be understood. [*She stops when N comes into the room. N assumes that the conversation is about C and her relationship with her boyfriend, who, incidentally, had been one of the first to leave the party. N realizes instantly that the conversation is a private one.*]

N: Sorry. Didn't mean to interrupt. The living room is finished. [*He leaves, and as he walks the few steps back to the living room he can't help thinking that for J to be giving advice on emotions to C is ludicrous. For it is J who is filled with emotional contradictions, emotional anxiety, and emotional timidity. Unbelievable.*]

Soon both girls get up, dress, and start on the rest of the cleaning. When J sees the living room, she compliments him on his work.

J: You really made quite a dent in here.

The room is virtually spotless, but J gets on her hands and knees to find the one spot remaining. Assuages her guilt, no doubt.

At last the mess has disappeared from The Flat and with it J's obligation to stay. The only chore remaining is to wash the glasses. C volunteers to do that alone, and N silently thanks her a thousand times over. Now J is free to give some attention to N. They head for the street.

DOUBLE-FAULT: What time is it now?

FAULT: Almost half past four. It took over three hours to clean the place despite the fact that N had already done the

224

living room. Although it was late afternoon when J and N left The Flat, the sun was still bright. It felt good to get out of the building and into the fresh air. No more party to think about. Freedom! They walk hand in hand. The streets are nearly deserted, the stores are closed. Once N maneuvers J inside the doorway of a shop, gives a quick glance around, and, seeing no one, kisses her. But she seems uninterested, so they continue walking. And then J starts to talk about her worries. She doesn't speak directly to him, but as if she wanted him to over-hear what is rankling inside her.

J: I can't see far ahead. The tour is coming up and I just can't see past it. Everything is so cloudy. I don't want you to feel obligated to wait for me. If you meet some-one else, I can't feel I have the right to ask you to wait. I would feel very guilty.

[*N is upset but fights to keep his control. "Calm, N, be calm," he tells himself.*]

N: What's happening, J? Remember when you wrote me you were dreaming of going over the hills with me? What happened to those dreams?

J: I couldn't get over the hills. I couldn't see over them. I tried.

N: What about our children? The little girls we both want?

J: [*Tears now*] I could see me as the Mummy but I couldn't see you as the Daddy. [*They are about four feet apart. J is nearly walking away from him. Fortunately they are standing on a very wide sidewalk on a nearly deserted street. N wants to talk things out but J doesn't— the less said the better. She looks distraught; her head is down and her eyes are searching the ground. To her credit: she knows she is hurting him, and she is trying to soften the hurt.*]

N: I don't understand. Of all the women I've ever known, not one didn't think I would be a good—forgive me for beating my own drum—a great father. You're the first one. And something else I don't understand. You told me the last time I was here that you would have married me three years ago if you had stayed on in my country to do advanced work in musicology. You also said that if it wasn't for this tour you'd marry me now. Why do marriage and musicology mix but not marriage and tour?

J: I've gone off marriage now.

N: I told you very explicitly that I wouldn't interfere with your career or come between you and your tour with C. In fact, I'd like to go on the trip myself.

J: [*Annoyed*] It's not my career—it's my hobby.

[*You must appreciate the error N had just made when he said "career." J was part of a cabaret act—a professional entertainer. When he used the word "career," he put J in the large class of people who make their living by singing. But J preferred to think of herself as a member of a smaller, more élite class of academicians who happened also to perform. Her choice of songs and her arrangements of them were the real reasons for her singing. This was partly true, but J also enjoyed the limelight, seeing her name in the papers, and—horror of horrors—even the money. She always wanted to be paid in other countries so that her taxes at home would be less. N didn't criticize these desires, only the self-deception.*]

N: All right—your hobby, then. [*J's protective anger is beginning to surface now. N is a logical person who normally prefers everything out in the open, to be discussed and mulled over. They are on a collision course.*] What about your feelings for me—don't you love me?

J: I love you—in my way. [*The extra phrase "in my way" qualifies "I love you" in such a way that it entirely negates its meaning for N.*]

N: What do you mean, "in your way"? [*He feels he is losing her and is becoming angry. Doesn't this woman realize what she is saying? But J is beyond answering any more questions, and she strikes back.*]

J: Oh, honestly, you'd think . . . Sometimes you bore me, just positively bore me.
[*N's anger is now vast, but he freezes it inside him. He stares at her, then stares away from her. He simply can't bring himself to hurt her. He repeats her last words slowly.*]

N: So I bore you. [*He becomes silent. No one speaks. They walk back to The Flat. N can feel the years of love turning rancid inside him, but he still loves her and the real possibility that he has lost her is like a knife in his chest.*]

DOUBLE-FAULT: But didn't J write N and say, "I want to be a mother and I keep dreaming of our children"?

FAULT: Yes, she did.

DOUBLE-FAULT: And how many times did she tell him she loved him?

FAULT: Countless times by letter; countable in person.

DOUBLE-FAULT: It seems so sad.

FAULT: An hour later in The Flat, each is apparently trying to rebuild the ties that seemed to have been destroyed in their last conversation.

J: I trust you. I feel I can trust you.

N: I'm going to be faithful to you while we are apart.

J: It doesn't matter. You can have a hundred women. It won't change the way I feel about you. I'll come see you after the tour is over.

N: I want you to come. When we left the hotel the other night, I thought that might be the last time we would ever sleep together.

J: [*Waving her arms in denial*] Oh, no. There'll be lots more time for that.

N: I hope so. I love making love to you. J, if you think there are ways I should change, please tell me about them.

J: [*Looking away, close to tears*] Don't change. Please don't change.

N: If you feel that I deserve criticism, by all means tell me, but do it gently and I'll try my best to fix what's wrong.

Later she comes to him and they kiss good night. Apparently they've talked out their differences. He feels he is loved again.

DOUBLE-FAULT: Is he happy?

FAULT: He wants to be. Monday, the last full day, can only be described as "unforgettable." In the morning he takes J to work. She says she will come home to have lunch with him and C. N goes back to the all-purpose store. He wants to buy C a gift that will start her thinking about becoming more independent—a half-month-premature birthday gift, because he is sick and tired of hearing J say, "I cooked—you wash up." He buys C a cookbook, and writes on the flyleaf, "One who sets one's own table determines one's own life. Anon." Propaganda. He goes back to The Flat, which is empty. He puts the book and card under C's bedcover, on top of her pillow. A short time later, both C and J arrive for lunch, and after they've eaten, for some reason or other they all go into C's room. N points to C's bed.

N: I saw something move under the bedcover.

J: There's nothing there.

C: Nonsense. I don't see anything.

N: I SAW something.

C: All right, I'll look. [*She doesn't believe him, but still she approaches the bed warily. N is smiling; he winks at J as if to say, "Watch this."*]

C pulls the bedcover back, and when she sees the package she is delighted. She opens the card, which she finds amusing. It's a big cutout of an ugly man, with the inscription "Don't be afraid if I come into your room tonight." She puts it up on her desk and then opens the package. The book pleases her tremendously, and she says she had been thinking of buying one herself. She stands there, touched—a moment in which N feels he is seeing right into her heart. She takes a step forward, puts her arm around N's neck, and kisses him on the cheek.

After lunch, J goes back to work and N spends some time walking in his favorite park—The Park. He wants to see all its beauty once more, in the hope that it will be firmly etched in his memory. Finally he goes back to The Flat to await J's return. He is leaving in the morning, and is very depressed. He has not, as he had vowed he would, got a firm commitment from J about marriage. "Yes" or "No"? She would have said "No." But she has promised she'll come live with him when the tour is over, and he believes that if she does, she won't be able to leave him, that her love for him will blossom. The clock ticks time away, and J arrives. Before dinner N offers to give her a massage—something she has never refused. He wants to touch her. They head for her room so that she can lie on the bed, but J is moving slowly and uncertainly. When they get there, she seems reluctant to let him unzip her dress down the back. N feels that C's presence in the nearby bedroom is preventing J from relaxing.

N: Well, do you want a massage, or don't you?

J: Yes. [*But the look on her face is the look of someone who is feeling trapped. N is not happy with the way things are developing.*]

N: How about my room? [*Further away from C and a flatter bed.*]

J: All right. I'll be there in a minute.
[*N goes down the hall to his room and waits. "Why didn't she come directly?" he ponders. He gets restless. He goes back to her room.*]

N: Well, are you coming? [*She very hesitatingly follows him back down the hall to his room. He closes the door part way after her, although this door is definitely still open. J* SEIZES *her opportunity. She interprets his partial closing of the door as an affront to C, who is in her own room behind a closed door. She turns around and runs out of the room and then scolds him in a voice sufficiently loud to be heard down the hall.*]

J: YOU CAN BE SO UNGRACIOUS AT TIMES.

N is absolutely furious with her—she has deliberately picked this fight. Why doesn't she just speak up when she's asked to do something she doesn't want to do? He waits a minute to calm down and then goes down the hall to J's room. She is sitting on the bed, her back against the wall. She looks distraught.

N: I feel absolutely miserable. What's wrong? [*He knows what's wrong, but he wants to hear her say it.*]

J: Tch. You know what's wrong! Why did you close the door? I don't ever want C to feel locked out. [*Using C again—but N doesn't want to tell J what he thinks of that tactic.*]

N: I pushed the door back to where it was partly for privacy and partly to keep drafts out of the room. The door was still open and C wasn't locked out. [*J turns her head away; she doesn't want to hear more. N is tired of making explanations.*] I'm leaving tomorrow and I'm going to pack now. [*Spoken matter-of-factly*]

He goes back to his room and opens his suitcase. He packs very slowly—almost in mechanical slow motion. He is more and more depressed; he cannot bring himself to go down the hall to J's room again and apologize. Something has to come from her. He takes his luggage into the living room—he feels he is slowly dying—to finish packing. It's roomier there. He is kneeling on the floor rolling up his clothes to make everything fit more easily when J comes in. He stands up and looks at her. "My gosh," he thinks to himself, "I still love her." She looks very unhappy.

N: Hello. [*He says it softly and tenderly. She comes forward and he moves to meet her. They embrace and without words they apologize to each other.*] I can't stand it when we argue, I love you so much. [*She nods her head as it rests against his shoulder.*]

J: I know. I don't like it either.

N: I'll be finished packing soon. [*She nods her head again.*]

J: I'll go back to my room and write you a letter, darling. You can open it when you get back home.

N: That will be wonderful. [*He smiles, and she smiles, too. They've made up. He finishes his packing and heads for J's room. She is almost finished with the letter and she smiles at him again. Tears in her eyes give her face a misty quality. Life is beginning to seem good to him once more.*]

DOUBLE-FAULT: It does remind one of hurricane weather—calm-storm-calm sort of thing. Very difficult to get comfortable in the calms because you know the storm is waiting.

FAULT: [*Introspectively.*] Yesssss. They sit and talk. J tells N that she will drink a lot of wine at dinner to knock her out so that she can get to sleep early. She promises N that she will come lie beside him early in the morning, half an hour before he has to get up. He is somewhat surprised, because C will still be in The Flat. If only every day could have been like that.

At dinner J does drink a lot of wine and goes to bed soon after. C is busy working on a nightgown she is making on her new sewing machine, a birthday present from Mummy and Daddy. N roams The Flat. He has little idea of his future at this moment, but feels strongly that everything must be made right before he leaves. The same old dilemma. How deep are her emotions? He goes to C's room, knocks, and enters.

N: I see you're making progress. How's it going?

C: I'm getting there.

N: C—two months ago I came in here for a talk with you and now I'm here again. A lot has happened since then, but things are really still the same as far as J and I are concerned. She loves me but can't decide whether to marry me. Anyway, I want to wish you the best of all possible years—in fact, the best of all possible lifetimes. I don't know whether I'll ever see you again. I hope I do. [*And he gives her a kiss on the cheek.*]

C: Thanks, N, and I hope things go the way you want them.

N: Do me one favor—the day after I leave, buy J some flowers.

C: Of course. [*N gives her the money.*]

N: Thanks. I'm really going to miss you. [*He goes back to the kitchen. Although it's close to midnight, it's too early for him to sleep.*]

232

He makes a sandwich and eats it and finally he turns out all the lights and goes to bed. C is still working at her sewing machine. N lies awake, not wishing to admit to himself that this may be his last night in The Flat—ever. He hopes J will come to his room early, very early. All night long he keeps waking up. In the morning he hears J get up and come down the hall. She comes into his room and into his bed. She feels so warm, N relaxes completely. J is still tense and shushes him every time the bed makes a noise under their shifting weight. They aren't making love, however. J no doubt thinks that all noise is funneled directly to C's ear. To N J's actions are almost pointless, because C must know—I mean, she *must*. In all too short a time, they get up to start getting ready. They have breakfast. The coffee is hot and N is sipping it rather noisily.

J: [*In a sweet, loving voice*] You're making noise, darling.

N: Sorry, it's rather hot. [*"She's so sweet to me now," he thinks, "last night was a century ago."*]

They dress and N says good-bye to C through her bedroom door. C is still in bed.

N and J get a taxi and are off to the bus terminal. J looks as if she's about to burst into tears. He puts his arm around her and presses her close to him.

J: When I'm on tour near here, I'll have more time. Things sort of loosen up, and you can come visit.

N: Do you mean that, J? I'd love to come see you during the year whenever I can get away.

J: Yes. Things are so hectic now. C and I will have to practice, but once we get our routines straight the trips are fairly relaxed in some ways. [*To hear her talk like this pleases N, but J has a habit of saying things to fit the occasion. Still, it's better that she's said this; there's a chance it will happen.*]

The taxi reaches the terminal, N hands his baggage over, and he and J stand facing each other for their last few words.

J: I don't want to wait around, darling. It's too upsetting. [*She is nearly in tears, but she holds them back. N comes close to her and is only a couple of inches from her when he speaks his last plea.*]

N: I'm going to miss massaging your back. We fit so well in so many ways.

J: It seems that way. [*But he sees she is not as emotional as she was the last time.*]

N: Find us, J, find us.

He hails a taxi for her, gives her all his change, and they say good-bye, waving to each other until her taxi is out of sight. N leans against the façade of the terminal, incredibly sad. His head sags, he is crying. He wonders if this is the last time he will ever see J. In spite of all her promises, he knows her too well. He has her promise to come visit him, and her statement that he can visit her while she's on tour, but she has disappointed him and other men so often before that he can feel no certainty about her. He has promised her he will be faithful to her, and that will be easy for him to do if she keeps reinforcing her promises to him and writing to him lovingly. Otherwise it will be a year of torture.

He makes his way back into the terminal and starts the long journey home. In his pocket is J's letter and he promises himself he won't open it until the day after he arrives. The trip seems longer than ever before—an unending nightmare of reminiscences that give him no peace. When he arrives home, he goes to bed but he can't sleep. He lies there feeling sad and decides it won't be possible for him to wait till the next day to read her letter. He opens it, and finds rose petals inside, together with the letter itself. It's a "nothing will ever keep us apart" letter, and she says that she feels she's being pulled in toward him as if he were a lovely whirlpool. But she adds that she can't predict the future—that's still nebulous. She thanks him once again for all he's done for her and ends it with an "I love you always—J" refrain.

DOUBLE-FAULT: I think it's a beautiful letter. It must have comforted N greatly.

FAULT: Yes and no. There were, once again, the conflicting themes running through it. The "I love you—always!" counterbalanced by the "What's to become of us?" She acknowledges what she has received from him and, as before in her letters, she sounds as loving as you'd want. But she also says his behavior is extreme.

DOUBLE-FAULT: Still, she will definitely come to him. He must feel secure in that.

FAULT: No. He doesn't. J had written him before and said, "It does no good to rake up old romances," or some such. If she completely goes off marriage to him, then it might logically follow that there's no sense in their even seeing each other again, these loving words to the contrary.

DOUBLE-FAULT: I judge from your last statement that N was still terribly unsure of his future with J.

FAULT: Yes, because he had little confidence in her ability to sustain emotion. Was she, once again, writing words to fit the occasion—or was this real? Again, the test of time would tell. And J had always failed that test.

DOUBLE-FAULT: Are you implying that J is false emotionally?

FAULT: We've talked about this before. Even if you assume she really feels the way she acts and looks and speaks—what does it matter if it all evaporates so quickly? You decide. I want to go on.

DOUBLE-FAULT: Well, go on, of course, but it looks to me as if it was a lovely beginning to N's summer.

FAULT: The summer—I'll summarize it for you.

As N saw it, there was to be no question of marriage until the tour was over, which was sensible, because there could be no answer until then. His expectations were that he and J would correspond, try to see each other sometime during the year as travel plans permitted, and that J would come live with him for a while when C went back to school after the tour. J said this was what she wanted and N wanted it, too. He could sense that J hadn't been as desperate or as tense about seeing him off this time as she had been the first time, and he interpreted this almost as relief at seeing him go, for with him there the issue of marriage always stood between them. He awaited her letters to see what direction they would take.

> J: I miss you, darling. I long to see you again. What's to become of us? But we needn't worry.

But N does worry when he reads that.

> N: I could come visit you in September, either in The City or at your first stop on the tour.

Which would be nice for two people who long for each other.

> J: Travel plans don't permit it. Sorry.

The correspondence continues. Despite all J's "lovely phrases," N wearily and warily eyes the troubling phrases that creep into her letters.

> J: Do you think I'm inconsiderate not to have made a decision? Something is shaky inside me. But I look for-

236

ward to seeing you. Nothing can ever keep me from coming to you. I am longing for you.

N: I can come to you over the year-end holiday.

J: Travel plans don't permit it. Sorry.

Mummy *vs.* Daddy ructions bring Mummy to daughters' door with tears in her eyes. She wants to live with them. J says it's all so sad. Mummy stays twenty-four hours—one day. Much time is spent on the telephone talking to Daddy. Peace is achieved; Mummy goes back home. Crazy coots, those two. But J is deeply affected. She is Mummy's protector, isn't she?

J: Marriage with all its quarrels and misunderstandings is not for me. It would be frightening to make a ghastly mistake. I love you, darling, but I've gone off marriage now, I just can't see it. I will come to you.

Consider N for a moment. Every few days he gets a letter from J that tears his insides apart. Keep in mind that whatever love he had for J before his two trips has been multiplied by the joys he experienced with her during those visits. Her dichotomous feelings have him running in circles.

N: Here I am, sitting here, waiting for her letters, and it's plain to see she's in distress. I've written her dozens of pages, I've sent her words on tape, and still she's pulling away from me. She tells me she reads my words, listens to my voice, loves me, but damned if I don't get a letter saying we're "moving in different directions," like the one she wrote me the first time I asked her to marry me. She's not responding to what's in my letters. It's like writing to a post office box, with nothing coming back. Only her own worries, decorated with "I love you." I'm not even asking her to decide now. All I want is for her to wait and then come live with me for a while. I'm sure if she does it will be so fantastic she won't want to leave. How can she write all this "longing for me" stuff and yet keep putting off any meeting while she's on tour? Communication between us takes so long now. I'm impatient. She writes that she's broken out in a rash all over her body. She's so damn nervous. She'll back away from anything that will make her more tense. Why does she keep writing about her fear of marriage? It will be at least a year before the question can be seriously considered. I've sent C the correct version of *Black Orpheus*. Glad to hear she likes it. I wonder how she's doing. Her exams came out all right, but I knew they would. Mummy coming to stay with the girls—what a joke. I wonder what those people said to each other over the phone. The girls are still having difficulty with their final business arrangements. What should be so hard about my visiting them while they're traveling? They're going to meet other people—perhaps see some friends. She's going near "current boyfriend's" home. When I asked her whether she expects to see him, she said she didn't know. That made me feel confident! I don't trust her. She writes and says she's finished with him. I believe it, but she always leaves me with a lingering doubt. Or is it me? Why am I having so much trouble perceiving things? Probably because I have to wait for her to make up her mind and I don't want to rush her and force the wrong decision. If I try to box her into a corner, she'll run away, the way she walked away from me on the street. Never would sit down and talk things out with me. My fault? I knew she wouldn't sit still for it. Funny, though— I told her to have a long talk with C, and she writes that she did and quite a few things were ironed out. I hope that means it's easier for C to live in The Flat. I really like that girl. Here's another letter from J. She tells me she loves me in the very sentence that follows "I'm just not cut out for marriage." What the hell does that mean? I know I'm

238

depressed, but now I'm getting tense, too. Using more four-letter words when I talk to myself. Can't J see herself? I know *what* she's doing, but not *why*. She tells me that in theory I'm a perfect catalyst for her, that I'm one of the best men she's ever been fortunate enough to know. Why does she run away from me? I've got lots of faults— she says. Never tells me what they are. You would think that for a woman who can speak as well as J, something could be articulated. Well, I'm not going to sit here any longer and lose her through doing NOTHING. It's fantastic how her letters look the same as the ones she wrote me years ago. All I have to do is change the dates. I NEED CONSISTENCY FROM J. I promised her I'd wait a year for her. That's a long time. I think it's possible I could wait the whole year and THEN have her tell me she won't come visit. Could she be so cruel? I think it's possible. I wonder what Daddy thinks of her. I want to talk to him. J's letters give me no peace. I don't trust her. I love her and don't trust her. That's terrible. I must do something to help me see the future more clearly. I'll write Daddy— maybe we can have a man-to-man talk. He must have some opinions. I don't believe all the stories I've heard about him. Maybe he'd even welcome a correspondence with me. Don't get carried away, now. This could be a very stupid stunt. Don't say anything concrete in the letter, work on his curiosity. I'll write him at his office. That way Mummy won't know he received the letter. Secret correspondence. J hates intrigue. But I feel compelled.

Dear Dr. Daddy:

I trust you are in good health and enjoying your summer. This is the most innocuous way I can think of starting this letter, which I hope will be a pleasant beginning for a STRICTLY PRIVATE, *very personal correspondence*

with you. There are some questions I would like to raise. They are the type of question that might seem rude if they were asked of a perfect stranger. Fortunately we are not strangers, but you may still think me rude and it may be poor judgment on my part to write you in this manner, but the truth is I am stymied in my attempts to figure out certain things that have a direct bearing on my personal life. The questions I want to raise may require some sharp inner searching on both our parts. They may also require a candor that may at times make us each feel that we are exposing too much of ourselves to the other. I can't theorize in a vacuum and I want to "talk" with you. I hope you are amenable to my suggestion of starting a correspondence. If not, for whatever reason, I hope you won't think me too out of place for writing you like this. I look forward to hearing from you, and if I don't hear from you, I will assume this letter has ended up in the trash basket.
Respectfully, N

No reply. [*N is in torment.*] Why doesn't Daddy write? Even J is not writing. Did Daddy show the letter to J? What's happening? Have I made a gross error? Surely he can see from my words that I'm a man crying out for help. No letter from J. "Only an act of God can keep me from coming to you." Has God acted and I've not heard about it? I can't make things worse. I'll write to C. Finally, a letter from J. She sends her love. Oh, no—Daddy showed her my letter— DAMN IT. Another letter from J. She's furious with me for writing C. Signed it "J." How dare she do that? Even if she doesn't like what I've done, if her love means anything she should be able to yell at me in a letter and sign it "Love, J." "Swarming" about the members of her family, am I? I am not. If she would write and answer my questions or comment on my worries, I wouldn't have to write elsewhere. I am

240

stranded here, and when she doesn't write it's like being on a desert island. Isn't C marvelous? She's written me a supportive letter. She's not surprised Daddy didn't answer my letter— the family motto is "The less said the better" where emotions are concerned. Wishes me well. I don't feel so depressed now. I would hate to lose her friendship. I'll write J a newsy letter. No more questions. J wants a free mind, but doesn't want to be "free" of me. Wants to see me sometime in the future. I can live with that, even if she says now that marriage wouldn't work. Who knows what the future holds? I'll gamble on that.

And so the summer came to an end. J and N were exchanging love letters once more, and they had an unwritten contract that had two clauses—no more talk of marriage, and she'll come to visit when the tour is over. There is absolutely no question about that—the promise has been reaffirmed.

DOUBLE-FAULT: So to N there's still the promise of love for life. How lovely!

FAULT: In September the girls take off on their tour. Weeks pass and no word from J. Finally a letter. J tells N where she is and where she's going. Everybody loves their act and wants them back. The adulation of cabaret owners. The ultimate adoration. She says she hasn't written before because they— C and J—haven't received any mail in a month. But now she got three letters from him all at once, letters that were waiting for her in some office. Her reason for not having written him makes no sense to N. He is sure she's writing Mummy regularly, and even if she doesn't receive mail from him until it accumulates, her letters would get to N immediately no matter where she mailed them. Wisdom born of experience tells him a time bomb is ticking away. He feels it, he is certain— ineluctable fate. One day he gets a letter from L-One.

DOUBLE-FAULT: L-One! Whatever became of her? I forgot all about her.

FAULT: During the time between N's March and June trips to see J, he and L-One drifted totally apart. When she returned N's car to his sister, all links between them were cut. Apparently, L-One felt she had to write a last letter and tell him she is married and now knows what it means to have each day happier than the last, with the next day sure to be even better. Her love is amply returned. N was happy for her. She asked him what he thought his future would be. He replied that he didn't think he would be married for a long time.

DOUBLE-FAULT: What about J?

FAULT: N didn't mention J. Obvious why, isn't it?

DOUBLE-FAULT: I suppose so. N had little hope left, or so it sounds from his letter to L-One.

FAULT: Quite right. He sent L-One's letter to J, and J wrote back that L-One still sounded insecure to her. N concurred, but he also felt that she would be happy. N still loved L-One. He was jealous of the love she would give her man. N would have settled for half of that from J.

DOUBLE-FAULT: That sounds like sour grapes.

FAULT: You don't know how much love L-One had in her. Half of it would still be twice as much as most people, happy people, get. Well—you know what happens. *The* letter from J arrives. It was four weeks getting to him. In it she says clearly and emphatically that she will never marry him. She has broken Clause One of their unwritten agreement. She sends lots of love and kisses.

N: Can the breaking of Clause Two be far behind?

N feels DOWN—DEPRESSED—DESOLATE. He had been suspended in limbo—now J has hanged him. She has strung him out—his vitals are in agony. How could she arrive at such a conclusion! She said she would put marriage out of her

242

mind until tour's end. What decided her? A few rounds of applause? Has he been sold out for that? Or a few "Come back again, J and C. There's always our stage for you to entertain our drinking patrons." N was sure J would never admit it was that. He is heartbroken. She had cudgeled him down for the third time—at least. He sits down and writes a letter to J.

October 21

My darling J—

I had a theory that I would sooner or later receive the letter you sent, though the letter shattered another theory I had about any mail you sent me reaching me in ten days at the most. It took twenty-eight days. Someone should check into the saying "Bad news travels fast."

As long as I'm talking—excuse me for writing about theories—I'd like to give you a few to ponder. However, I promise no more twenty-page letters. I think this will be somewhat shorter. I am sure it will.

Theory One: You see yourself as the savior of your family. As long as you stay single, your Mummy will be happy—provided, of course, you keep on with your entertaining.

Theory Two: You have a little niche in The Flat, especially with C, and you feel safe and secure there. And as long as I mentioned C, in the future please give up that "I cooked—you can wash up" litany. She knows that if you cook, she should wash up. Reminding her is an insult to her intelligence.

Theory Three: You, yourself, love the adulation of approving audiences.

Theory Four: You say you don't, but you really want to be a "star."

Theory Five: You hope to make it big financially.

243

Theory Six: You are really concerned with my welfare and are trying to be as kind as you can be.

It is clear to me, as it is to you, that our love would flourish if you wanted it to. I have no delusions about that. I have a firm belief about something else that might surprise you. If I thought I would make you unhappy in marriage, I would tell you to forget me. But I happen to believe I am the best thing that could possibly happen to you. I could and would make you happy. Which brings me to Theory Seven: You don't wish to marry now because you're afraid you'll get into a marriage like Mummy and Daddy's. By putting off marriage, you avoid this possible unhappiness. Do you really believe that by marrying late in life you improve your chances for a good marriage? How about children? Do you want your children to be raised by a mother who will by then seem like a grandmother? Children should have comparatively young parents. You're the ideal age right now, or just past ideal. Don't you consider that?

Theory Eight: You get into deep emotional relationships with men you like, and reinforce them, and then when it looks as if marriage will pop up, you back away and look for all sorts of excuses. How else could you go out with "current boyfriend" for a year and a half? What did you think would happen after that time? And how could you, at your age and in your situation, not want to live with him?

Theory Nine: The time isn't right for you yet. I don't believe this theory at all, but I include it anyway.

Theory Ten: You're so cautious you won't put yourself in a position of not having an excuse not to marry. You promised me you'd visit me and decide then whether marriage was right for you. You're afraid that if you come you'll love me so much you won't be able to leave. So you're trying to avoid coming.

As you see, I have lots of theories, one firm belief, and nothing with which to choose one theory as opposed to another except my experience and my prejudices. I have brooded over these theories so often that I run around in circles. I had to stop, in fact, because the more I thought of them the more I was destroying not my love for you but my respect. So I stopped. This last letter of yours has destroyed me. Before I got it, I was in suspended animation and quite content. Now I feel as I did after my phone call to you from Boresville. Low, sinking feeling. I called you the other night—halfway around the world—to tell you "I love you." I hadn't received this letter then. I wouldn't have called had I known it was on its way.

I still love you. I always will. I am extreme about that. I have a theory about that, too—but it's not worth mentioning.

Take care. I love you. Lots of love and many kisses,
—N.

DOUBLE-FAULT: My, he really spoke up to J and defended himself, didn't he? But what ego—"I am the best thing for you."

FAULT: He was.

DOUBLE-FAULT: You don't believe that, do you? Granting he's smart, and good-looking, if he is, and kind, and all that, he's still not the last man on earth for J. My word. There are so many. Anyway, what did she write in reply?

FAULT: "Would that we could see ourselves as others see us." She said she was sorry she had made him unhappy, but her

245

feelings were not likely to change. Even though "I still love you but love doesn't make a marriage" appeared in the letter, "I will come to you someday for a visit" did not. J no longer mentioned coming to see him. Clause Two is not only unwritten, it's unwritten about.

She did away with all of his theories by talking about the *form* of their presentation. And love doesn't make a marriage. Well, what the hell—if you have security, time, respect, *and love,* why doesn't it?

DOUBLE-FAULT: J doesn't think so and if he doesn't see that, there's no use explaining it. N is blind.

FAULT: Let me tell you what N decided to do as soon as he got N's letter.

He decided he had to act. His promise of fidelity had to be reconsidered. This was a big question for him, because it is almost emotional suicide to climb into bed with a woman when you love someone else. On the other hand, to stay faithful to someone as fickle or cowardly about love as J would be sheer physical torture. Life is short enough as it is, it shouldn't be wasted. Besides, J was telling him not to remain a monk—an attitude he felt might work two ways.

DOUBLE-FAULT: What does that mean, if you please?

FAULT: J said that she would be all wrapped up in traveling and so on, but maybe if she wanted a man, she wouldn't feel too guilty about it.

DOUBLE-FAULT: Did N believe that? Be honest, now, and don't slander J.

FAULT: No, he didn't think she'd sleep with anyone, although she did say she would be singing in "current boyfriend's" area and didn't know whether she'd see him or not. Remember how it was when N came to see her in March? She said she had wanted to sleep with N that first Saturday, but also that she felt like an adulteress. Maybe she did want to sleep with someone. A year and more without sex is very wearying. Perhaps she would crawl into bed with someone and try the same "I feel like an adulteress" gambit again. Who knows?

DOUBLE-FAULT: He decided to break his promise, didn't he?

FAULT: Yes. N gave considerable thought to how he should break his vow. He was opposed to paying for sex, he was opposed to just picking up someone with a hot bottom requiring deactivation, he was opposed to having one-night stands. He thought an affair should last a couple of weeks, that the attraction should not be merely physical but should include interest in the girl as a person, and most important, it should involve no love at all. No "I love you." Because he couldn't. And with these criteria N decided he would try to break his vow with—care to guess?

DOUBLE-FAULT: I haven't the slightest idea.

FAULT: I'll bet. Well, it was L-Two. N wrote to J and told her that for his year-end holiday he was coming back to The City. He wanted to see The Park and walk the streets.

DOUBLE-FAULT: Why didn't he try to see J? Wouldn't he have preferred that?

FAULT: Oh—sure. In fact, he did try to make plans to be with J, but though at the start she sounded interested, as the time drew near she found the usual assortment of excuses. Anyhow, she would be out of the country. When he wrote her that he was coming to The City even though she wouldn't be there, she wrote back that she thought it sounded a trifle "sick" to want to walk the streets. N laughed at that. He had never done a "sick" thing in his life—he had a reason for everything. And she also added her expected admonishment,

"Don't you 'swarm' around my family. Remember, what I said earlier still goes. I mean it."

The time came to fly to The City and N did.

DOUBLE-FAULT: But didn't he try to contact L-Two first? He didn't just up and go, did he? That's bewildering, if he did —not like N at all.

FAULT: What are you talking about? N has a flare for adventure. L-Two or no L-Two, he still wanted to make the trip. He would of course let Mummy and Daddy know he was in The City, and if they were coming in for the holiday, he would invite them out to dinner.

DOUBLE-FAULT: But J expressly warned him not to "swarm" around them. Doesn't he listen?

FAULT: How do you figure that his inviting them to dinner is equivalent to "swarming" around them? They could always decline the offer.

DOUBLE-FAULT: A technicality. N knew what J meant.

FAULT: He sure did and he didn't give a damn. He was certain even if they didn't come to The City, they would invite him to spend a day with them.

DOUBLE-FAULT: How could he be so sure? After all, his mysterious letter to Daddy got no response. Perhaps they would have considered themselves interfering in J's affairs to invite him out.

FAULT: Good thinking. All right. It wasn't certain. But if these people wanted to talk to him, they'd invite him. Comment?

DOUBLE-FAULT: No. But he just doesn't listen. No wonder J is off marrying him.

FAULT: Thank you for the "No" comment.

N arrives in The City. Nostalgia hits him in waves, but he

repulses the waves like a breakwater. He will first see how things go with L-Two before he gets in touch with Mummy and Daddy. In short order, N stands before L-Two's flat. From the street, he sees a light in her window. He walks up the one flight of stairs and very calmly rings her bell. He knows that L-Two will be shocked to see him. He hopes she is alone, for he knows nothing of her personal life. Everything will have to be in his favor if he is to succeed. Her footsteps approaching tell him that the adventure will begin momentarily.

N prepares himself. He will present himself matter-of-factly and explain his desire matter-of-factly. But first he will explore whether there is any chance of success.

The door of the apartment opens and there before him is L-Two, looking ever so delightfully tempting. She is absolutely stunned to see N.

L-Two: Why, N! What are you doing here?

N: Well—that's a long story. May I come in?

L-Two: Yes. Of course. Do come in. I'm just making tea. Would you like some?

N: Oh, yes. It's rather wet outside.

L-Two: Here, let me take your coat. [*He slips out of it. He's smiling and she is smiling, too. She's almost laughing, she's so surprised to see N.*]

N: Glad to get out of that thing. It keeps in the cold.

L-Two: Here, now, come this way into the kitchen. [*N follows her. So far, he feels calm and lucky.*]

N: You have a nice cozy place here.

L-Two: I manage in it. It's comfortable. Now, tell me what brings you to The City? And to my door? [*They are in the kitchen now, and N still refrains from answering her questions.*]

249

N: Shall I sit here? Is this all right?

L-Two: Yes, that's fine. I know J is out of the country, so that can't be why you're here. [*It is exactly why he is in The City.*]

N: The last time I saw you was the night of the party.

L-Two: That's right. It was a lovely party.

N: Unbelievable party.

L-Two: Here. Lemon? Sugar?

N: A bit of both, please. [*They both have their cups now and are sitting at a table.*]

L-Two: Well—tell me, why are you here? I'm over my shock now and my curiosity is overwhelming me.

N: I'll be happy to tell you why I'm here but I have to work up to it slowly. I hope your curiosity can stand it. First, let me ask you, how are things going for you?

L-Two: Everything's going fine.

N: Good. Am I interrupting any plans you have just by being here? I know I came unannounced.

L-Two: You certainly surprised me. But, no. I have no plans. In fact, I thought I'd spend this holiday sort of relaxing and resting. [*"Beautiful," N thinks.*] But come on, now, stop stalling. What brings you here?

N: I'm getting to it.

L-Two: How'd you get my address?

N: Trade secret. If you think about it, it isn't hard to get, is it?

L-Two: I suppose not. Go on.

N: A few more questions. Not hard ones, either. Now suppose you wanted to do something that was sort of

250

unusual, something you felt might not succeed. Would you try it?

L-Two: That's a cryptic question. I suppose so, but it would depend on what it was, of course.

N: Naturally. But suppose there's a good chance you'd come out looking like a fool, regardless of success or failure. Would you try it then?

L-Two: Oh, I don't know. I might.

N: Good. O.K., now suppose—

L-Two: I wish you'd get down to it!

N: Patience, patience, patience. Now suppose you meet someone you like—what do you do about it? A man, I mean.

L-Two: What kind of question is that? There are so many variables involved there. Surely what brings you here isn't that complicated.

N: No. But if given the chance, I'll complicate matters. Look—suppose you meet a guy you're really physically attracted to. That's certainly possible, isn't it?

L-Two: Yes, of course.

N: And you want to meet this guy more often. What do you do about it? Go home and hope he'll call, or forget him, or what?

L-Two: I don't know. I would hope he'll call. Perhaps I might have a friend who knew him and could make a suggestion. What are you getting at?

N: Well, I'll tell you. My problem is I've met a girl, really a lovely girl. I don't love her but I do like her. I even admire her, and by that I mean I think she's something special. I've decided to ask her directly whether

251

she'll have an affair with me, and I thought I would first ask someone whom I consider to be an attractive woman —please don't blush—what she would say if some man approached her that way. I mean, do you think it could possibly have any chance of success?

L-Two: You're not talking about J are you?

N: No. No. J is completely out of this—completely.

L-Two: I thought you were very high on her.

N: J is halfway around the world at present and I'm here, asking you a question. Let's forget J—as if she didn't exist.

L-Two: O.K. Well, I don't honestly think there's much chance for you with this girl. Does she know you?

N: Yes.

L-Two: What does she think of you?

N: I don't know. I never asked her.

L-Two: You can try, but not much chance, really. Why do you want to try in the first place? I thought you were stuck on J.

N: J is "past tense" as far as the present is concerned. She doesn't control my behavior. [*A lie of sorts!*] That's the way it is. Regardless of how we got this way, that's the way we are. Perhaps she'll remain "past tense"—I don't know and I don't think about it—at least, not too much. I feel certain—well, as certain as one can be— that I'm doing what I want. My eyes are wide open. [*L-Two has listened silently, sipping her tea, while N talks.*]

L-Two: I think I understand what you're trying to say. [*"Understand?" N's thoughts flash. "What does she un-*

derstand? About J and me, or why I'm here? It won't be long now before I know."]

N: So what do you think—is there a chance, even a small one?

L-Two: Probably quite small. There's always a chance, I suppose. [*She smiles and N doesn't know whether she can't guess it's she, or whether she knows and wants to be asked, or whether she knows and doesn't want to be asked. He didn't come this far to be timid. He takes the plunge.*]

N: If you haven't already guessed, I'll put it bluntly and, I hope, politely. [L-*Two is silent. He asks the question calmly as if he were requesting a refill for his cup of tea.*] Are you for it? Do you need time to think about it?

L-Two: I don't need time. Are you sure this is what you want?

N: Yes.

L-Two: My answer is—much to my surprise—[*when N hears those words, he knows what the next word will be*] yes! I'll tend to your desires and be your paramour. Hmm. I think I'm going to enjoy it very much.

N: [*Feeling bullish*] If I have anything to do with it, I'll almost give you a written guarantee.

"Tend to his desires," she had said to him, and that she did. They were together two weeks solid, day and night.

DOUBLE-FAULT: What about L-Two's job?

FAULT: What kind of question is that? It was vacation time. Are you ill, do you feel all right?

DOUBLE-FAULT: I have a slight headache. I'll be all right. Go on, please.

FAULT: As a paramour, L-Two was ideal. When they weren't making love, they talked, or they rested, or they walked the streets of The City arm in arm. Sometimes they would come back to the apartment, and the moment the door shut behind them, they would look at each other—irrepressible smiles would break out—and fling themselves into each other's arms, kissing and stimulating each other, throwing their clothes off, and make their way to bed.

DOUBLE-FAULT: Sounds disgusting.

FAULT: Now, now. Everyone has his own little ways of getting pleasure out of life. What could be more honest than their behavior? They did what they felt, and each was glad the other was uninhibited. It was a joyous binge for both of them.

DOUBLE-FAULT: It still sounds disgusting.

FAULT: If you want to look at it that way, that's your choice. But these two were giving each other—

DOUBLE-FAULT: Giving! That's not giving. That's lust, if you ask me.

FAULT: Lust that's reciprocal isn't lustful. What am I saying? Lust that's reciprocal is grand. Too bad you don't appreciate that. And it was a giving on both sides that sustained their interest. "Not giving" one day and "giving" the next—that's not giving. Don't look so glum.

DOUBLE-FAULT: I think N's a horrible person.

FAULT: Why? For doing what J suggested?

DOUBLE-FAULT: No. For doing it with an acquaintance of J's. She introduced them. It's not fair.

FAULT: Fair! There's a fine word. Let's get off this topic or we'll end up yelling at each other.

DOUBLE-FAULT: I DON'T YELL.

FAULT: Of course you don't.

N and L-Two are lying in bed, both naked. He's lying on his back, his head propped up by two pillows, his arms around her. She's lying alongside him, her head on his chest, one hand under his neck, the other running patterns over his stomach, et al. One sheet covers them—that's all they need.

> N: Did you ever stop to think what life was like about three or four hundred years ago? Whether men and women had the same fetishes in their love-making back in those days as we do now?
>
> L-Two: I sometimes think about the past, but I much prefer to be me alive in this century.
>
> N: Yes, I can see why—being emaciated—excuse me, emancipated, as women are.
>
> L-Two: Pretty poor pun—rather puny!
>
> N: Poor puns are the best kind. The worse the better.
>
> L-Two: Well, then, I was wrong. That was a good one. As for love-making styles, I would say that modern technology hasn't taken us that far from the past. Desires don't change, stimulation doesn't change. It's probably much like it was and will stay that way. Oh, I'm sure there are a few cultures which have different styles, but within a culture things haven't changed much.
>
> N: I'm not so sure. All the modern developments and inventions weren't available in olden days. They have a liberating effect. Here we are, going at it hot and steady, day and night, with never a fear of your getting pregnant. Every burst is anguish-free.
>
> L-Two: Yes, that's true, but that only frees you to perform. It doesn't necessarily bring about a change in style.
>
> N: Perhaps. But suppose you consider this. Say it's that time in your cycle when you're most potent for reproduc-

tion. I would have to splatter you or the bedsheet instead of collapsing inside you if we made love at all. That means I would have to be in a position that made it easy for us to disengage. So it could change our style.

L-Two: Yes. I suppose it could, in that sense—and I like you collapsing in me. But getting back to the point. That doesn't mean that a new style would be introduced. Just the same ones used at different times.

N: I guess I would agree with that. Maybe modern love-making isn't so different, after all. Just easier.

L-Two: Oh—better also.

N: You think so?

L-Two: I think you're quite advanced.

N: Do you?

L-Two: Of course I do.

N: You're something else, you are. Guess what?

L-Two: Fine with me.

Time passes. They are serene—no bickering. Maybe this is because they both know it all ends when N leaves. Their conversation is pleasant, and filled with laughter at the right time. They enjoy themselves. N can make L-Two laugh almost at will. He mocks, mimics, and impersonates L-Two at auspicious moments when they're alone. She thinks his charades are uproarious.

DOUBLE-FAULT: What about J?

FAULT: J's name was never mentioned after the first conversation over tea. That was mutually understood, and it was good. N never got in touch with Mummy and Daddy, either. He couldn't leave L-Two. That is, he didn't want to. So he left them in their "unswarmed" state.

DOUBLE-FAULT: Maybe he was afraid of J's wrath if he did get in touch with them.

FAULT: You can believe that if you want to, but it's simply *not true.*

In two weeks N and L-Two solve the world's problems, only no one is listening. When it's time for him to leave, he stands, bag in hand, at her front door.

> N: It's been interesting and I've enjoyed every minute of it. I'm sorry to see it end.
>
> L-Two: Me, too. It's been so easy, so unpressured, so natural.
>
> N: That's the way it should be. I don't think people in love could get on together as famously as we did.
>
> L-Two: Possibly because there's been no crisis. I find myself thinking how remarkable our being together has been. I'm glad you shocked me at the front door two weeks ago.
>
> N: Maybe our paths will cross again, but if not I hope all goes well for you. [*He laughs at this and then adds:*] I hope all goes well for you even if we do meet again.
>
> L-Two: I hope everything works out for you, too. Don't worry about my saying anything to J, or anybody else.
>
> N: Thanks. It's been our two weeks.
>
> L-Two: Yes. I don't want to share them with anyone— not even in talk. They were glorious and I shall be self- ish about them.

He opens the door, smiles at her for a long moment, she grins; he ducks his head in a nod, steps out, and hears the door close behind him. He bounces jauntily down the steps to the sidewalk. She has given him back his zest for life. L-Two has been absolutely fantastic.

257

DOUBLE-FAULT: Just an ordinary tryst, if you ask me.

FAULT: You followed that part of the story pretty closely.

DOUBLE-FAULT: Yes. The disgusting is always interesting. But the whole affair was stupid, simply stupid.

FAULT: How so?

DOUBLE-FAULT: N didn't have to travel so far just to have an affair. And what did L-Two get out of it? N used her like a slave.

FAULT: Now wait a minute. She had her eyes wide open. She could see what was going on. She said she'd tend to his desires—she didn't have to say that. No one was forcing her. She said she enjoyed herself. Sounds like she wasn't disappointed. You're talking nonsense.

DOUBLE-FAULT: Don't you dare say I talk nonsense. The whole thing was stupid, simply stupid.

FAULT: Two people spend two weeks together, enjoy each other's company and conversation, and you say it's an ordinary tryst and stupid. Explain that to me.

DOUBLE-FAULT: L-Two accepted N because she was jealous of J's relationship to N.

FAULT: *What?* J spurns N and L-Two is jealous of that?

DOUBLE-FAULT: L-Two *did not know that.*

FAULT: True, maybe. But she certainly knew that things were off between N and J, or why would N be knocking on her door? And also why did she promise to keep the whole affair a secret? If she were jealous of J, she would in all likelihood want it known that she had stolen N's affection, or had his attention for two weeks. A little bragging, you might say.

DOUBLE-FAULT: Preposterous. L-Two was jealous of J—of J's ability and so on, of J's apartment, and J's boyfriends.

FAULT: Are you suggesting that all women of J's acquaintance are jealous of J?

DOUBLE-FAULT: They probably are. That's why they sometimes make remarks intended to hurt her.

FAULT: So you would have it that L-Two fell prostrate at N's feet just because he was emotionally involved with J? That she felt that if he was good enough for J—even in the past—he must be good enough for her?

DOUBLE-FAULT: I did not say that.

FAULT: That's weird thinking.

DOUBLE-FAULT: Weird! Look, the whole affair is stupid, simply stupid.

FAULT: It's more than stupid. It's imaginary. I made it up.

DOUBLE-FAULT: You what? That's even stupider than the whole incident.

FAULT: I made it up to see how you would react to it.

DOUBLE-FAULT: Are you playing a game with me? I won't tolerate it.

FAULT: [*He fixes Double-Fault with a stare.*] Is that so? Well, then, I'll continue with the original story.

DOUBLE-FAULT: That would be much better. It's sadder but not as stupid.

FAULT: J's letters turned into infrequent postcards. Half the words on the cards were his address, and this annoyed N. Furthermore, postcards aren't really private. Anyone could have read them. And she always wrote the same things—sometimes about the weather, hot or cold, sunny or not, wet or dry—and something about how much everyone liked the act. Never an "I miss you" or "I love you."

259

DOUBLE-FAULT: Oh, honestly. Cards are not private, as N said, so why put private thoughts on them? And besides, he knew things weren't going well between them.

FAULT: True. But he loved her, and the thinness of her communication was distressing to him. He would think that the next time he heard from her it would be a letter saying an eternal good-bye. He was a mass of contradictions. He didn't like not hearing from her, didn't like getting cards, and yet he would feel relieved when a card came instead of a letter. Finally she did write him a letter—wishing him a happy birthday.

DOUBLE-FAULT: That was nice.

FAULT: Was it now? She had forgotten the date and was two months ahead of time in her "happy birthday." When he informed her of that in a letter completely devoid of anger and, in fact, full of humor, he also reminded her of his real birthday. On that occasion he received nothing—not even a card.

DOUBLE-FAULT: Maybe she was busy.

FAULT: Come on now! Come on! [*Fault is agitated over what he considers an exceedingly lame excuse offered by Double-Fault. He composes himself and continues.*] N could just imagine J's reaction when she got his letter telling her she had the wrong month. "If I can't even remember his birthday, I evidently do not love him," he thinks she thinks.

DOUBLE-FAULT: That's too much imagination. He can't possibly know why J didn't respond a second time. Maybe she felt that to do so would be to hurt his feelings by reminding him that she had previously forgotten the date.

FAULT: That's amazing reasoning. And I thought I'd heard everything! Anyway, J has isolated N again, and left alone with his thoughts, N despairs. The more he thinks of J and C, the more starkly clear it becomes to him that he wishes J were more like C. And then he takes the next step—HE WISHES IT WERE C IN LOVE WITH HIM AND NOT J.

DOUBLE-FAULT: Why, the man's a lecher, and that proves it!

FAULT: It proves nothing of the kind. Day after day of rehashing the circumstances that have led up to his present situation have made him not only unhappy but also aware of what it would take to fulfill part of his dream. And he sees that C has in her emotional qualities he wishes J had. The transference of love from J to C is more an easing of a tortured mind than a reality, but N discovers, the more he thinks about it, that he could love C without limit. It surprises him that it could be so. N is not a lecher, by any rational estimation.

DOUBLE-FAULT: You're aiming some very tart cracks in my direction and I wish you would cease immediately.

FAULT: So you think I'm being tart, do you? Well, stop making such idiotic pronouncements and listen.

DOUBLE-FAULT: You asked me to comment whenever I wished, and I resent your judging my opinions. If you don't stop—

FAULT: All right. All right. Accept my sincere apologies, please. Let's go on.

DOUBLE-FAULT: I accept them, but you could sound more sincere.

FAULT: N was well aware of the mental gymnastics he was putting himself through, but it was the unavoidable result of contrasting the two girls. All the bickering, arguments, eruptions, and explosions that were part of any projected future (no matter how much he desired it) with J vanished for him when he thought how it would be to have C's love. Also he could see in C all the qualities he admired in J, plus modesty and reasonableness. His dreams reflect his new fantasy.

Dream Sequence Number Three:

The tour is over. J and C are once again living in The Flat. J is lapping up the adulation of her friends which she feels she so richly deserves while at the same time she is complaining that all the phone calls are such a bother. N returns to The City unannounced and unexpected. He stays in a hotel. He immediately goes to The Park. He knows that C will be there, and she does appear. She walks with her head down. Presumably she is unhappy. N walks toward her and she is flabbergasted when she recognizes him.

C: N! What are you doing here?

N: I want to talk to you. Can you come with me?

C: Yes, I'm not busy now. Where to?

N: I have a room nearby. We can talk privately there.

C: I didn't know you were coming. Does J?

N: No. I didn't tell anyone I was coming. But I had to come. [*They go quickly to his room. There is little conversation between them on the way despite C's surprise at their meeting. Once there, they sit in chairs facing each other.*]

N: I don't know what kind of year you've had but mine's been hellish.

C: Mine, too. My boyfriend and I had a falling out and we no longer have any attachment to each other.

N: I'm sorry.

C: I'm not. I think it's for the best.

N: Oh!

C: And J was simply unbelievably difficult. [*N nods his head, since he can well understand how torturous it has been for C. She tells her story. N tells his.*]

N: . . . and so it boils down to this. I am here because I love you, C. I had no idea of how things had gone for you, and if you say it's for the best that you've broken with your boyfriend, then I happily accept that. The contrast between you and J has made me want you more than J. That probably sounds callous. It always does when one became clinical about feelings. But I can truthfully say that if I can't be your husband, I would like you to think of me as a brother, and if you can't do that, I would like you to think of me as a friend, and if you can't do that, I pray you to forget me completely. I never want to be associated in your mind with misery and hurt. I've begun to feel too much for you, and I want you to be more than happy. I wish it, I hope it, I pray it. [*He has spoken softly. There is no doubt in C's mind of the sincerity of his words. She has just been proposed to and she sits there silently, dismayed but not repelled.*] C—if you can find it in your heart to love me, or even if you can't—will you marry me? [*She stares at him, speechless. He waits silently, his life passing in review before him. How strange! He has just proposed to a woman he has never so much as held hands with. Irony of ironies. His momentous question awaits her momentous answer. C is still staring at him and N reads her eyes. She is seriously considering his proposal. He wonders if it's the first time the thought has occurred to her or whether she dreams, too. Her breathing is heavy.*]

C: I've decided YES, N. I'll love you with all my heart. [*She rushes into his arms and he hugs her close to him. He* KNOWS *she will love him with every fiber of her being and he* KNOWS *that their love will grow every day of their lives. It could be no other way with C.*]

N: Let's go get the necessary papers. We can be married within the hour.

C: Absolutely. I'm so happy now I can't stop the tears.

N: Let them flow, they're tears of promise. [*They kiss. They rush off to be married. The ceremony consists entirely of signing papers. When it's over, they rush back to N's room. Their honeymoon night starts with the promises each makes to the other—words they will remember for a lifetime. They*

263

*say to each other what they find in their hearts, not some
printed, recited vow. They completely neglect to tell J or
Mummy and Daddy what's happened, but next morning agree
they should go back to The Flat to pick up some of C's clothes
and to make their announcement to the family. Their faces
glow. It has been a good night. They make their way along
crowded—or were they empty?—streets and up the familiar
stairs to the door of The Flat. C produces her key and they
enter, C first. A minute later N follows noiselessly after her.
Down the hall a shrieking J is abusing C. All three meet at the
kitchen door.*]

J: WHERE HAVE YOU BEEN? I'VE BEEN WORRIED SICK
ABOUT YOU. [*J would never first ask if C was all right. Then J
sees and recognizes N. She bellows.*] N!!!! [*J almost stumbles.
She apparently senses that something is radically altered. N is
calm. He holds all the trumps. He knows that J is about to
receive an emotional blow that will shatter her—not losing
him, you understand,* BUT C. *He doesn't want to appear as if
there's satisfaction in it for him. Last night he was blessed;
he hopes everyone can be lucky and happy as he. C is his wife
now and he is prepared to put the facts of life plainly to J. He
will not shrink from it, but he will not enjoy it, either.*]

N: Hello, J. Before you say another word, C and I wish to
inform you that we were married yesterday.

J: YOU WERE WHAT?

C: We're married, J. [*J is in shock.*]

N: It's rude not to congratulate us. [*Why did N say that?
He took it as an affront to C that J wouldn't or didn't wish her
well. Then he was sorry he had said it.*]

J: [*With an implausible smile*] Well, congratulations, of
course. How nice. [*Weakly said*]

C: We want to call Mummy and Daddy and tell them.

J: Yes, of course. [*She is speaking mechanically, but her
eyes keep darting back and forth from N to C. N has the ex-*

264

pression of a stoic. He is keeping back his happiness.] I called them last night when you didn't return. They're very worried, too.

N: Our joy made us selfish. We only thought of ourselves last night. Incidentally, we'll be living in The City. Either you move out and we take over The Flat, or you stay and C and I will find a place. Suit yourself. [*J looks crushed.*]

DOUBLE-FAULT: This is an obvious acting out of a subconscious wish on N's part to hurt J. You can see what would follow from the premise of the dream. As C's husband, N would say no more tours for C, and J would be the loser. It's not a very edifying dream for one who claims to be giving and unselfish.

FAULT: Is that so? Well, the fact is that if N had his choice between C and J, he'd pick C.

DOUBLE-FAULT: I don't believe that. I simply don't believe it.

FAULT: I don't care what you do or don't believe. It's obvious you haven't got a feeling for the differences and similarities between C and J. J is a vixen, C is—well, C is C.

DOUBLE-FAULT: Again we don't agree. I see it differently. C is nice, I suppose, but she has her faults, too, you know.

FAULT: [*Exasperation has made Fault silent. Then he finds his voice and speaks.*] Let me tell you of another dream N had. Because in this one you actually may find evidence to back up your opinion that N is trying to hurt J.

Dream Sequence Number Four:

N is in J's room in The Flat. J sits at her make-up table applying cosmetics. The tour is over and it's been sixteen months since they've seen each other. J is giggling and laughing and elaborately painting her face for no reason at all, as no plan has been made to leave The Flat. N starts to speak— slowly, gravely.

265

N: Listen to me, J. I have something to say, something I must say to you. I've loved you since we first met and I've loved you the years we've been apart. I love you now before I say what I must, and I'll love you just as much after I say it. My love for you has made me miserable before and I shall probably be miserable again after I finish speaking. You're laughing and giggling now just as you used to do when I was here last, and you act as if nothing of consequence or importance has happened between us. I don't know now as we sit here whether you realize just how bad you made life for me and whether you want to make things up to me from this moment forward, or not. If you do, then what I say here will only increase your compassion for me and your desire to do what you intend. If you don't, then in any case I shall be miserable, for there seems to be no peace about you inside me, and my insides still accompany me wherever I go! Although your life has been no bed of roses and you've suffered, all your life you've been a BITCH, a vain, arrogant, selfish, self-centered BITCH who—

[ABRUPTLY, *the scene in the dream changes. They are now in C's room, J sitting on C's bed. N is sitting in a chair not far from the bed and C is there, too, on the far side of the room, by the window, her hands raised to her face and tears trickling down her fingers and falling to the floor. N is still speaking.*]

N: All your life you've been a BITCH, a vain, arrogant, selfish, self-centered BITCH who—

J: [*Screeching*] I have had quite enough of this! [*Rises and walks to door, pointing her finger at N.*] You're not perfect, you know. You have plenty of faults. [*She's on her way to the door, about to run out on the confrontation, when N stands up, takes one step toward J, and with his right hand grabs her right arm. That hand which used to massage J so lovingly, that hand which had squeezed the hard wooden handles of so many tennis rackets until the rackets seemed to complain, that hand*

266

seizes J's arm—so soft an arm—with a grip that freezes her in position, makes her immobile. From N's eyes comes a glare which instantly transmits to J a fear for her own safety. Which is precisely what N wanted. Quietly and resolutely, as if a pontifical proclamation were being issued, he addresses J.]

N: Sit down, J. You will listen quietly and very, very, very attentively. [*He releases her and J meekly goes back to sit on the bed. Her arm was almost bloodless and now the color starts to come back. C is still quietly crying. N continues.*]

N: All your life you've been a BITCH, a vain, arrogant, selfish, self-centered BITCH who—[*J starts to whimper. She looks lonely and uncomfortable. She doesn't want to listen to what N has to say because, as she herself has said, she respects his wisdom, and the words he says may well be too true for her to bear hearing.*]

N: All your life you've been a BITCH, a vain, arrogant, selfish, self-centered BITCH who . . . [*N keeps repeating himself, and as he does so tears pour from his eyes. All three are crying now, C quietly, her hands still covering her face, J convulsively, and N with tears streaming down his cheeks as he continues.*]

N: All your life you've been a BITCH, a vain, arrogant, selfish, self-centered BITCH who . . .

DOUBLE-FAULT: Of course this dream reflects an obvious desire to hurt J. N is just striking out at her with his name-calling. Even the quality of his love becomes suspect now, if you ask me.

FAULT: This was a dream. He never said those words to her—at least he never called her a BITCH to her face. His letter of theories did suggest, of couse, those other attributes—the unflattering ones. But why does his love become suspect even if, I grant you, the dream attests to his anger?

DOUBLE-FAULT: I can't be bothered to explain such a clear fact. If you don't understand, then you simply don't understand—and you probably never will.

FAULT: Well, I'd like to point out to you what N told me. He said it was funny that he still loved J as much as ever but could also see himself loving C.

DOUBLE-FAULT: That proves my point. If you love someone N's way, there is no emotional room for loving anyone else. Isn't that what you implied?

FAULT: I thought you were listening. Even when N loved J, he loved L-One. Because there was no future in loving J at that time. But then things changed. And now it seemed to N they were changing again, for the worse.

DOUBLE-FAULT: Let me guess what happened. N had written to J asking to spend the summer with her, and she had said her commitments would make it nearly impossible for them to spend any time together.

FAULT: Close. Very close. He wrote her that he had two options. One was, as you said, to spend the time with her, and the other was to visit a place N considered the most beautiful spot in the world. But he didn't put it that way to J. He said he would spend the summer in a place he liked. Care to guess what J did now?

DOUBLE-FAULT: Ahh . . . J ignored the letter.

FAULT: Riiight. You're catching on. And N wrote again asking her for a decision. And J offered the excuse you gave before. So N wrote J that he was going on his vacation to the place he liked so much—not The City, incidentally—and he would spend his vacation playing tennis and writing a novel.

DOUBLE-FAULT: What would he write about?

FAULT: Ahh, yes. What would he write about! Well, you see, N was well aware that C—that's right—C would never be his wife, so he decided he would write a story which would be exclusively intended for C to digest—a digest for C.

DOUBLE-FAULT: Groan.

FAULT: N also had to get it out of his system, because he was certain that someday in the near future J would write and say she would not be coming to visit him. N would make that letter the detonator to the time bomb he was assembling for C. N was sure that no matter how he reported the events or slanted the characters—that no matter what—C WOULD SEE THE TRUTH.

DOUBLE-FAULT: Spoken like a missionary.

FAULT: Precisely. It would be N's mission to unfold for C's eyes much of his own life as well as another view of J.

DOUBLE-FAULT: [*Aghast at the prospect*] But that's—that's . . . that's totally unfair. J's private life should not be divulged to C. N would have to be incredibly mean to do that. [*Tears come to Double-Fault's eyes.*]

FAULT: There, there, now. I didn't realize you were in such sympathy with J. Hang on. There's not much more to tell. Before N left to do his writing, he received a postcard from J. The usual. He wrote to her and gave her his new address, and he settled down to his new routine. Write in the morning, play tennis in the afternoon, and write at night. The courts where he played tennis were surrounded by beautiful gardens and they had a soothing effect on N. Every day he would check his mailbox, but never even a card from J. C's birthday was coming up and N wanted to hear something from either J or C, so he sent C some pictures of the flowers that he saw every day and wished her well on her birthday, reminiscing about the last time he had seen her.

DOUBLE-FAULT: He only wrote to her to get a thank-you note in exchange.

FAULT: Not at all. Here he was, writing a novel expressly for C, and he did wonder how things were going for her. He told her that he was writing the novel: "I spend my time writing a novel, and if there's anyone in the world I would like to have read it, you are the one. Possibly because of the enormous number of books on your shelves, I suspect you to be a worthy critic. But there's more to it than that."

And he went no further in explaining.

DOUBLE-FAULT: What could he possibly hope to gain?

FAULT: Information, for one thing, and an indication of how C was doing. It was nearly a month since he had last heard from J, and that was depressing him.

DOUBLE-FAULT: What did C do with N's letter?

FAULT: She answered it and raised his spirits just as she had a year before. N redoubled his efforts to finish his novel for C.

DOUBLE-FAULT: Aren't you going to tell me what she wrote?

FAULT: Of course. She thanked him for his present and said she'd welcome reading the novel and that she would make a special place for it on her bookshelves. She told him she would be going to school in September, so N knew for certain when the tour would be ending. C wished him well. It was a cordial letter.

DOUBLE-FAULT: She really likes him, doesn't she?

FAULT: Yes, and he her. The letter also took care of one excuse that J might use for her silence—not knowing his address. So N's love-hate for J grew stronger. He loved her, but it suited his writing to hate her a little—made him work harder. He vowed he'd finish it, and J's ignoring him was like a sharp-pointed pole poking him on. A very effective stimulus.

DOUBLE-FAULT: I am sure he must have enjoyed it.

FAULT: Not according to N. It was hard work, very time-consuming, and it opened up old emotional wounds again. Sometimes when he wrote about L-One, he would have tears in his eyes. And recalling that March-to-May correspondence with J was like losing the promised land. And again when he reread J's correspondence from the period just after his return in June, he saw it in a different light. He could see J being thoughtful of his feelings. And he wondered whether he was doing the right thing. He'd become overwhelmed with guilt. But he went on, and J herself with her continued silence convinced N that he was right to do so. J could change like a chameleon, and N couldn't let the "good" in J blind him to the "bad." C had to see, and that was final. N is a stubborn man—persistent to a fault.

DOUBLE-FAULT: Did N finish his novel?—probably a piece of trash anyway.

FAULT: Yes, he finished it, and don't be so generous with your compliments. Every couple of weeks he would write J his news, and tell her that his novel was progressing nicely. She never answered, but at the end of the summer she sent him a card saying she was glad to hear the writing was going so well.

DOUBLE-FAULT: Did she know what he was writing about?

FAULT: No one knew. N was going to make sure that nothing J asked of C in the future would interfere with C's happiness. No plotting by J or scheming by Mummy or Daddy, for that matter, no "How could you do this to me?" from J to make C feel guilty, no anything to prevent C from seeing clearly that she should put herself FIRST.

DOUBLE-FAULT: Sounds like make-believe altruism on N's part. He's being mean and he knows it.

FAULT: When N finished his novel, he thought about sending copies of the manuscript to Mummy and Daddy, too. Nothing like a good family fight. Now *that* might be considered mean.

DOUBLE-FAULT: N wouldn't dare!

FAULT: Young lady, don't dare N anything now!

DOUBLE-FAULT: Very well. So when N finished his novel, did he send it off to C to read? What happened?

FAULT: Since the novel is finished, this can only be told in an Epilogue.

The Epilogue

The gardens surrounding the tennis court are more beautiful now than at any other time of year. Fault, carrying a large envelope, makes his way past row upon row of roses in search of Double-Fault.

FAULT: Double-Fault, where are you? There's still more to tell. Come out, come out, wherever you are. Are you hiding?

DOUBLE-FAULT: I am not hiding; I am over here. [*Said with the realization that there is no use in not answering Fault's call, for she knows he will persist and locate her sooner or later.*]

FAULT: Why didn't you answer when I called?

DOUBLE-FAULT: Oh, honestly . . . What do you want?

FAULT: Well, I thought you didn't like the ending of the story I told you, and so I was looking for you to let you know the final outcome.

DOUBLE-FAULT: You needn't have bothered.

FAULT: It's no bother. Oh, incidentally, the tennis match is still going on, if that interests you.

DOUBLE-FAULT: I couldn't care less. It became altogether boring.

FAULT: Ohh. Too bad. I thought it was spectacular. Well—are you comfortable?

DOUBLE-FAULT: Yes—go ahead. [*She is momentarily resigned to listening to what will follow.*]

FAULT: Don't look so petulant. Wasn't it the least little bit interesting to you? No answer. Well, let's see. N finished his novel—a task with few moments of joy—

DOUBLE-FAULT: You've already said he finished it. Can't you be less wordy?

FAULT: Probably not. Well, as I was saying, he finished the novel and went back to Expectancy to await J's decision.

DOUBLE-FAULT: Decision! What decision?

FAULT: She had promised N that she would visit him after the tour was over. Though her correspondence was sporadic, even nonexistent for long periods of time, N thought of J as basically inconsistent, and it was still possible she might write and say she would visit, and thus keep her promise.

DOUBLE-FAULT: How absurd. That's the most twisted piece of reasoning I have heard in ages. It's perfectly clear that J has gone off N and doesn't want to have anything to do with him. The card she sent toward summer's end made no mention of seeing him soon, did it?

FAULT: That's right, nothing was said.

DOUBLE-FAULT: Well, it's perfectly obvious there's nothing left between them, so far as J is concerned.

FAULT: You sound so secure about that conclusion. Would you care to make a wager about its correctness?

DOUBLE-FAULT: I don't gamble, thank you.

FAULT: I would have bet on that, too! Anyway, N had his one last hope. He tended, on the practical side, to agree with you, but his incurably romantic inclination toward J fostered in him this one last hope.

DOUBLE-FAULT: I still say it's stupid.

FAULT: Never mind what you say. A long time ago—the previous summer, in fact—N had written in one of his long letters to J that he felt he was playing out a part in some morality play where everyone knows the conclusion, but he can't stop doing what he does. So he wasn't dumb and blind. He could hear the future.

DOUBLE-FAULT: That's the first sensible statement you've made concerning N's awareness. And don't you dare speak to me in that insulting way you just—

FAULT: Never mind your lecture on manners.

DOUBLE-FAULT: You'd better be more courteous or I'll . . .

FAULT: I apologize. I was rude. I shall exert great care and not let myself be rude again—I hope.

DOUBLE-FAULT: It's poor breeding to be so much on the offensive.

FAULT: [*In great anger*] Really, now! [*Fault suddenly breaks out in a smile.*] I am reminded of a book title N once thought up—a title for a book he thought J should write. It goes like this: "The Ultimate Writings and Last Words on the Rules of Manners and Formality Making It Unnecessary for Anyone Else to Ever Write on the Subject Again," by J. Perhaps you could write the text.

DOUBLE-FAULT: How viciously sarcastic of both you and N.

FAULT: You think so. Then it must be so. Please, let's get back to N in Expectancy. He sends J a birthday card with a note to the effect that her present is waiting for her when she comes.

DOUBLE-FAULT: What did he buy her?

FAULT: He didn't buy her anything. He wasn't going to buy anything until she said she was coming. I told you he was partly practical.

DOUBLE-FAULT: I don't know why I listen to you at all. I have so many better things to do than listen to your drivel.

FAULT: Look. Let's agree to a few ground rules. I will try to be courteous, really I will, and quick in what I have to say. You have to listen, so make the best of it.

DOUBLE-FAULT: There's no other way, is there?

FAULT: Apparently not. As I told you, N had done some writing which he intended to send to C if—and this is a big if—if J failed to keep her promise to come live with him. If J came and they parted in a manner that would allow him to respect her, he vowed he'd burn it. And if J came and wanted to marry him, he would let her read it so she would understand how much he loved her.

DOUBLE-FAULT: Burn it, after all that work? Not likely. And if N was as smart as you say he is, he would have decided to let her read it if, on parting, he respected her, and he would never have decided to show it to her if she said—I can't imagine this either—if she said she would marry him.

FAULT: I won't argue with you over what would have been wisest. The fact is that N continued writing J every two weeks —a bit of news and a little philosophy and no barbs about her failure to write him. N felt that eventually J would answer.

DOUBLE-FAULT: What did he think she would say?

FAULT: He thought she would say something like "It's useless to continue writing me. It's all over. J."

DOUBLE-FAULT: He thought she would write that?

FAULT: Yes.

DOUBLE-FAULT: Then his last two choices of what to do with the manuscript were strictly academic. He knew he would send it to C.

FAULT: Yes.

DOUBLE-FAULT: Well—did J write?

FAULT: No. She didn't. And after two months of waiting N decided to send C the manuscript.

DOUBLE-FAULT: Then he gave up on J?

FAULT: Yes, except for a miracle.

DOUBLE-FAULT: Why was he doing this? I mean, what did he hope to accomplish at this juncture by sending C what he had written?

FAULT: Why? It's obvious. He was going to hold J up to C so that C would never become the mirror image of J. We went through this before.

DOUBLE-FAULT: He should have let the past die, I say.

FAULT: Let me read you part of the letter from N to C which accompanied the manuscript. [*Fault pulls out a sheath of papers from the envelope and starts to read.*]

> *Dear C:*
>
> *Some time back, you wrote me that if I ever completed my novel you would read it and put it in a "place of pride" on your bookshelf. I don't know whether you will do the latter, but I want to hold you to the former promise. I hope my words will prove meaningful to you and I await your criticism with a forced patience.*
>
> *Love to J. I mean that. I haven't heard from her in a long time and I didn't write this letter to get information from you about her. It's best if you don't become involved. For what it's worth, I am not wasting away.*
>
> *My fondest regards, N.*

DOUBLE-FAULT: "Love to J" indeed.

FAULT: He meant it.

DOUBLE-FAULT: What did he mean, he wasn't "wasting away"?

FAULT: Probably that although he despaired about his situation he wasn't giving up on his life—even if J was not to be a part of it. At least, I think that's what he meant.

DOUBLE-FAULT: Woman's intuition tells me there's more to it. But let's not get into that. What did C respond?

FAULT: She wrote N a letter he cherishes. She refused to make any comment about N and J. Said she hoped to see him the next time he was in The City, wished him well—and most importantly, told him that she was saving his manuscript for the weekend. She wanted to "read it in one sitting. I enjoy books best that way."

DOUBLE-FAULT: I suppose it was a nice letter for N to get. She certainly is enthusiastic, but it's gruesome to think of her going in and out of her room, seeing The Package on her shelf, and not knowing what's in store for her.

FAULT: An interesting consideration. It was nice of C to let N know The Package had arrived, and to tell him in a nice way that she could not tell him anything about J.

DOUBLE-FAULT: It's quite conceivable to me that C might not tell him anything *even* if she *can* finish reading his novel.

FAULT: There can be no doubt that once she starts it she'll finish it. Could anyone pass up a novel which so closely concerns her?

DOUBLE-FAULT: What did he think C's reaction would be after she read her own special novel?

FAULT: N suffered over that. He was not proud of what he was doing. It was something that had to be done. He agonized over what she would think of him for telling her about his love affairs and J's, too. He didn't think he depicted himself as such an admirable character.

DOUBLE-FAULT: I thought C was supposed to know the truth no matter what. Was he doubting his own judgment?

FAULT: Good point. No, he always came back to believing that C would see things most clearly when she reached the end of the novel. The more he thought about that, the more he mistrusted any queasy apprehensions on that score.

DOUBLE-FAULT: Wouldn't it be wonderful for J if C rejected his work as boring?

FAULT: Are you daydreaming, Double-Fault, or am I? Don't look so frightened. The next day, N received another letter.

DOUBLE-FAULT: From C so soon. Fancy that.

FAULT: Your sarcasm goes unnoticed. And your conclusion is incorrect. The letter was from J. Does that surprise you?

DOUBLE-FAULT: That depends on what it said.

FAULT: N felt its weight. It was light. He knew what it would say. J told him she didn't want to see him again or hear from him again. "Sorry to be horribly frank. J."

DOUBLE-FAULT: I expected that. How did he take it?

FAULT: He sat in his chair and read it a couple of times. In former days, he might have picked up a pen to answer her immediately. This time he didn't. He wasn't numb; he wasn't overjoyed, either. He went out to a rose garden that even this late in the year had some roses in bloom, though most of them were dead, with fallen petals lying about. He talked to them:

> N: Well, my dear roses, this will be my last soliloquy. I've talked so much to myself these past few years I can't believe it. In some respects my life parallels yours. I bloomed when I saw J and she accepted me. I fell to the ground when she spurned me. She was like the sun to me. I couldn't resist her. Now there are to be no more bloomings. I knew it would end this way. Long ago I knew it. Spring lies ahead for you, and I hope to have a rebirth, too. I shall succeed, I must—for I still live. [*He walks*

279

silently along the rows, stopping to smell and admire the roses which remain.]

You're beautiful, and I've enjoyed knowing you. I hope when I come back to see you again I'll bring someone else with me. If I don't or can't, that will be acceptable, too. And if J should come by, remember that it couldn't be any other way. Be beautiful for her, be beautiful for everyone.

And he left.

DOUBLE-FAULT: Such a mushy oration. Still rationalizing.

FAULT: Yes, but in truth J's letter hadn't hit him as hard as one might think it would. You know how it is when you've thought something over and over for a long time. At the end there's no feeling or sensation—just an awareness that the future will be different from what you've dreamed.

DOUBLE-FAULT: Should I feel sympathy for him?

FAULT: It's not necessary. He was really all right. Oh, and he answered her letter, despite her "request" that he not get in touch with her again. He thought the way she had treated him was totally unacceptable. A rebuke was in order. In his letter he tells J she hasn't been "horribly frank" but "horribly false," that she only "took from him" and "wasn't giving." It's the strongest language he has ever used toward her, and he does it without getting any pleasure from it. The letter is not long and he sends it off the next day. Any comment? No? Please don't feel that N abused J in that letter. She was not the most gracious of lovers, and N—may someone support his view—felt J needed to hear a few words of truth.

DOUBLE-FAULT: Oh, nonsense. Needed to hear words of truth! I can just imagine N taking on that holier-than-thou attitude. No woman who doesn't want to love a man and doesn't want to see him could have hinted more strongly than J did. The kindest thing we can say for N was that he was blind. "Totally unacceptable"—what rot. And I can easily imagine him deriving considerable pleasure from giving C The Package.

FAULT: N can't really imagine it, but he agrees it looks that way. He didn't deserve *hints*, he deserved honest consideration. Anyway, now he waited to hear from C. I imagine it was a time for N to pause and think back on his life.

DOUBLE-FAULT: Oh, don't start talking like an overstuffed shirt. Did C write or didn't she?

FAULT: Yes, she did. And her letter—which I have here among these papers—arrived one month and one week after the weekend on which she had said she would read the novel. N understood why it took so long; she probably had to gather her wits together for a good think.

DOUBLE-FAULT: Stop talking and read the letter.

FAULT: Here it is.

December 11

Dear N:

It's very difficult for me to write this. I've always been a closed-in person and it's not easy for me to write about feelings. Several days ago I was still of a mind not to write, but the more I thought about not writing you, the more I realized that my failure to communicate with you would be exactly like my family's unspoken motto—the less said the better. I don't think it would be right for me to apply that policy toward you. I also feel that I should apologize to you for any hardship my family has caused you.

I am not sure where I should begin but it might be easiest to adopt a chronological approach. Much like your novel but not so far back in time. When I opened The Package and removed the manuscript, I felt great curi-

osity about what your work would be like and I wanted to give it a good critical reading. The front page was a small shock to me when I saw the letters "N," "J," "C" in the title. And your pen name, J. J. sephoJ, with the prominent "J"s. I wondered then why you didn't use your own name. The dedication, "To C to see," was another surprise. I felt flattered, and some apprehension about what was to be unfolded before my eyes. After reading a few pages I realized that a critical assessment of your style, or anything pertaining to the writing, would be beyond my editorial capacity, because I was too involved myself. I'm quite sure that you're not interested in my editorial appraisals anyway.

It's a strange feeling, and I must confess somewhat fascinating, to get to know someone in such an intimate way —someone you've known for a short period of time in a place called The Flat. Please don't interpret that as my saying I enjoyed reading "L-One, etc." because, as you probably imagine, "enjoyment" or "pleasure" could not be my reward as a reader. I don't regret reading it, however. How valuable a book it will become on my bookshelf is hard to judge. I think I appreciate how difficult it was for you to put on paper so much of your past. I must say that the "N" I lived with day to day in The Flat was very easy to live with. You distorted yourself in the novel and I think you did it deliberately, to shock me. I know that people aren't always how they appear. I know you to be a very giving, strong-minded man—possibly the only kind who could love J over such a long time.

Perhaps it would have been best for you if L-One had made you forget J. I can understand your fears about her but still think you consider yourself fortunate to have known her. I know I'd like to meet her and I hope she is as happy as she indicated to you in her last letter. Some aspects of your life seem very ironic to me. In spite of L-One's obvious difficulties—I do hope she's over them— she is a loving, giving, and I would venture to say a ro- mantically inclined person. Much like I know you to be. And yet you didn't believe you could find happiness with L-One. J rejected you, and you were unhappy about that and fought to get her to change. L-One had the same re- lation to you as you had to J. I wouldn't suggest it to be poetic justice, but it is irony.

It seems to me that you're a dreamer who tries to face reality, and J is a dreamer who runs away from it. You've loved J for too long, and in too romantic a fashion, which I would say was unwise and impractical. Yet you seemed to sense that it never was going to be. I can't make ex- cuses for J, just as I can't make excuses for your attitude toward the love you fought to keep and sustain for J. I admire such deep commitment to love, and your roman- ticism. Pity that it wasn't matched, from your point of view, by J, but it wasn't.

J is my sister and I feel a loyalty and allegiance to her that I am sure you can understand, and whatever faults she has are well known to me. Whatever happens to us, I can assure you that she won't destroy my independence or use me for her ends. You said you wanted to give me all the support I would need to withstand any pressure from her. I thank you for your effort, but it wasn't really neces- sary.

Whether I was aware of your amorous doings with J in The Flat or not, I don't know. I didn't give it any thought at the time. But I was mortified to read about your noc- turnal conversation with J concerning A. Dick. If Mummy and Daddy know about a rape, I've never heard them mention it. But they wouldn't know if J didn't tell them. In this way, all members of the family let the others keep the image they want in the eyes of the others. Just as I haven't mentioned to J what your novel is all about, and she hasn't asked.

Two weeks ago, when I was home for the weekend, I went for a walk in the park up the street from our house. A. Dick was there alone, pushing his baby in a stroller. He's married now and he looked happy. Perhaps your novel had an effect on me, for I went over to him to talk. Usually when I see him, I nod hello and keep going. It seems unreal to me now, actually, but I blurted out to him that I heard he had arranged an abortion for J to terminate a pregnancy he forced on her. I couldn't believe I had said what I said. HE DENIED IT. I won't give you the details of the talk we had, but he said it was impossible for J to have had an abortion in a local hospital without Daddy knowing about it and he was sure Daddy wouldn't stand for that. He said my accusation was "positively shattering" and he wanted to know where I had heard it. I refused to tell him, and he said if anyone made such an accusation in public he would be very quick to make use of the libel and slander laws. He asked me if J had made the statement, and I said, "No. She doesn't even know I've heard the story." Incredibly, he told me to go have a talk with J—that she would tell me "it simply isn't true." We parted after a while. I was in tears. He was so believable.

This is another reason why I decided to write this letter to you, N. I don't know who's telling the truth and who isn't. But it does no good to keep on hating A. Dick, if you still do, or to develop a hatred for J. It's no good dredging up the past. You should know that better than anyone. Leave it, N.

I don't think I should make any comments about much else in your writing, except to say that your memory is phenomenal.

N—please don't love me in any way. I want to believe that paragraph on how you would love me—whether as wife, lover, sister, or not at all—was a piece of literary fantasy you invented for that section. I think it's best if all concerned go their own ways. Perhaps after many years we may encounter each other again. Till then, thank you and good luck.

Bon accord, C

DOUBLE-FAULT: An incredible letter. She thanked N and in effect said good-bye forever.

FAULT: That's how N sees it, too. The entire letter was very difficult for C to write, but the confrontation between A. Dick and herself was extraordinary. The elusive truth . . .

DOUBLE-FAULT: The truth doesn't seem to matter now, does it? C told N to leave the past alone. Will he take her advice?

FAULT: I think so. J was a big part of his life, but now if he says he "loves" her he means love without passion or hope. A love without pain.

DOUBLE-FAULT: I expect he should be able to go on from there. I think he might feel some satisfaction not so much in guiding C but in awakening her more to what life has been around her.

FAULT: Quite so. She is armed now with facts and details. It will be up to her to live her life. You seem to be—if I may say so—much calmer now than when I found you here. How come?

DOUBLE-FAULT: I feel rather pleased—C, J, and N all finally seemed to make the best of their situation. Life going forward isn't a bad ending.

FAULT: Speaking of forward, shall we catch up on the tennis match?

DOUBLE-FAULT: It's not so amusing sitting there forever just to see things stay even, do you think?

FAULT: Would you like to go to a party instead?

DOUBLE-FAULT: That would be splendid.

They both rise and start walking out of the gardens, out past the roses. And carrying from the umpire's chair in the stadium comes the sound of a rich, resonating voice intoning,

"THE SCORE IS DEUCE."

A NOTE ON THE TYPE

The text of this book was set on the Linotype in a face called Times Roman, designed by Stanley Morison for *The Times* (London) and first introduced by that newspaper in 1932.

Among typographers and designers of the twentieth century, Stanley Morison has been a strong forming influence, as typographical adviser to the English Monotype Corporation, as a director of two distinguished English publishing houses, and as a writer of sensibility, erudition, and keen practical sense.

The book was composed, printed and bound by The Haddon Craftsmen, Inc., Scranton, Pennsylvania.

Typograpy and binding design by Christine Aulicino.